TAGGED

AMY ADAMS

7-17

TAGGED
Copyright © 2014 by Amy Adams
All rights reserved.

Cover illustration by Paul McPhee
Cover layout and design by Scott LaFortune

First edition

Published by Yellow Dog Printing LLC
Stuart Borton, Publisher
905 S. US Hwy 1
Malabar, Florida 32950
321-508-8550
www.yellowdogprintingllc.com

International standard book number 9780984291656
Library of Congress Control Number: 2014942092

Printed in the United States of America

For
Alexa & Samuel

Showing his support of white shark research and education, renowned marine artist Paul McPhee generously donated the cover illustration for TAGGED.

Visit him at www.facebook.com/public/Paul-Mcphee.

A portion of the profits from TAGGED will be donated to the Atlantic White Shark Conservancy, a non-profit organization established to support white shark research and education programs to ensure that this important species thrives. Conservation of white sharks is a key factor in the ocean legacy we leave to future generations.

For more information about white sharks, visit:
http://www.atlanticwhiteshark.org/#welcome

ACKNOWLEDGEMENTS

Family means everything. Without the daily encouragement and patience from my husband Doug and our children, Alexa and Samuel, pursuing my goal to write would be out of my reach. Further, my grateful thanks to Doug. Without him sharing his expert knowledge of sharks, tagging, telemetry and fish biology, this book would never have been possible.

Extended thanks to Paul McPhee for his generous donation of the book's cover illustration.

Thank you also to the team at Yellow Dog Printing LLC for making the Tagged eBook and printed book a priority.

Finally, to you, the reader. I am honored you've selected this story to read, the first of the *Great White Adventure series*. Without your support there would be no stories.

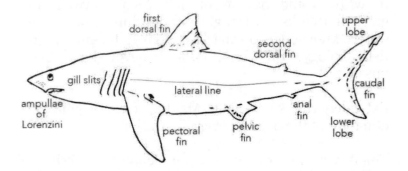

GLOSSARY

Ampullae of Lorenzini–special sensing organs called electroreceptors, forming a network of jelly-filled pores found in sharks and rays.

Biopsy punch–removing tissue from a living organism using a punch or an instrument for cutting and removing a disk of tissue.

Caudal Peduncle–the part of the body which attaches the caudal (tail) fin to the body.

CFO or Chief Financial Officer–reports to the president and manages the company's investments, income and expenses.

Gray (Grey) Seal (*Halichoerus grypus*)–marine mammals found on both shores of the North Atlantic Ocean, a large seal of the family Phocidae or "true seals," the only species classified in the genus *Halichoerus*. Its name is spelled gray seal in the US; it is also known as Atlantic grey seal and the horsehead seal.

Gurry–the innards of fish or whales; the waste parts left over after cleaning fish.

Longfin Mako Shark (*Isurus paucus*)–a species of mackerel shark, a large lamniform shark with a probable worldwide distribution in temperate and tropical waters of both the Atlantic and Pacific.

Moribund–approaching death, that is, about to die.

Necropsy–the examination of a body after death; autopsy.

Nictitating membrane (from Latin *nictare*, to blink)—a transparent or translucent third eyelid that can be drawn across the eye for protection and to moisten it while maintaining visibility for some reptiles, birds, sharks and a few mammals. Unlike the upper and lower eyelids, the nictitating membrane moves horizontally across the eyeball.

Ops Boss—a USCG Response Chief who coordinates all station responses to calls.

PSAT or a Pop-off Satellite Archival Tag—an archival tag that also has the capacity to transmit the stored information to a satellite. It is used to track movements of usually large, migratory marine animals and fish.

ROV—a remotely operated underwater vehicle, which is usually untethered and acts like a robot fitted with sensors and sampling tools to collect various types of data. In this story the fictitious VSAT resembles a tiny ROV and is tethered to the white shark by a barb at the end of the tag.

Serotonin—a hormone that is found naturally in the brain and digestive tract of human beings and animals.

Tonic immobility—a natural state of paralysis which animals enter, often called animal hypnosis.

Veterinary pathologist—a veterinarian with specialized training in diagnosing causes of disease and death in animals through studying bodily tissues, organs and fluids. Veterinary pathologists diagnose illnesses and determine reasons for death in everything from family pets to herd animals to zoo animals.

VSAT or a Video Satellite Archival Tag—a fictitious archival tag made up by the author of this book. It has the capacity to transmit its stored information to a satellite. It is used to track and video record movements of usually large, marine animals.

White Shark or Great White Shark (*Carcharodon carcharias*)—also known as the great white, white pointer, white shark or white death. It is a species of large lamniform shark, which can be found in the coastal surface waters of all the major oceans. The white shark is mainly known for its size, with mature individuals growing up to 26 feet in length and 7,300 pounds in weight. It has a life span of over 70 years.

NOTE: Definitions have been compiled from many different sources.

PROLOGUE

Cape Cod, Massachusetts
Ten years earlier

Kyle Kelley would never have thought this fish, of all the fish in the sea, was vulnerable. Man-eater? *Yes.* Mysterious? *Yes.* Nightmarish? *Yes, definitely yes.* What young boy wouldn't? But *vulnerable?* That wasn't the word that came to mind, until he stopped at the town fish docks with his father one steamy summer afternoon.

On that cloudless August day, Kyle ran to catch up with his father, a local shark biologist, who had slipped through the back alley next to Kyle's grandfather's fish house just steps from the commercial fish loading dock. Kyle hopped the swinging chain that held the EMPLOYEES ONLY sign and rounded the building at a feverish clip.

He nearly collided with his older brother Jack who was rigid and staring at one captain's monstrous catch.

"Kyle, come here!" Jack said. "Isn't it the coolest thing you've ever seen? Dad works on some pretty bad fish, but this one—this one is BADASS. Look at its teeth. How'd you like to go nose to nose with him in a wave?"

At sixteen feet and easily 2,500-pounds, a female

great white shark hung from a pier stanchion by a thick, bloodied rope wrapped tightly around its gills. Slightly shorter than a two-story building, she was gigantic and undeniably magnificent. Her head and jaws folded grotesquely over the rope cinched just above her torso. Her white, laden abdomen drooped downward, so swollen, she was either robust with a recent meal or carrying pups. Her crescent-shaped tail swayed an inch off the deck.

Kyle couldn't take his eyes off the massive fish.

"Caught the old girl off that wreck about twenty miles north of here," a man in a captain's cap was saying in a loud melodramatic voice. "You know, the one they say is the pirate ship lost in a wicked nor'easter in 1720. Word is the shark was a regular around the wreck. Some called her The Warden who protected the ship's buried treasure. Others hailed her The Executioner. One bite and you were gone, swallowed whole!"

Boys younger than Kyle gasped at the captain's exaggerated words. One even turned and buried his eyes into his father's trousers.

"For decades no one but those with a death wish would dive the wreck, not even with a lookout. Can't say I blame 'em. This old girl was ruthless, ran my line out like a scalded dog. Nearly spooled out."

Kyle was appalled yet riveted by the story and moved with the crowd as they pushed closer to see the shark.

"Put up a heck of a fight for two solid hours. But she was no match for me! And news travels fast," he added, his chest puffing out. "I've already got collectors bidding against each other for her jaws, and I'll be able to sell her teeth for a pretty penny."

The smug look on the captain's face sent a surge

of anger through Kyle. Why would anyone want to take the life of such an awesome animal?

Sloshing sounds below the dock caught Kyle's attention. Through the warped boards he glimpsed two gray seals struggling for position. They were jockeying to catch the stream of gurry, the guts and blood oozing from the shark's jaw and streaming down to its tail and into the water. The heat of the day, a mental picture of the shark fighting for her life only to have seals gorging on her innards, and the smell of diesel fumes from a passing boat mixed with his anger caused his stomach to cramp as if he'd been sucker punched.

Tasting bile, he turned and ran as fast as he could to the parking lot, where he heaved his lunch into a bush. He couldn't get the smell of the gurry out of his nose, and he hurled again. As he stared down at the contents of his stomach, he brought his fury under control by mulling over the idea of marching back to the pier and telling the captain what he thought of his dead trophy.

The monster-size shark deserved more; she deserved a better fate than to have its jaws hung above some trophy hunter's fireplace, her teeth sold as jewelry and her fins sold in the Asian market for soup.

He stood up and, wiping his mouth on his sleeve, looked around the parking lot, hoping his brother hadn't seen. He'd never hear the end of it.

He also discarded the idea of confronting the captain and headed to his father's truck. Who would listen to a nine-year-old anyway?

As his stomach settled, Kyle glanced around the inside of truck. He eyed his father's filet knife in its leather sheath lying on the bench seat. Next to it was one of his father's favorite treasures, a homemade keychain his father had made when he was a kid not much older than Kyle. Grampa had helped wrap wire around the base root of a longfin mako shark tooth from a fish they had landed aboard one of the Kelley fishing boats.

The clatter of fishing supplies landing in the truck bed jolted Kyle from his thoughts. His father was a marine biologist who had grown up on the water, helping his father and grandfather on board their family owned commercial vessels.

"Hey, Kyle, c'mon." His father waved toward the docks. "Want to show you something amazing one of the captains caught by hook and line today."

"No. thanks. Seen it."

"Really? Hmmm. Well, that's one heck of a rare catch . . . for any fisherman." There wasn't a father on Earth who would let his son or daughter miss seeing that type of catch, especially a shark biologist.

"Yeah, way gnarly." Kyle shrugged off his father's enthusiasm. He knew by this time tomorrow the carcass of the shark would be in bottom of the dock dumpster, decapitated, jawless and finless. He wanted to get as far away from it as possible.

His dad climbed in the truck. "You okay?" he asked.

"Um hum," Kyle lied, turning to look out his window. "Where's Jack?"

The elder Kelley turned the key and the engine roared to life. "He saw Annie from the bonfire last weekend. Said he'd catch us at home. I sure didn't think he'd go girl crazy this soon."

Kyle blew out his breath and rolled his shoulders back, thankful for the reprieve. He still hadn't figured out what he would've told Jack had his brother harassed him.

As the truck pulled away from the docks, Kyle saw that the crowd had not dissipated.

"Why?" Kyle pounded a fist on his knee.

"Why? You mean why is Jack interested in girls all of a sudden?"

"No. Not that."

"Then what?"

"Why would anyone want to kill something that cool?" Kyle stared out the windshield.

"Oh. The shark." His father's voice turned thoughtful, and Kyle waited silently for his answer. "I suppose some do it for money. Others because they think they're ridding the world of monsters. And then there are the self-important showoffs like that captain back there, who do it to feel powerful and mighty."

"To prove what? That he's a tough guy?"

"Maybe. To show that he hooked and killed one of the world's great predators. In my experience as a marine biologist, I haven't come across any other animal that is more 'cool' than the great white. Problem is if people keep killing them, the world will one day be rid of them. On that day we will be less one more awe-inspiring creature—not to mention, devoid of one of its top predators, and the world's oceans will be completely out of balance."

Kyle's jaw flexed in frustration as he pictured the world without sharks.

"What will people kill then to prove their dominance?" His father tossed the rhetorical question out.

Kyle didn't answer. Instead he sucked in a deep breath to suppress another pang of rage at the captain and others like him. Salt pricked his eyelids, and his nose stung.

"You okay, son?"

Kyle could not meet his father's gaze. "Uh huh," he lied then bit his lip.

He pretended to look out the side window, and soon the scenery blurred from tears that welled up and overflowed. He thumbed away the tears, hoping his father would not notice.

People called sharks vicious. But were they as ruthless as people believed?

Maybe, just maybe, they were vulnerable.

ONE

Big Betty

The ocean was a dark cobalt, expansive and ominous beneath the sliver of pale yellow sunlight creeping along the horizon's edge. The air, leaden with salt spray and humidity, was unusually warm for the first week of June on Cape Cod.

Nineteen-year-old Kyle Kelley climbed the dune crossover, his surfboard balanced on one shoulder. Sporting a few days of blond beard stubble and a head of tousled yellow hair, he was tall and broad shouldered with a muscled back above the slim hips of a well-toned athlete. No surprise that his image had embellished many surf magazine covers in his early competition days.

He squinted in the predawn light as he searched for his girlfriend, Lucy Wharton, who had agreed to meet him on the beach at sunrise. She was late.

Until Lucy arrived, he'd be alone on the beach this early in the season, sharing the morning with the occasional flyover of a herring gull. As a fourth generation Kelley to reside at the southeastern tip of the Cape, Kyle didn't care if the beach was dimly lit and desolate. Often described as a flexed arm jutting outward from the eastern side of Massachusetts into the north Atlantic, this beach was where he was most comfortable; it was home, the sound of the wind and waves calming him, especially in the shadowy gray-blue predawn light.

He unraveled the towel from his neck, tossed it aside, and dropped his board on the cool sand, waxy side up before glancing back at the crossover. Still no sign of Lucy.

Looking out at the water, he stripped off his hooded sweatshirt over his bare chest and stood with the top half of his wetsuit hanging from his waist. The horizon glowed with pink and yellow streaks, reminding him of the beachscapes he had painted as a child for Mother's Day. The rest of the page he'd colored deep blue-gray.

He and Lucy only had three weeks of high school remaining before they'd fling their graduation caps to the sky and relish their final summer together before college. Together, they would enjoy the festive atmosphere of summers on the Cape where a few penny wise tourists would arrive early to take advantage of the shoulder-season rental rates. The seaside village would not balloon into full summer until the arrival of its wealthy summer residents and the usual swarms of tourists in late June. During these ten picture perfect weeks, business owners often amassed enough earnings to carry them through the rest of the year.

His father's ringtone interrupted Kyle's thoughts. He dug the phone out of his rear pocket, along with his surfboard wax. Pinning the phone to his ear, he rubbed the wax onto the board's midsection.

"Hey 'sup?"

"Your chores, son?" His father wasn't calling to say good morning, and Kyle braced himself for the familiar rant on responsibilities.

No surprise, given that it was the third consecutive day Kyle had gone AWOL at sunrise. An avid surfer himself, his father never put pleasure before work. Having Kyle finish chores prior to school was far more important than enjoying a morning wave.

"Yeah, yeah, I know. It's still early," Kyle said. He frequently anticipated his father's reactions, so he waited for the inevitable query about the exact time his chores would be finished.

But Kyle missed his father's muffled query as he caught sight of a slow moving, dark dorsal fin slice the surface between two waves. The large, triangular fin moved parallel to the shoreline in a slow glide. As the next wave rose, Kyle forgot about the phone, his hand dropping to his side as he watched the shark's impressive profile and length illuminated against the light green water. The massive, torpedo-shaped fish rolled back into the curling wave, exposing its stark white underbelly before it flicked its crescent-shaped tail. Another 20 yards and the fin reappeared. Kyle watched it move away from shore and descend until it vanished below the surface.

"Kyle, Kyle? You still there?"

Dr. Griswold Kelley hated not knowing what his son was doing. A world renowned marine biologist, he listened for his son's voice while his computer pinged to life. He was impatient for his state-of-the-art satellite tag-tracking software to update the latest coordinates for each of the 42 tagged great white sharks moving along the Atlantic coast.

Known locally as Gris or the Shark Doctor, he was a well-published researcher who had a gift for relating complicated scientific information in terms the public could easily grasp. Born and raised in the quaint seaport town at the Cape's elbow, Gris maintained a cautious eye on newcomers moving into town. They had a knack for getting into trouble.

A week ago, Gris had received a call from another shark biologist south in New Jersey with news that several tagged great whites had been spotted traveling north. The New Jersey crew enthusiastically reported they were experiencing their best tagging season on record, having tagged seven white sharks so far with many more moving into their region. The New Jersey tagging coordinator, Al Yates, reported the new high-tech video satellite tags were performing better than anticipated and were proving to be one of the most useful tools available to marine fishery scientists studying sharks.

Gris looked at the new coordinates. Two tags lit up the screen. Big Betty's satellite tag blinked in a green dotted line. The 15-foot female white shark tagged two summers earlier had traveled north overnight from Long Island Sound. She was now moving into one of her frequent feeding areas which she had regularly inhabited during the last two summers. The second tag belonged to a 10-foot male great white dubbed Larry, tagged only two weeks earlier by the New Jersey crew near Hendrickson Canyon, one of the vast undersea ravines off the coast of New York. Both sharks were swimming along the shore in 20 feet of water adjacent to where Kyle was standing.

"Whoa. That's the fattest white pointer I've ever seen!" Kyle breathed into the phone to his father.

Gris was about to warn Kyle of Big Betty's movement north when his son cut him off. "Look, I need to find Lucy. She should be here by now. I mean, she could be here, but I haven't found her. Call you right back." The phone went dead.

Gris hit the 'Call Back' button and waited. No response, not even a dial tone. He looked at the phone's screen. A bright spinning disc whirled in the upper left hand corner. It stopped. 'No Service' blinked on the screen.

"Not now! Piece of useless junk." He enunciated each word. Snatching his truck keys and a plastic insulated briefcase, he rushed to his truck, gunning it down the driveway. He redialed Kyle's number. Still no dial tone.

Kyle hurried to the shoreline, scanning the water for any sign of the fin. He cocked his right ear forward. Amid the constant sound of crashing waves, he caught the rhythmic sound of paddling. Scanning the foaming white water, he spotted a girl struggling to steer her surfboard toward the beach. He did not recognize her.

He cupped his hands to yell when he spotted a dorsal fin rise above the surface. Based between the dorsal fin and upper lobe of the tail, he guessed the fish was at least 10 feet long. The upper portion of the shark's snout poked through the surface, gliding toward the girl.

Kyle watched with astonishment as the fish nudged her ribs in an almost playful movement with its nose. The girl flipped sideways off her board, plunging below the surface as the shark veered away from shore into a curling wave. The shark then flipped to its back and stayed in that position, still swimming, its white belly exposed to the sky for another 30 yards or so. Kyle had never seen any shark swim in an upside down position for such a great distance; it nearly resembled a circus act.

The girl surged up and out of the water, her chest

heaving as she coughed up seawater. Her head darting from one side to another, she caught sight of her surfboard and stroked toward it. After hoisting herself back on the board, she rubbed her side which was scraped and bleeding from the shark's sandpaper skin where her rash guard had been torn away.

Kyle yelled to get her attention, but the breaking waves deadened his words. He watched as the girl lay flat against the board and resumed paddling. Only 15 more yards, and she'd be safe.

Kyle ran into the surf but froze at the sight of a shark rising out of the water beyond the girl on the surf board. The fish lifted and held its head and gill slit area partially out of the ocean, like a person treading water. Kyle gasped at its size.

Could there be two sharks in the same vicinity? The shark he'd seen nudging the girl was nowhere as big as this one.

Unlike moments earlier when the first shark had abnormally traveled upside down for nearly 30 yards, this present behavior was familiar. Called spy hopping, white sharks and killer whales occasionally engaged in such behavior to view above-surface activity or prey at a distance.

The white shark held its elevated position with its eyes slightly above the surface. Slowly, it rotated its body until it caught a glimpse of the girl who was jabbing her arms in and out of the water.

"Get. Out. Now!" Kyle screamed. He waved his arms and jumped up and down in the surf to attract the girl's attention.

This shark's behavior was predictable. When Kyle's father had first gained the satellite tagging software, he'd noted that two huge tagged females avoided one another by using different coves and shorelines. They didn't like to share their food supply.

No doubt this mammoth spy-hopping shark would not tolerate the smaller shark moving in on its prey.

The only question was which shark would reach the girl first?

TWO

Wiped Out

Kyle glanced again at the beach parking lot entrance to check for anyone coming. It was deserted.

He looked left up on the dune crest for any lights on at the weathered-grey cottage. It was dark, with boards still covering the front windows from the winter season.

He was alone.

Kyle raised his hands to resume yelling when the smaller shark's pointy, black nose broke the surface five yards away. Moving in a direct line, it steadily glided toward the preoccupied girl. Two yards from the side of her surfboard, its head rose above the surface, drew its protective membrane across its pitch black eyes, and extended its tooth-rimmed jaws.

This time the shark didn't display any nudging or prey-testing behavior. It clamped down on the girl's right thigh, lower back and board, penetrating her skin with its powerful jaw.

Once in its grasp, she fought for a breath, twisted her head and thrashed her fist toward the shark's right eye. Her efforts had little effect. With momentum, the shark's weight plowed her under, leaving a swirling eddy spiraling at the surface where she disappeared.

Kyle froze, his mouth agape. She was gone. Only her vacant board remained, drifting in toward shore with the wave that rolled over the vanishing whirlpool.

He was suspended in shock for long moments. Then he came to his senses and ran toward the eddy, yelling his loudest for the girl. There was nothing below the spiral.

Nothing surfaced . . . not a fin . . . not the shark . . . not the girl.

Kyle frantically paced the shoreline looking for anything to break the surface. Suddenly, shockingly, a harrowing scream pierced the air to his left.

The girl floated to the surface on her back with her arms outstretched ten yards from shore. She was struggling to stay afloat.

Among the garbled screaming, she coughed and gasped for air.

Wondering how she was still alive, Kyle ran straight toward the water and dove head first into the breaking waves. The white water of the surf around her was tinged pink. He swam a distance to reach the girl. It was further than he expected.

When he grabbed her limp body, blood gushed from her right thigh where the skin was torn back and teeth swipes scored her skin.

Clutching her in a lifesaving hold, he began the arduous swim back to shore. When he was finally able to stand, he dragged her through the shallow breaking waves and beached her gently on the sand.

Kyle heard someone screaming out his name and looked toward the dunes where saw Lucy. He pushed himself to his feet.

As their eyes locked, Lucy dropped the hot chocolates on the sand and lunged off the crossover onto the beach toward Kyle. Barefoot, in a bikini top and sweat pants, she sprinted across the sand. When she reached Kyle, she threw her arms around his waist, and he stumbled back a couple steps.

"Oh, my God, Kyle, oh, my God!" She couldn't

think of anything else to say. She pulled back. There was so much she wanted to say, but right now all she wanted to do was touch him to reassure herself that he was alive.

She had arrived just in time to see the girl mauled by a white shark. She'd also seen her boyfriend's terrifying plunge into the ocean to rescue the girl.

Lucy wrapped her arms around Kyle again and pressed her cheek to his chest. His heart beat like thunder beneath her ear, and she swallowed the fright lodged in her throat. She squeezed his arms for another long moment before leaning back to see his face. The thought of losing him terrified her. She did not even want to contemplate what her life would be like without him.

She let her beach blanket and canvas bag roll off her shoulder. She wanted to tell him so much. She wanted to tell him what she'd thought as she watched his selfless rescue. She wanted to tell him what she'd been thinking, of what would have happened if the shark had turned and bitten him.

But they were on a beach where a girl was moaning and bleeding out on the sand.

"Need help?" Her voice came out as a croak.

Kyle did not speak; he went into action, and together they dragged the girl to drier sand where they lay her on her side. Panting, he collapsed to his knees.

Lucy pressed a hand to his back, and her warm touch immediately helped quiet his labored breathing. She, too, dropped to her knees beside the girl, gripping her wrist, counting beats. She listened to the girl's rapid respiration. *Inhale, exhale, inhale, exhale, inhale, exhale.*

Thin rivulets of blood seeped from her rib cage and hip where the shark's sandpaper skin had ripped her rash guard when it nudged her off her board. Bone and flesh were serrated from the backside of her right thigh. The shark's teeth marks ran horizontally across her thigh, leaving deep swipe marks through her upper layer of skin, exposing an under layer of tissue, but no bone or veins. Her femur was broken but the bone hadn't yet pierced through her skin. Instead, it bulged outward at an awkward angle.

"We need to stop the bleeding," Lucy said. "Compression," she added, remembering first aid class. "Find something we can use for compression."

Kyle stood and peeled down his soaked wetsuit, thinking he might be able to use it for compression. He looked at the damp lump of slick quarter-inch neoprene on the sand and shook his head.

"My shirt, where's my shirt! Dammit. Maybe this will work!" He tore off the rest of the girl's rash guard and ripped it into long strips. Then he wrapped the girl's thigh tightly to slow the flow of blood.

"My beach towel!" Lucy handed it to Kyle who tore it into pieces and wrapped some of the strips tightly on the girl's upper thigh. He used the remaining pieces to dab the blood flowing from the swipe marks across her lower back.

Lucy pulled a beach blanket out of her bag and threw it over Kyle's shoulders, using a corner to rub gently at the congealed blood rimming his neck and in his hair to see if he, too, was injured.

Satisfied that he was in no immediate danger, Lucy pulled her cell phone from her back pocket.

"I'll call 9-1-1." She tapped the screen to life. "No signal!"

"You'll have to get to the top of the dunes," Kyle said.

Lucy was about to head out when a moan from the injured girl stopped her. She dropped down to the girl's side and checked her pulse again.

"She's getting weaker," Lucy said under her breath.

"Let me have your phone. I'll call 9-1-1."

"No. I got this. You rest," Lucy said, rising to her

feet and looking toward the dunes when a ringtone jolted both teens back to reality. Lucy looked at Kyle and then leaped across the sand to grab his phone off his beach towel ten feet away. She tapped it on.

"Hey, Kyle, what's going on?" his father asked.

"Um. . . Dr. Kelley? It's Lucy. Ah . . . um . . ." She didn't know what to tell him first. "Kyle just rescued a girl. From a shark attack. Pulled her from the water. She's lost a lot of blood. She needs an ambulance."

"Say that again?" Gris said at the other end of the line.

Taking a deep breath, Lucy repeated the information at a less frantic pace. "Kyle and I planned to meet before sunrise. I was late. When I got here I saw the shark grab her. She screamed and went under, and then Kyle dove into the water to help. He got her to shore and wrapped her leg to slow her bleeding. It bit her bad! She needs to get to a hospital."

"I'm in my truck. You call 9-1-1 yet?"

"No. Can't get a signal."

"I'll call. They should be able to get there in five, maybe six minutes. Tell Kyle that Brodie called, and he tried to text, but the message bounced back. He said he'd see him at school." Then he was gone.

Lucy turned to Kyle. "Your dad is calling 9-1-1. And Brodie's not coming. I didn't know he was going to join us."

Kyle didn't answer; she wasn't even sure he'd heard her.

Kneeling on the sand next to the girl, he assessed her condition. Her face was pale, and her body shook with tremors, but though her breathing remained shallow, it was steady.

He looked toward the beach entrance for paramedics. No one was in sight. He yanked the beach blanket off his shoulders and draped it over the girl's back and legs to warm her. But she continued to tremble. He took her small cold hand in his.

"Hang in there. You're doing good." He hoped his words were reassuring. He hoped she could hear him.

Her eyes opened, and she looked into Kyle's eyes. A surge of relief that she was conscious rushed through his body.

He held up two fingers. "How many?"

"Two," she whispered, moving her gaze back to his. "You have blue eyes."

"See, you're doing great. Just keep your eyes on me. Open, right?"

She didn't answer, but another minute passed while she held his gaze. Then her eyelids started to droop.

"What's your name?" Kyle asked quickly.

"Annie," she murmured through purple-blue lips.

"Okay, Annie. I'm Kyle, and this is Lucy. Help is on the way. You're going to be OK."

"Kyle? Jack's little brother?"

"Yeah!" Kyle looked closer and recognized her as Jack's first girlfriend.

Lucy bent over and wrapped the girl's damp hair behind her ear. She squatted beside her and tucked the blanket edges under her hip above her broken leg. Annie immediately squeezed her eyes shut and winced.

"Sorry," Lucy said.

"Hey, Annie," Kyle said. "I know that probably hurt. But remember what I said? I need your eyes on me. Can you do that?" The girl jerked her eyes open again. She focused on Kyle, but her eye lids drooped from exhaustion and pain. Her face was white, her lips bloodless.

Kyle shifted when he heard sirens wail into the parking lot. Two paramedics jogged toward them. One carried a rolled up stretcher, and the other carried two red medical kits. Squatting in the sand, the first paramedic rested his hand on Kyle's shoulder.

"I'm EMT Jones. Either of you know her name?" He moved closer and started assessing her condition.

"Annie," Kyle and Lucy spoke at the same time.

"Annie. Okay . . . Annie what?"

"Morris, I think," Kyle replied.

"She live around here?"

"Yeah, she's a friend of my brother's."

"Can you tell me what happened?" The paramedic looked from Kyle to Lucy then back to the girl.

Kyle shifted his weight back and tried to stand. His legs felt immobile, like they were stuck in cement. His stomach was queasy. He was in a nightmare, unable to wakeup.

"You all right there?" the second EMT asked as he gripped Kyle's arm, helping to stabilize him.

"Sure," he lied and bit his bottom lip to keep the nausea at bay. Pounding footsteps drew everyone's attention away from Kyle, who caught sight of his father running toward them, a waterproof supply case gripped in his hand.

"You hurt?" Gris asked, moving directly to his son where he dropped the case and enveloped Kyle in a hug.

"Dad, I'm fine. She's the one who needs help," Kyle lifted his chin in the direction of the girl. "It's Annie."

The paramedics worked on her with urgent efficiency.

Gris studied Annie then focused on Lucy. "How 'bout you?"

"I'm okay," Lucy said.

A shout had them all looking in the direction of the parking lot where a police officer waved as he trudged toward them through the sand. Kyle heard the officer's keys bounced at his belt as he approached them.

"Who pulled her out?" the officer asked.

With a deep breath, Kyle straightened his spine,

cleared his throat and said, "I did."

Lucy reached for Kyle's hand and gave it a squeeze because she knew what an ordeal the telling and retelling of the rescue would be for Kyle. He'd dealt with enough press during his competitive surfing days.

Rubbing his hands over his face, he straightened to his full height, threw back his wide swimmer's shoulders and in clipped words relayed the story of Annie and the two sharks.

THREE

Talk To Me

After a few minutes, the paramedics lifted the wounded girl to a stretcher. Dr. Kelley stepped forward and asked if he could photograph her bite wounds for fish identification and to estimate the fish size. The medics obliged and allowed several measurements of the slash lengths with Gris's calipers before they carried her off the beach.

"Hey," Kyle's father called to him.

"Yeah?" Kyle answered.

"You were right to dive in after the girl."

Kyle looked into his father's eyes and let his words sink in. Then he turned away to grab his board.

"Sometimes life leaves us with few choices, son. You considered your options, even the option of walking away," Gris continued.

"No. I couldn't, not after I heard her scream," Kyle said, shaking his head free of the flashback.

"I know, and you made the right choice, Kyle."

Kyle scooped his damp beach towel and wet suit off the cool sand. He draped them over his board. "Yeah, right. That's what I'll tell myself in the middle of the night while reliving this." His voice was nearly a whisper.

Lucy moved closer, and Kyle tucked her into his shoulder. She was the ideal height to fit into the notch under his arm.

"Ready?" he asked her, and she nodded. "You coming?" Kyle asked his father.

"Not yet. Need to stay a few minutes and then hit the hospital. Get the girl's story and take some more measurements of the bite marks."

Kyle nodded and began to head away.

"Hey?" His father called after him; Kyle paused. "You didn't happen to see a tag on that shark, did you?"

"Yep."

"One of the new ones with the long antenna whip, or was it a shorter whip used on the older tags?"

"It had a long whip."

"One of the newer ones," Gris confirmed.

"The shark—it was pretty big with serious scars on its head right back to its first dorsal. One deep mark looked like a the letter A on its dorsal."

"Humph. Well, they get all kinds of marks on them. Those body scars and other natural markings are what help us separate one individual from another. Sort of like fingerprints."

"Didn't know that," Kyle said. "So does that go for behavior, too?"

"Say again?"

"Behavior. Does each individual shark have its own imprinted behavior? Because this one sure had a bizarre approach to the girl." Kyle ran his free hand through his damp hair to wring out excess water.

"Bizarre approach? What'd you mean by bizarre?"

"Before it came in for a typical test bite, it took a pass and bumped the girl off her board. Playful like, you know?"

His father listened.

"Then it did this weird thing. Or maybe it's weird because I've never seen a shark do that," Kyle added.

"What?"

"It rolled back into the next wave, like away from the girl, and swam with its white belly side up for maybe half a football field."

Gris' eyes widened. "Kyle, half a football field is a long distance for any shark to swim on its back, never mind a white. Are you sure it was that far?"

"Yeah, I'm pretty sure."

"Because it's not only unusual, it's completely abnormal for this species."

"Truly, Dad, I didn't even know they could do it. I mean, I've seen you flip a shark on its back to take a blood sample. But I've never seen them flip upside down and swim around on their own."

"They can do it on their own, and there's nothing to physiologically prevent a shark from swimming upside down. It's just not common behavior and actually quite dangerous for whites."

"Doesn't seem like anything could be dangerous for these fish," Kyle murmured, remembering the girth size of the larger spy-hopping shark.

"Turning any shark upside down has an unusual effect as the fish enters a state of tonic immobility or induced paralysis. After a short time, the shark is essentially rendered immobile and helpless, unable to move and reducing the ability to use any of its senses."

"Humph," Kyle tilted his head. "So if it stays like that, will it die?"

"It can. When on its back, large amounts of serotonin are released into the shark's brain. That's what delivers the calming to let it pass through the unusual experience. But too much time on its back and the shark gets excess amounts that can act like an incredibly strong anesthetic."

"So it can actually overdose from swimming upside down?" Lucy exclaimed.

"Swimming for very short periods and the paralysis doesn't usually grab hold of them. They can right themselves quickly and regain their senses and continue as normal for most species. But a white shark swimming upside down for any significant time doesn't bode well. Being immobile for extended periods would cause respiratory problems for these fish. Even short periods can lead to suffocation. It just isn't beneficial to the fish; it offers no predation advantage or anything along that line."

"So have you seen these sharks swim on their own like that? Upside down, I mean?" Kyle asked.

"I've seen white sharks swim upside down, but only for a few yards, never over any great distance. And it's always been when they're coming in for an attack on a porpoise or moving in for a bite angle on a dead pilot whale or other whale carcasses. But in the last 35 years, I can count the number of those times on one hand."

Kyle nodded slowly, his shoulders slumping and his eyes glazing over.

"Damn, son, you're coming off the adrenaline that's kept you going since the attack! Go home, clean-up and get some rest. I'll look up the tracking movements from this morning. If this shark had the long antenna whip, then it's a recently tagged fish with the new video function tag. If so, I'll look for its behavior on video." Gris raised a hand in farewell and moved further down the beach.

As Kyle and Lucy trudged to the parking lot, images from the last hour raced through Kyle's head. The only place he wanted to go was into a hot shower to wash away the morning's ghostly visions. He also needed some fuel in his stomach before he turned into a bear. He'd be late for school. "You headed to school?"

Lucy shook her head. "Word spreads fast. Pretty sure we'd never make it in the door past the press frenzy and attention."

"And here I thought you liked being the center of attention?"

She looked into his eyes. "Only yours."

Only mine . . . nice. "Okay, so we skip. How 'bout

breakfast? I need some fuel in me, or as you say I'll be 'impossible' to be around." Kyle raised his brows at her. "Promise to keep you hidden from the press," he added. He propped his surfboard against his 1970 restored Bronco.

She shook her head.

"Luce, what 'sup?" He hooked his arm around her waist and pulled her close, her face now a couple inches from his. He searched her eyes and leaned in.

Lucy turned her face so that his lips brushed her cheek.

Dating since eleventh grade, Kyle and Lucy knew each other's quirks by now. He could be bossy, but usually his observations assured her that she had his full attention, and his demands made her feel safe.

Lucy was on the naïve side, so Kyle sometimes needed to step in. But he also loved that about her. To him she was untainted with a sweet side he found hard to resist. Today, though, she was upset over the attack.

"Kyle, I got to go," she said through tightened lips. She promised herself no tears, but the enormity of the morning was now roaring through her head.

Kyle wrapped his arms tightly around her but was careful not to stifle her. He was content to breathe in her scent. "Talk to me," he demanded in a soft voice.

Lucy shifted her face away, but he gently thumbed her chin, drawing her back. "I know it wasn't the best morning. In fact, it sucked." Kyle waited. His gaze drifted over her face.

"Yeah, I know. I just. . . I need. . ." Her voice now a whisper, she didn't finish. Instead, she pulled out of his grip and ducked under his arms to face her car door. Kyle stepped back and pulled the handle open for her. She slid into the driver's seat and immediately started the engine.

He would never hold her against her will, but Kyle needed her to tell him she was all right. "Luce, what you need is to turn off that engine and talk to me, yeah?" His voice was firm over the sound of the engine.

Kyle laid his forearm across the doorframe and looked down at her. She looked away. Tears pooled in her eyes.

"Luce, seriously. Don't run away into your head." It was something he said to her when she got that distant look, like she was afloat in a daydream far away. Only she wasn't in a daydream. Her mind was swarming with the nightmarish scene from an hour ago.

An only child, Lucy had become proficient at engaging the steps of retreat while her divorced parents exchanged hurtful words with each other.

Kyle leaned into the car. He ran his hand along Lucy's jaw and moved his lips closer. Her cheeks flushed hot as she let him kiss her. His touch was tender, yet possessive as he cupped her jaw.

Kyle was making sure she didn't drive away an emotional wreck. But she didn't want to share her tears and wasn't about to rehash what happened that morning, at least not now. She needed time to study things and assign reason.

When they parted, she cleared her throat. "Really, Kyle. I got to go."

But he stayed there, just a couple inches from her and searched her eyes. "Yeah, you mentioned that," he said with his lips against her head, speaking the words softly into her silky brown hair.

"I'll be okay. Really." She pressed her head back into the car's headrest and lied.

Kyle pulled back. "I don't like you to go like this. But, you know that. And you also know I'm not going to hold you here if you want to leave."

Lucy kept her eyes on the edge of the steering wheel and bit her lower lip. She wasn't going to respond, not while her head was spilling over with the chaos of the morning. That would just open her up to him to discuss it, sort it all out. She wasn't ready to go there, and Kyle knew it.

Kyle stepped back and let the car door swing shut. The engine revved into reverse. Lucy slowly eased her car back over broken clamshells dropped by gulls on the sun-bleached pavement. Kyle watched her pull away until he lost sight of her brake lights and then he watched longer.

Back at his house, Kyle took a shower and got some food into his still queasy stomach before he texted Lucy who didn't respond. Two more times, and still no response.

At noon Kyle switched gears when his best friend Brodie texted him to meet at a lunch counter where they served a local favorite, seafood salad on Portuguese sweetbread.

"Hey man." Brodie said, shaking Kyle's hand and leaning in for a light chest bump.

"You picked the wrong morning to bail on me, Brodie," Kyle said.

"Yeah. Heard you been busy playing hero all morning. You know me. Didn't want to show up and steal your limelight." Brodie spoke with mock seriousness.

"Yeah, right. If I know you, you've been sleeping off a hangover. Am I right?"

Brodie grinned at his friend and didn't answer.

"So what's the real reason you bailed? One of your ladies keep you out on the town late?" Kyle raised his eyebrows suggestively.

Brodie shook his head, diverted his eyes to his sandwich and held a wide grin as he listened to his friend's interrogation tactics. With Kyle's two older brothers at college, Brodie had filled in the sibling gap during the last three years.

"You keeping your father up late springing you free again from our local jail?" Kyle waited.

Brodie shook his head and continued to grin.

Reading Brodie's response, Kyle asked, "So, she got a nice rack or what?"

Brodie looked straight into his eyes. "How do you get there from no answers?"

"Because I know you better than you know you. Seriously, Brodie? What'd you do, graduate from high school, grow up and get soft on me? If you like this girl, do her a favor. Don't get her hopes up just before you head off to boot camp in six weeks. It'll just break her heart."

Brodie's playful smile was now gone. Kyle's comments were sinking in.

"I think that shark attack turned you soft. You're one to talk with your little hometown honey headed off to college with you. You know, the first girl you lay eyes on or flirt with, and she's going get hurt," Brodie said.

Kyle held up his hands. "Okay. Okay. You're right. I'll shut mine now if you shut yours. But I'd still bet my first week's paycheck that you'll meet some hot Coast Guard babe within three weeks at Coast Guard boot camp, and this girl will be smoke."

"Dude, shut up," Brodie said. His grin was back.

"All right. All right. So what's her name?"

Brodie remained silent.

"Great. You finally find a girl you like, and you won't even trust your best friend with her name? You think you can hold back details after all I've shared? C'mon, Brodie. Let's hear it."

Brodie was back to shaking his head, eyes on his sandwich.

"So give me the short version, Kyle. What the hell happened this morning?" Brodie switched the subject.

Kyle shook his head and pressed his mouth into a thin line.

"Okay, okay I'll share some about my date if you first give me the quick version of the morning's shark attack."

Kyle's mouth curved into a genuine smile. Finally his day was improving.

~

Later that evening, Gris headed into the local tavern for his Friday ritual to knock back a few drinks with his older brothers.

"How's my nephew," Jim asked as he gripped Gris' hand.

"No injuries. A little shaken. He'll have some nightmares tonight."

"Do your boy a favor; leave a bottle of cold medicine on his bathroom counter. If he asks, tell him to take some before he hits the hay. At least he'll get a solid four hours before the nightmares kick in."

"Hey Gris, nice of you to finally show up," his brother Dale called out. "What, are the sharks keeping you out late? Or maybe I should ask, waking you up early these days," he asked as he crossed the tavern's wide plank floor and slammed a frosty mug on the varnished bar top. He gave Gris a light punch to his shoulder. "Tell me about my nephew. He pick up any scrapes this morning when he decided to dive into that bloody mess?"

"No," Gris said. "Like I told Jim, no injuries, just future nightmares. He'll survive."

"No doubt there, little brother. He's a Kelley. There isn't a fish alive that would hold down a Kelley." Dale repeated the words their grandfather had frequently uttered after rolling ashore from a long offshore haul when Gris was a boy.

"Hey, Gris," a yell came from across the bar. It was Gray O'Connor, a commercial herring fisherman. "Did you hear how one of your golden-boy great whites attacked my mid-water trawl yesterday?"

Gris shook his head.

"That 12-footer made fringe out of my net. Lost all of my haul and most of my trawl after fishing the eastern canyons off Georges Bank. Only part I could salvage was ten feet of net and my cod end. Damn fish!"

"Sorry to hear that, Gray. So, what happened?" Gris asked as his brother moved in to listen.

The herring captain didn't acknowledge Gris' apology but continued his story. "It was late afternoon when I heard one of my crew screaming to me in the pilothouse from the stern 'Shark at 3 o'clock. Starboard rail.' Then I saw it, swimming white side up. I had fish jumping out of the net from every angle. It was a mess. My guess is the fish rammed the trawl's starboard side going 20 knots before it flipped over and swam away on its back. Weirdest damn thing I've ever seen.

"When it finally rolled back to the surface, one of my crew said he saw one of those big tags fixed to its back near its dorsal. That's when I knew it was one of yours."

Gris rubbed his chin as he contemplated the fisherman's claim.

"It wasn't at the surface for long before it disappeared. Finally I thought we were in the clear. But I guess we got no such luck. The damn shark came back out of nowhere and breached out of the water. Cleared six feet above the surface and landed smack down next to my starboard rail. This time I saw its head and black eyes. There were scratches all over its head. One of my boys took a picture with his cell before it moved away."

O'Connor fished his phone from his pocket and showed Gris the photo.

"After it surfaced, it did that swimming on its back thing again for about 20 yards. So Gris, what's with that swimming upside down thing anyway?"

Gris looked closer at the photo and noticed at the

fin's base some scratch marks that resembled the letter Z or letter N. He made a note to share it with Kyle later.

"Not too sure. It's not a normal behavior. My son reported similar behavior this morning from the shark involved in the attack on the girl. That kind of swimming on its back can actually asphyxiate a white shark."

O'Connor cocked his head. "Well, I guess you haven't heard the rest of the story."

Gris shook his head and waited.

"This morning while our crew worked on my torn trawl, I heard Geoff Harrington talking on the radio. He was calling in the location of an 11 to 12-foot white shark to the Coast Guard. It had a lot of cuts on its head and open sores near its gill slits and was floating belly up on the outside of Georges.

"Then about three o'clock today I heard Geoff back on the VHF. He was telling the Coast Guard that he nearly collided with the same fish while setting his herring trawl. It was floating belly up and submerged about two feet below the surface. He said it must have died and floated with the current about two miles north."

"So do you know if the Coast Guard ever got hooked-up with the shark?" Gris asked.

"No. A few minutes after Geoff called it in, he was back on the VHF telling the officers that the fish was sinking quickly. Then he patched back in and told them it was out of sight," Gray finished.

"That's too bad. Would have liked to get my hands on its carcass." Gris nodded.

Jim signaled the bartender for drinks as each brother pulled out a barstool.

Still early in the evening at the tavern, the bar was crowded with dinner patrons waiting for tables. Some people even sat on the large raised hearths of the two massive stone fireplaces at opposite ends of the bar.

As Gris watched the bartender set down three whiskey shots and beer chasers, he caught sight of two new oversized framed photos. One was an aerial photo taken last summer by a spotter plane pilot of Gris standing with a harpooner tagging a great white shark. Less than two football fields away, beachgoers lined the shore watching.

The other photo was a close up of Gris with a dozen microphones pointed toward his face. He was answering reporters' questions after a day of tagging last summer. Jim watched Gris' reaction.

"You're getting to be quite the celebrity, little brother," Jim said.

"Yeah. Do me a favor. Don't mention the prints to Audrey. She's pretty fed up with all the attention."

His brother held up his hand and nodded.

Jim handed both Gris and Dale a shot glass then grabbed the third for himself. He held up one finger then two then three when all three brothers tossed the smoky-flavored drink to the back of their throats. It was a good way to end the first day of white shark season that began with a ruthless shark attack on one of his son's childhood friends.

FOUR

Three-ring Circus

The night of the shark attack, Kyle made a point to fold into bed early. The hot shower he'd taken washed away some of the gory images flooding his head. He hoped extra sleep would wipe the rest away. But he realized that wasn't going to happen as he tossed and turned and tossed again through the hours.

A loud banging on the screen door jolted him awake just a couple hours after he finally dozed off. He peeked one eye open in the sunlight, then buried his head in his pillow and hoped whoever it was would go away. But the banging continued.

"What idiot shows up on a Saturday this early?" he mumbled, aggravated by the nine o'clock wake-up call. The house must be empty.

Kyle slid to the side of the bed, checked his one text message from Brodie and was adjusting his boxers when he heard the screen door creak open. He heard his father greet George Harland, the town's mayor. Their voices rose upward from the family room as the two exchanged small talk.

When Gris' voice rose, Kyle tiptoed to the top of the stairs and peered through the spindles.

"What the hell does that mean?" Gris said in a loud voice.

When the mayor did not respond, Gris said, "No, I can't make up some bullshit story about yesterday's shark 'interaction' and dish it to the press. You think these people are idiots? It's the press. Their job is to investigate! And I'm not going to risk my reputation for you or anybody!"

Regularly sought for shark identification and behavior questions, Dr. Kelley had granted hundreds of interviews over his career. Despite the fact that his father and grandfather had served as state senators, he only tolerated public figures and made it a habit to distance himself from foolhardy ones.

Raised on the stern of his grandfather's and then his father's commercial fishing fleet vessels with his two older brothers, he had been regarded a rebel in the family when he decided to study science and the biology of fish instead of harvesting them with the two older boys. Gris had always known that the Kelley fleet would be in good hands under the leadership of his oldest brother Jim.

Gris' early years as a young fish researcher were complicated as he shook free from his family's stoic reputation as loyal commercial fleet owners. During those years, Gris was looked upon as a non-conformist with a far-reaching intellect and quick-witted sarcasm. But he soon learned from his father that a show of tolerance accompanied by charisma would ply his way toward easy funding for his research on the white shark.

A scholar, his goal was to uncover answers to how the sharks live, feed, interact, mate and reproduce, because so little was known. He speculated that what humans didn't understand, they feared and would eventually annihilate. But better understanding could yield respect and maybe allow coexistence.

His father's vetted approach had worked. With funding for research, his labors led to several states adopting laws banning the possession and sale of shark fins taken in a practice called finning, and the classification of the white shark as a protected, 'vulnerable' species, landed only with a special federal permit.

Now the mayor was asking him to risk his carefully built reputation.

"Look, George," Gris softened his voice. "I know you think this incident will be bad for town businesses."

"I'm not convinced it's necessarily bad," the mayor interrupted. "But at the same time, I have Joseph Bigelow breathing down my neck, threatening he'll blame any economic losses in this town on my lack of leadership."

Gris tilted his head back as he rolled his eyes to the ceiling. "Every year that man gets on his soapbox at town meetings and rants about how sharks will be the destruction of the world as we know it. I don't get it."

"Who, Bigelow? He's a multimillionaire. Who knows how they think?" George shrugged with a lack of understanding. "He apparently got bored after retiring two years ago from being CFO at one of the large biotechnology companies in Boston. He bought that posh, 80-acre, five-star resort on the hill overlooking the harbor as an investment. I guess he's protecting his investment to a degree," the mayor assumed.

Gris shook his head. The tale was all too familiar. Out-of-towners come to town. Out-of-towners buy property. Out-of-towners then think they have the clout to demand changes to how the town works, like zoning, spending and if they could, the weather.

"Honestly," the mayor continued, "I think he purchased it as a place to attract the people he has shown off for over his whole career. You know, to show that he's still successful, even in retirement. For him, I think the resort represents a venue where he can surround himself with all the players he's known and schmooze."

"Man must have a bundle of cash if he can finance a play room to invite 'friends' so he can gain attention to stroke his own ego." Gris spoke quietly.

"I agree. But I think it's more than attention he craves. Its attention and the chance to rub elbows with the elite," the major finished.

"Amazing how people think if they are seated in the same room with the rich and famous, then they *are* one of the rich and famous." Gris rubbed his forehead and ran his hand through his already tangled hair. "So for him the sharks are . . . . ?"

"The sharks?" the mayor interrupted. "That's simple. They're an obstruction, the bulls in his china shop. They threaten havoc, loss of control. I don't think Mr. Bigelow likes losing control. It's pretty hard to control a wild animal in the water. A bit like trying to control asteroids in space."

"Sounds to me you have a good read on him—like an open book," Gris observed.

"Yeah, well, it's pretty clear that he sees himself as a player, very sophisticated and complicated. But after you've sat through as many of his presentations and arguments as I have, you realize he's pretty transparent and maybe even petty. I've got to hand it to him though. He's persistent and will stop at nothing to get what he wants."

"For a person who reveres himself as refined, I guess he doesn't get it," Gris added.

The mayor looked at Gris quizzically. "You lost me."

"These fish are actually having the opposite effect on tourism."

"Come again?"

"Think of it this way. Most people are rubber-neckers. They're voyeurs. I'd say many are fiercely interested in the plight to save our planet's large predators, the mega-fauna, whether it's the lion, the rhino or the great white shark. Sure they come here for R & R and ocean air. But some also come with the hope for a glimpse of these elusive sharks." Gris broke for a breath.

"Do you think that's the majority of our tourists, or just a few people in the mix?" the mayor asked.

"Have you any idea how many tourists asked me where they could go to see the sharks last summer? Like we have them penned in some Sea World tank near the beach."

Kyle slid down another step as he listened to his father's line of reasoning. The mayor now looked down at the patterns ingrained in the wood floor. Kyle knew he wasn't studying their design as much as he was trying to understand his father's point.

"Humph," the mayor paused. "You may be right about that assessment, Gris. But I'm fairly sure Bigelow would be the last to admit that the world's most ferocious animal is bolstering our economy."

"Yeah . . . well, I'll agree with you on that," Gris finished. The two men stood quietly for a moment as they watched several vehicles pull up to the front lawn.

"Looks like you may not be our only visitor this morning," Gris said.

Several television news trucks parked on the roadway near the house.

"I . . . ah . . . I just want to get something straight. For the record, I never asked you to lie about the 'interaction,' as you call it, Gris. But I would appreciate you keeping your answers, well . . . brief to the press." The mayor's voice was tight and controlled.

"This will blow over," Gris assured him. "It's not like we're trying to hide anything, quite the opposite. The town is acting smart by using the whites' presence here as an opportunity to educate people."

New signs posted earlier in the week at all the beach entrances warned *USE AREA AT OWN RISK* in large reflective letters at the top of the sign and an outline of a white shark at the bottom.

"So you'll keep it short?"

"You bet, George."

During the last two summers, Gris had worked with local biologists, identifying and tracking a white shark population on the rise. Though historical records showed the fish hugged the Atlantic coast, moving from Maine to Florida, hunting large prey, very little was known about them. Until the last two summers only a few had been spotted along the town's coast.

With a seal population exploding from 1,200 to 12,000 in the last three years, the town had become a white shark buffet. In fact, local fishermen dubbed a sandbar at the harbor's entrance, a spot where hundreds of gray seals sunned themselves, "The Raw Bar" due to almost daily white shark attacks on seals.

Gris opened the front screen door, then shut it abruptly. "You might want to use the back door." He herded the mayor to the kitchen door, while an onslaught of press swarmed the front yard.

"I knew it was just a matter of time before they'd get wind," the mayor mumbled, shuffling toward the back door where he ran into Kyle's mother, Audrey, carrying an armful of groceries.

"George," she greeted him.

"Audrey," he nodded.

Audrey's cheek muscle quivered from pressing her teeth together.

"I just want you to know I had nothing to do with this," Gris was quick to explain, holding his hand up.

"Really? How fortunate for you," Audrey responded as she glared at her husband.

"Yes," Gris feigned, holding the door for the mayor.

"We are so fortunate to have, what four or five television crews with us this morning?" she continued with sarcasm as she looked over to Gris for an answer.

She slid the bags onto the counter.

"Oh, and I bet they're walking all over my spring flowerbeds," Audrey added.

"We can plant new ones," Gris said softly, trying to make light of their squabbling in front of the mayor.

When the door retracted behind George, Audrey cracked open a soda can, looked at her husband and calmly asked, "So, why are they here—again?"

Gris averted his eyes to study the groceries and didn't respond.

"I thought we agreed—no interviews at our home, right?"

Gris lifted his eyes but still didn't respond.

"Our discussions—earlier this week, remember? No three-ring circus, like the last two summers."

Gris put the half gallon of milk in the refrigerator.

"Or did you forget?" Audrey folded her arms over her chest.

Gris held his silence and her stare. He was uneasy knowing the press was congregating on their front lawn. She was right, they had agreed, not just last week, but at the first of the year and at the end of last summer. He reached for Audrey's hand, but she stepped out of his reach and tilted her head in a gesture that said she wanted his answer.

He gave none.

"How is it a brilliant man like you can recall the most minute details of a research manuscript read months ago, and yet forget a conversation with his wife just a few days ago?" Her mouth formed a thin line.

"I didn't forget. I just didn't think this would happen again. At least not today. I thought they'd go to the hospital. To interview the girl."

Gris was hoping Audrey would yield. But from her grim expression, he knew it was a long shot. And honestly, she was right. This was not a new exchange for them. They had been over this not once, not twice, but many times in the past two summers as the press inevitably invaded their privacy once the first white shark of the season was spotted.

"You didn't think they'd be at our doorstep? After two years of relentless phone calls, knocks at our door at all hours, even intrusions on our meals while we're dining at a classy restaurant? You didn't think they'd be here?" Her words mocked him.

"Audrey, I know you're upset . . . "

She cut him off. "You didn't think they'd come here—to our doorstep?" she repeated, punctuating her observation with a short sharp laugh as she realized how absurd her question was. "I guess a better question is why *wouldn't* they come? Have you told them that they're not welcome *here*? That they're not *wanted*? That our home is *off-limits*?" Her voice rose another notch.

"Audrey, I know what we agreed. And I know you're annoyed," he started again. "And you have reason to be. But, this—well, this is a fluke, unexpected. The sharks, they arrived early this year. Just let me handle this. The reporters probably just want a quick word with Kyle about yesterday. Then they'll be gone. I promise."

"Kyle? Kyle?" Her voice cracked. "You're going to let them question our son?" She blew out her breath and stared at her husband. He'd made up his mind without her! He had every intention of allowing their son to speak to the press, providing Kyle agreed.

"Audrey," he raised his voice to gain control of their quarrel. "Look, Audrey, I know you are frustrated with the loss of privacy . . ." He began to concede her feelings when she interrupted.

"Frustrated? Frustrated?" Her voice came out in a controlled clip. "You've already decided to continue on with the press. You don't want my input. You're fine with a repeat performance of the last two summers.

It's your job! Your responsibility to educate everyone about the plight of the great white shark! Your duty! Who else will save the species?" She slammed her soda on the counter and watched as the liquid spurted out and splattered on the floor.

She squared her shoulders and took a calming breath. She wasn't finished. She placed the soda can in the sink and turned back to her husband.

"So where's that leave the rest of us? Where's that leave the boys? Where's that leave me?" She looked him in the eyes and waited for his answer.

Gris stared at Audrey. She rarely raised her voice, and he could count the number of times she'd lost her temper during 26 years of marriage on one hand. One of which was when a particularly tough reporter had questioned her and the boys.

Yet, despite her venting, Gris clung to the belief that she'd give way. A high-level finance professional herself, Audrey would back him in the long run. She had always been his most fervent supporter, and she knew providing white shark research updates was part of his job. They were a team.

Gris finally broke his long silence. "Audrey... please. You know this is part of the job. I know you don't like it and it's intrusive, but—" He quickly raised his arm to stop her from moving toward the screen door. "We need to talk this out."

Her eyes were darker than he'd ever seen them, almost smoky with confusion and disappointment. Maybe he was wrong. Maybe he had finally pushed to her limit.

"I can't do this anymore." Her voice was low and controlled. "The interruptions. The exposure. The frenzy that takes place every time an 'interaction" occurs. Goddamn it, Gris! I thought you understood how I feel, and the fact that you don't take me seriously, makes me angry!"

"I know. I know. I know. You've made that quite

clear. What do you want?"

She looked at him with amazed bewilderment, parting her lips to answer him then closing her mouth before speaking again. "Don't you know? Haven't we discussed this?" She rubbed her fingers against her forehead and temple. "I want our boys to be more important to you than them." Her voice started softly but ended loudly as she pointed to the front lawn. Then she tapped her own chest. "I want to be more important to you than them."

"C'mon Audrey. That's not fair. Don't you think you're blowing this out of proportion just a little bit? I mean seriously, you know you are more important. You make it sound like talking to the press is the end of our world. You know I'll be brief. It'll be over before you know it."

She shook her head and turned to walk toward the door.

"Hey, where you going?" he asked.

"Out for some fresh air. I'll be back when . . ." She broke off to collect her thoughts. "I'll be back later," she finished, pressing her lips into a tight line.

Gris looked into her eyes. They were heated and threatened tears. "You sure? You just got here. Don't you want to just go upstairs? Maybe have a bath, or better, take a shower. You know, get away from this mess while I handle it?" He raised his eyebrows trying to convince her that she didn't need to leave her home to avoid the press.

She didn't answer.

"I know . . . I know what we talked about," he acknowledged. "I *will* make it right. I *will* tell them. I'll tell them never come to our home again. Any information from today forward will be provided through the Marine Fish Lab. Okay?"

Again, she didn't answer. Her expression was more placid, devoid now of frustration and anger and even sadness. She looked still, almost static. She looked . . . she looked defeated.

She had reached the end of her rope and Gris knew he had brought her there. They had quarreled about this in the past. But he realized this time was different for her.

When she didn't answer, Gris quickly glanced away to check the front door where he now saw a large crowd gathered on the front steps. He turned back when he heard the slap of the screen door, then the sound of an engine turning over. From the back door, he saw her turn her car around and drive to the end of their driveway. He watched her pull away and stayed there, waiting until her taillights were out of sight.

"Shit. Shit. Shit," he cursed quietly to himself, running both hands through his uncombed hair. *Smooth moves. She tells you what she wants, and you tell her to wait a moment, that you'll be right with her. You sure blew that.*

FIVE

Untamed Animals

Gris Kelley cleared his throat and strode through the kitchen to the front door. He took a deep breath to prepare himself for facing the press and slowly turned the knob. Bulbs flashed and microphones pushed toward his face. Three reporters shouted his name.

In a bold maneuver, one reporter stepped onto the first step to the porch, "We would like to speak to your son. He is the young man who rescued the girl from the giant great white shark yesterday, right?"

Gris pressed his lips into a flat line. This was exactly what Audrey didn't like, and he didn't much either. "Step off my porch," he ordered. "I'll see if my son is available." The entire group took two steps back.

Gris closed the door on them. The white shark curiosity had turned their lives into a spectacle. He and Audrey had never argued so much in their entire 26 years together. The invasion of privacy, continuous questions from the press, and Gris' long hours made their once-beloved summers unbearable. No wonder Audrey now dreaded the summer season.

Gris turned to find Kyle dressed and sitting on the bottom step.

"I heard you and Mom arguing."

"I'll talk to her, make things right," Gris assured him. "I suppose you overheard the reporter?"

Kyle let out a heavy sigh and spoke softly, "Yeah. I

know I owe them my story. But I also know they'll twist my words and make me look like a fool."

It was a familiar drill for Kyle. At age eleven, he had caught the press' attention as a tween on the surfing circuit when he landed the New England Invitational title. That same year, two major surf companies signed him on, paying for his travel, contests, and gear. With the sponsorships came the obligation to provide access to the press. The circuit routine was easy in middle school and even during the first couple years of high school. But by junior year, the attraction had waned. His priorities had shifted. He decided to decline sponsorship offers and step away from the pressure to go professional.

"You don't have to talk with them. You don't owe anyone," his father corrected. "Look, son, this is up to you. You know from competing, the press can be relentless. I find it easier to give them a story early before it turns into a manhunt."

Kyle considered his father's words.

"If you decide to talk, I will stand by you," Gris reassured him. "If at any time you feel a question makes you uncomfortable, look at me, and I'll handle it."

"I knew they'd be here," Kyle blew out. "This really sucks." He waited a minute to gather his thoughts. "I guess it's now or never, huh?"

Gris walked to the door and stepped out onto the porch, first leaving Kyle inside. He held a hand up to hush the group and spoke in a firm, booming voice that caught the attention of each reporter and cameraman.

"We are going to do this one way and only one way. My son is a teenager with little press experience. I have advised him that he does not need to answer your questions or relate his story. But he has agreed to do so anyway.

"If at any time I feel the questioning is getting out

of hand, or any of you are disrespectful or disorderly, we will leave. I see eight of you here with your crews. You each get one question."

The reporters whispered to each other.

"These are the ground rules. Agreed?" He waited for answers from all the reporters. "I can't hear you. Agreed?"

The reporters all piped up with confirmations.

Kyle eyed the doorframe while he waited for a pause in his father's voice. On his second step through, he held up his hand to adjust his eyes to the glaring lights and bulbs flashing. His kneecaps were jumpy and stomach tense.

Gripping one shoulder with a warm squeeze, his father looked into Kyle's eyes to see if he was ready. Kyle nodded. His father looked to his right, and the first reporter fired a question.

"The police report said that a girl was mauled yesterday morning by a shark. Kyle, when you dove into the water, weren't you nervous that whatever mauled the girl would come after you?"

Kyle wrinkled his brow and considered the question. He thought for a moment about his comfortable pillow and bed and sucked in a deep breath before answering.

"The sun was on the horizon when I first saw the dorsal fin. I looked around and saw I was alone on the beach. There was no one. A few moments later when I heard her cries, I knew I had to do something."

"That was brave, son. Don't you think?" the reporter added.

His father's eyes narrowed. He was noting the first reporter had already broken his rule of one question each.

Kyle thought about the comment and decided to ignore it. He looked to the next reporter.

"So you weren't scared when you saw the shark bite the girl?" the next reporter followed up.

"What kind of question is that?" Kyle rumbled. He rolled his shoulders back and took a long breath. He adjusted his voice. "Maybe surprised when I saw the shark push her under. I remember I froze, but not because I was scared. I was more concerned than scared. I didn't want to lose track of where she was. It was ultimately her screams that jolted me into action and made me dive in for her," he answered.

"Do you know if it was a great white shark that attacked her?" another reporter interrupted.

"Pretty sure. It wasn't a mammoth one. Maybe about nine to ten-feet in length with a big girth like four to five feet wide and had the classic conical nose. I saw its fin and then its profile when it rolled back into a wave after it nudged her off her board."

"Wait a minute, I thought you said it bit her?" the fourth asked, his notepad flipped open with his pen ready.

"It did, but it took two passes. The first time it approached her, it bumped her off her board with its nose, then sloshed back into the wave. When the girl got back on her board and began paddling to shore again, it came in for a second pass. That's when it came up out of the water and took a test bite."

"A test bite? You mean the shark was testing her, like sampling her?" the fourth reporter continued. Again Gris's eyes narrowed as the reporter fired off a follow up question to his first, but he allowed it.

"Yeah, a test bite. White sharks are different from other shark species that do the wolfing down first, ask questions later. Dad once found part of a toilet seat in a Tiger shark's stomach."

Laughter erupted from the back of the press crowd.

"White sharks have super sensitive snouts and mouths that they use like we use our hands, to touch and test things before they scarf them down."

"So you think this shark was just testing her for a

meal item?" another asked.

"Probably. I mean I'm no expert. I think it found the hard surfboard and boney surfer different from its usual prey, like a fat seal. So it moved on."

There was silence. Someone yelled from the back. "Just to recap. You thought the shark found the girl as an unsuitable prey. So do you think the shark left the area to hunt for seals?" the sixth question came out loudly. The reporter's statements made Kyle feel as though his theory sounded more like a farce.

"All I'm saying is that whites are smart fish. They've been known to test bite buoys and lobster traps and moorings to see if they are potential prey. People are not an ordinary food for them. So yeah . . . it's possible the fish moved on to dine on one of the thousands of seals nearby," Kyle finished his thought.

His father lifted one brow, realizing how much information his son had absorbed from family dinner discussions over the years. He could also tell Kyle was growing tired of the repeated questions and backtracking on answers. Gris noticed his son's expression, much like his mother's. He was near the end of his rope with the interview.

"So you thought the shark had moved on. Is that why you weren't scared when you rescued the girl," a new reporter near the front backtracked to a former question.

Now Kyle felt like the reporter was feeding him lines.

He considered his previous answers and wondered whether to continue. *Did he owe this group any more explanation? They didn't seem interested in the sequence of events. They were now fishing around for his feelings. He thought about what a waste of time this was.*

He swallowed his irritation and took a shot at answering the scared question, one more time.

"When you have a few seconds to react, you aren't really weighing all the pros and cons of the scene. I reacted to her scream. I'm sure there are some people who would have reacted the same and others who would have reacted differently. I can't give you a tabulated list of reasons why I ran to help her," his voice was exasperated.

"Would you say you had a knee-jerk reaction?" another question came from the back.

Kyle had a vision he was encircled by a pack of wolves and they were closing in on him. He considered a cynical response to the man's question. Then reconsidered.

"Knee-jerk, that's your question? Where do you guys come up with these questions?" He looked at the reporter with disbelief and heard whispers from the back.

"You know it's probably smarter for me to provide yes and no answers at this point. You all talk like the shark was acting unnaturally, like the girl was paddling around in a swimming pool at resort." He weighed whether to continue and sucked in a deep breath.

"Look . . . I've been surfing here since I was six. As a surfer you learn quickly that the ocean is not a place where you can tune out. When you're floating out there, waiting for that perfect wave, you get the message quickly that you're in a natural, wild habitat where untamed animals live. Animals you can't predict.

"So no. I don't think my reaction was knee-jerk or impulsive. If anything, it felt like time moved slowly as I thoughtfully considered the situation." Kyle shot his father a look that said he was finished.

Gris turned immediately to the press. "Thanks for your questions. My son has to leave now, so that's it for questions."

The two ducked back through the screen door and

closed the heavy front door behind them.

A few reporters shouted their names to lure them back outside, but Gris ignored them, urging Kyle toward the living room at the back of the house.

He reflected on the mayor's request. This round was about Kyle with little information provided by him.

Kyle collapsed into one of the leather chairs facing the fireplace and ran both hands through his hair. He was drained from the interview.

"We done here?" he blew out as he dropped his arms onto the chair's rolled arms.

"Absolutely," Gris said.

"Cool." Kyle pushed forward and stood to his full height. "I'll be in my room texting Luce."

SIX

Are You Listening?

Lucy avoided Kyle's texts and calls all weekend. This was the longest time they hadn't spoken to each other since the first day of school when he asked her out for a soda. That was two years ago at the start of eleventh grade. A new girl in town, she had moved from Boston.

He'd seen her walking into their first period class when he bumped into her at the door. She blinked her brown lashes. They looked so soft on her fair complexion. She lifted her gaze to look at him. His stomach flipped and all his muscles tighten. The pull was there. He smelled her light, sweet scent and barely croaked out a hello.

She studied him for a few seconds while other students stepped around them. Her cheeks flushed pink and one corner of her mouth curled up into a crooked smile revealing a dimple. She swept a piece of her dark brown hair out of her eyes and tucked it behind her ear and nodded hello. Then she took her seat.

Kyle couldn't take his eyes off of her.

That was it. She didn't actually speak to him, but he knew he had to find out who she was. For the rest of the day they shared classes, but never spoke. As a new girl at school that first day, she didn't speak to other students or volunteer to answer teacher's questions. So he was surprised when he caught up to her after school that she agreed to have a cold drink with him that afternoon.

The weekend passed without a word from her. He had swung by her house twice only to find no one home and hit the beach Sunday morning with Brodie in his restored candy red Manx dune buggy. They'd surfed for four hours then headed to Brodie's where they gorged on dinner party leftovers from the previous Saturday evening.

Now it was Monday and Lucy averted all looks from Kyle in school. She ducked into the girl's room when he walked to her locker. She had her mother pick her up after school, instead of their usual ride together.

Concerned with her distance, Kyle finally called her from his father's office phone, hoping she wouldn't recognize the number. She answered on the second ring.

"Lucy?" he choked out. "It's me, Kyle," he continued. He heard her softly gasp. "Hey, are you alright?" She was quiet.

"Luce, you there?" he waited. She gently breathed out. It wasn't a smooth breath; in fact, he thought he heard her body shudder when she realized he was on the other end.

"Luce?" he spoke softly. "You okay? Can you tell me what's going on?" His voice was patient with a hint of frustration. She didn't get to answer before he asked another question.

"How come you didn't return my texts?" Kyle asked. He heard her breathe again.

"Kyle, I . . ." she stopped. He waited for her to finish but she didn't.

"Look Luce, I'm not sure what I did to upset you. But you . . . I mean this . . . this is crazy," he declared. His voice was gaining strength and volume. Without her in front of him he couldn't read what she was thinking and her silence was driving him mad.

He gave her a moment and then heard her softly groan. *Okay, probably a sign she was either unhappy or confused.*

She blew out a deep breath and said, "Meet me under the town pier in an hour, I think."

"You think?" he restated.

"Yeah, I mean yes, meet me there. For sure, meet me." She hung up.

Okay. This was good. She hadn't asked him, she'd just told him. An approach she had only used one other time in their relationship. He shrugged it off. *At least she was talking.*

Lucy Wharton had a wide, white, even smile that could light up a room. With silky, long brown locks that turn lighter with blond streaks in summer, she was likely one of the prettiest and friendliest girls in school. With a petite build, she had curves that attracted the attention of far too many guys, at least from Kyle's perspective. But for him, it was her dimples that intrigued him, and Lucy knew this from the way his face softened each time her dimples appeared. One glimpse of even a single dimple, and Kyle was toast.

Street smart, she was not. She was one of those girls who would saunter down a busy street completely unaware of guys walking into telephone poles because they were gazing at her from across the road. At school, she was oblivious to the looks and stares from most of the school's male population.

Often taking things at face value, she was confounded by why so many people turned to crime in the world. But what Lucy lacked in street smarts, she made up for in book smarts. She read constantly—anything she could lay her hands on. For pleasure, she gravitated to mysteries or suspense novels because she liked using clues to find solutions and diagnoses. The only mystery she couldn't solve was her parents' relationship. Lucy was an only child whose parents had divorced when she was eight, citing irreconcilable differences. Her mother, a pageant beauty queen had married three times since. After each subsequent divorce, she returned to Lucy's father, thinking this time it'd work. The rekindled romance would last about three weeks before she was off to another distraction. She was now working on husband number four.

Kyle arrived at the pier a few minutes early, hoping his punctuality would reassure Lucy. He waited by a pier piling and glanced at the boats gently bobbing at their slips. Closest to him was the boat that had landed the mammoth shark at the fish docks when he was a boy. He remembered the massive female white shark dangling from the pier's stanchion and his father's explanation about why anyone would kill such a great fish. The memory made the hair stand on the back of his neck.

The sound of feet crunching through the sand and shells brought Kyle from his thoughts, and he looked up to see Lucy right on time, dressed in faded jean shorts, a halter-top and her hair down. She descended the sandy beach path from the pier's parking lot.

Earlier in the year, Lucy's father had asked Kyle to help pick out the right car for his daughter over spring break. When Kyle picked out the make and model car Lucy had talked about for months, her father protested, saying it didn't suit her, that she would prefer an Audi or Volvo.

"Mustangs are too rebel, too fast, too unsafe for my little girl," he explained to Kyle in the showroom. "Don't you think a Volvo would be safer? Better for her?"

Avoiding an argument with his girlfriend's father, Kyle acceded to his opinion and rode out to the Volvo dealership. After an hour of perusing the lot, Mr. Wharton folded, "I give up. You're probably right about the car choice. It's just I would prefer she be in a less eye-catching vehicle. You know?"

Kyle did know. Lucy turned heads. At times when she crossed the room, Kyle had trouble thinking straight.

Despite his concerns, Mr. Wharton bought Lucy the car of her dreams. The first day of spring break when Lucy first set eyes on the Mustang, Kyle knew the car and color were perfect. She had squealed with excitement and jumped up and down, which told them that her father had made the right choice. After she gave both parents hugs, she had turned to Kyle with an impish smile that conveyed her gratitude for saving her from yet another safety-first argument with Dad.

Now, Kyle drank in the sight of her striding toward him. He'd gone three days without seeing her, and nothing short of a tsunami could make him break his gaze. He enjoyed the wait, leaning casually against a pier piling, his arms folded across his chest, his feet out in front on an angle. The closer she came, the warmer his chest got as his speeding heart pumped blood and adrenalin through his body. *Damn, did she have any inkling how she affected him?*

Lucy's arms hung by her sides as she plied through the soft sand barefoot. Her jaw tight, she nibbled her upper lip. Kyle dropped his arms when she stopped a few feet away. He locked his stare on her dark brown eyes which were red and puffy and devoid of makeup.

Lucy folded her arms across her chest and shifted her weight to her right leg. Her eyes turned steely black in the early evening light.

"Babe, what's wrong?" he whispered, extending a hand to her.

"Don't!" She took a half step back. "I mean, I want . . . I need to say something, but . . ."

He quirked one eyebrow upward. *Damn if he*

knew what was bothering her!

"Arghh!" Looking down, she scuffed her foot across the sand. Her fists opened, then closed.

Kyle remained silent. He'd never seen her cross and troubled at the same time.

Lucy rarely got angry. Frustrated, sure. But Kyle had only seen her get worked up one time when the daughter of his mother's friend asked him to her private school prom. Lucy was green with jealousy, red with anger, and definitely embarrassed of her feelings. Kyle didn't attend.

Lucy lifted her gaze and swallowed hard. "I . . . I want to tell you . . . what you did for that girl the other morning . . . how you risked your life to save her, another person, I am incredibly amazed and proud of you. But—" She drew in a shaky breath and looked away.

Kyle reached for her hands. This time she let him pull her toward him but kept a couple feet between them.

"But what, Luce?" he repeated her last word.

"But, I was . . ." She pulled in another deep breath and finally met his eyes.

Kyle's heart clenched at the sight of tears pooling in Lucy's eyes. He had never seen her so serious, yet skittish. Was she breaking up with him?

"You were . . . ?" Suspense killing him, he encouraged her to finish her sentence.

"Look, Luce, I don't mean to rush you, but not seeing or hearing from you in three days, and now your hesitation at telling me what's going one is—well, making me a little crazy. Honestly, I'm pretty clueless where you're going with this. You're troubled, and I want to understand. But you need to just tell me."

She wiped a strand of hair from her eye, tucked it behind her ear, and swallowed her feelings with a nervous clearing of her throat.

"I was scared to death. There, I said it—" She tried

to pull her hands away, but he tightened his grip. She turned her head away, then just as quickly, turned back to him. "The truth is, I was scared to death when you dove into the water where that—that gigantic shark was. I was so scared it would get you, too," she stammered, her voice quivering. "How could you?" Her throat turned dry and the question came out no more than a whisper. She swallowed hard as she waited for his answer.

Was she accusing him of something?

"How could I?" he repeated.

"I mean, it was an incredibly courageous think to do, but I was just so frightened that you would die, and I would lose you." The admission came out in a rush. Tears welled in her eyes and slid down her face as she swallowed back her emotions.

A rush of relief attacked Kyle's body. He finally knew the reason for her silence. She had been brooding all weekend, battling the visions in her head. He couldn't blame her. That first night in bed for him was rough as scenes from the morning's attack replayed over and over in his head.

He pulled her into his arms, cradling her head with one hand, sliding the other around her hips. She leaned into his chest. Exactly where she belonged.

"Okay, Luce. I'm here . . . shhhhh," he said, hushing her soft gasps while she tried to maintain control. She pushed her head under his jaw and pressed her cheek against his chest. He tucked a loose hair that fell again behind her ear, then tightened his arms around her back. "Deep breath. I'm right here," he whispered in her ear. Her tears began to subside.

She doesn't want to break up! But she was upset and frightened, a bit proud and definitely scared. Afraid for his life!

Memories of that morning on the beach washed over him. No one else was on the beach when the girl appeared out of the water. He replayed the shark

71

rising up through the waves. Biting down on the girl's leg and her board. She was gone, and then he heard her screams. *Did he really have a choice?*

Lucy had arrived that morning just in time to see him dive into the water. She'd yelled something just as his arms broke the surface, but her words were muted.

"When you dove in, I yelled to you." Lucy was on the same wavelength as he.

"You told me that. But you never told me what you yelled, even when I asked that day. Luce, regardless of what you think, I can't read your mind. You want to tell me now?"

"No, don't."

"No, don't go after the girl?" He wanted to make sure he understood her meaning.

Shoulders slumping, she nodded and dropped her gaze as if to study the grains of sand beneath their feet. "I was just so terrified I'd never see you again." She spoke rapidly, for if she didn't say it fast, she'd never get her thoughts out.

Kyle slid down the piling and sat in the sand against it. He reached for Lucy's hand and pulled her down onto his lap, drawing her close to his chest. He ran a hand up her back.

The tears that had subsided welled again and tracked over her cheeks. He took his thumb and wiped away the wetness, then lightly kissed her hair. She pushed her face into his chest and let out a soft cry. As he slowly ran his hand up and down her back, her breathing slowed, and she began to collect herself.

"Before last Friday, our life was so laid-back. Most trouble we got in was four-wheeling in your Bronco on North Beach with that wine your Mom loves." She paused. "Remember, during nesting season with that bottle of wine from your parents' cabinet . . . ?" She sucked in a breath. "But a shark attack—Kyle, that's not laid-back. That's violent. That's harsh." Her voice rose in renewed strength.

When she finished, Kyle pushed back an inch and tilted his forehead against hers. He listened as she drew in shaky breath and waited for her to settle some more.

"Yeah, you're right." His voice was steady and calm. "It was all those things. Violent. Harsh. Intense." He paused for a moment. "So—so we work our way back to laid-back. Luce, sometimes life dishes out stress. It's inevitable." He spoke softly as he looked into her eyes. "But we can take it. Right?"

Kyle waited for her to say something, and in the silence, he could almost hear the gears switching in her head. His stomach growled.

"Let's head back to grab a sandwich for dinner. Dad and Mom are gone and. . . "

"No, wait," Lucy interrupted. Kyle's eyes widened at the sudden strength of her tone.

She pushed herself out of his lap and kneeled in the sand, facing him with squared shoulders. She sniffled once, cleared her throat and wiped her face clean of tears.

"Kyle, promise me something from now on." Her words came out wobbly, but her voice gained strength.

"Okay," he agreed, not knowing what he was promising her.

Lucy looked into his eyes. "First thing," she held up her index finger. "If you see a person being threatened by a shark, you stop and call for help." Lucy took a deep breath.

"Luce, it's not that simple. You know that."

"Second," she continued, speaking over his objection and reigning in his attention. "You don't run into the water while big sharks are swimming around."

"Right. But Luce—"

"No," she cut in again. "That's like running into a burning building. You don't know what's going to happen. You can't predict." Her voice was strong now.

"Got it?"

"Sweet—"

She cut him off with a frown and pushed her face closer to his. "Are you even listening to me?"

He was completely surprised at the power in her voice. How had she gone from fragile to tough-guy within a matter of seconds?

Kyle locked eyes with her and slowly nodded, focusing on maintaining the seriousness of the situation while holding back a grin. She was as solemn as a determined kitten flexing its new claws. He bit the inside of his cheek to keep from laughing with delight and relief.

"And the third thing," she paused to moisten her lower lip, "please, Kyle, tell me you will think twice before doing something dangerous, I'll admit courageous, also somewhat insane where you could die right in front of me . . . while I stand by and . . . "

He leaned in to hold her and put an end to her imagining the worst, but Lucy pulled back. "Tell me you get what I'm saying?" Now she sounded almost grumpy.

He brushed his knuckles over the place where her dimple showed when she's happy.

"Please, tell me!" She demanded his answer in a gentler tone now.

"Yes, yes, I get you, Luce!" He really did.

He dropped his head to meet to her forehead. She gulped in a breath of air, as if she'd been afraid to breathe, then exhaled a hiccup.

Kyle could not hold back a laugh. "And here I thought you were trying to break up with me."

She leaned back to let him see her eyes and offered him a twisted smile. "My mistake. You are insane. And yes, that was the worst wine we've ever tried. I can't believe your Mom drinks that Sake stuff." She finished the earlier story with a decided smirk.

Kyle laughed again and watched Lucy's face

soften. It was only a matter of seconds before her dimples would appear, and when it happened, he'd know he had his Lucy back.

SEVEN

Sonic Sophie

Swishing her tail back and forth to propel her sleek, torpedo-shaped body through the water, Sophie used her other fins only for stability and maneuvering. She was satiated from feeding on a wounded right whale calf near the Cape Canaveral shipping lanes.

As she'd done for decades, Sophie hugged the coast, moving north along the east coast of Florida. She was still a distance from her next marker, the muddy-grey, warm river plume that flowed into the Atlantic from St. Mary's River on the state's northeast coast. That marker would signal her to swim due east toward the azure waters of the Gulf Stream Wall before turning north into the warm current en route to rich northern feeding grounds. The Wall, known as a permanent oceanic convergence zone where a sharp vertical temperature gradient on the coastal side abutted the warm water of the Gulf Stream, was a magnet for sea life. Due to the speed, about four to five miles per hour, and the depth of the Stream, 600 to 800 feet deep along Florida's coast, upwelling along the Wall regularly occurs and draws many migratory species like tunas, swordfish and marlins to the abundant prey concentrated there.

Sophie had spent the last two years roaming the deep Atlantic far from major white shark feeding areas like those found in the Gulf of Maine and Cape

Cod waters during her pregnancy. Having birthed her pups, she was now on course to return to those rich feeding grounds for the summer months.

Earlier that morning the floating calf had become separated from its mother when it strayed into the port's shipping lanes. Confused by ship traffic and sonar activity from a submarine returning to Port Canaveral's Navy facility, the calf was struck and wounded by a citrus freighter leaving port. Though not fatal, the hit maimed the young whale, leaving it floating at the surface where it was quickly caught up in a southerly current. Commercial fishermen eventually called in the wounded whale's location to the Coast Guard.

After several hours, the 16-foot great white crossed paths with the injured whale while swimming in shallower waters that hugged the coast. The smell of the whale's blood from more than a mile away lured Sophie further inshore. Once she zeroed in on the waning whale, she cruised in concentric ovals around the animal and scanned the area for other predators and threats.

Sensing none, she turned sharply, looked left and right and sank below the surface. When she was less than a meter from her prey, she lifted her head upward and rose slightly from the water's surface. Sophie retracted her third eye lens and plunged her teeth into the fatty tissue for a test bite. She then backed off, circled the area and decided the flesh was familiar. She returned, this time to the whale's caudal fin area. She bit down and shook her head from side to side to tear way a chunk. The mouthful was likely the final blow for the calf, as it severed the caudal artery that carried blood from the heart to the tail flukes. In the first 45 minutes, Sophie consumed roughly 300 pounds of meat from the calf's carcass. The fatty tissue presented the perfect meal to replenish Sophie's energy stores before her long trip north.

An hour after first intercepting the calf and chasing away a smaller bull shark, Sophie sensed a change in her surroundings and detected sound and turbulence moving toward her. She paused to identify the threat, backed off her prey and cautiously circled the area twice while she waited for the approaching vessel to pass by and leave her to her meal.

But that didn't happen.

Once there, the 45-foot marine research vessel stayed and moved in on her kill, irritating her.

She continued to circle the metal boat to discern its interest. Using the miniscule jelly-filled canals at the front of her head to sense the vessel's magnetic field, she slowly approached it. The men aboard throttled back their engines and used the current to float down onto the whale. A large-handed man leaned out from the portside and jabbed a long gaff into the side of the whale to guide it near the boat. He pushed and pulled the whale into position and finally tail wrapped it for towing. Sophie eyed the muscular man as she passed by. The situation was similar to something she had evaded earlier in the week where she was chased with another long stick; a different stick with a long cord attached; she had tired of the game and dove deep to search for squid, all the while thinking how she didn't like the boat interfering with her meal.

As the man tightened his knot, Sophie took a second pass toward the boat. This time she flicked her large tail toward him, sending an impressive spray over the rail. She darted back at an angle and noticed she'd gained the attention of not only the man but also the other crew members on board.

Aware of eyes on her, she circled again, turned sharply and pumped her tail vigorously side to side. Gaining speed to 20 knots, she set a course to strike the vessel's port rail. As she thrusted closer and closer, the crew moved back and braced, only to see Sophie dive at the last instant. Not finished, she slithered under and forcefully whacked her tail against the vessel's underside as another warning.

The men stood along the center beam of the ship and studied Sophie's movements. After ten minutes, the crew decided the threats were of minimal concern, so they resumed work. But Sophie was not so quick to stand down. Instead she continued to investigate. Only after a half hour of no further attention, and identifying no other threats nearby, did she return to her meal, chunk by chunk.

When the vessel began to tow the whale back to shore, Sophie didn't deter. Instead, she followed, keeping pace, all the while consuming one chunk after another. Relentless, this white pointer wasn't about to surrender her meal.

Over the next 40-minutes Sophie continued to feed, tearing away bites, falling back to swallow and reposition, then sprinting forward to catch the whale that was moving at three knots. Occasionally, she glimpsed the marine biologists watching her. To their surprise, the movement didn't seem to bother Sophie in the least. Large prey like the whale was not easy to find. It was a meal that would sate her for the next four to seven days and supply her energy to swim north to more abundant fishing grounds for the summer months.

Repeating the pattern, Sophie continued to feed, fall back, even drafting in the prop wash current and sprinting forward until biologists partially beached the whale on Cape Canaveral's barrier island to begin their necropsy and removal of the skeleton for exhibition at a national museum. Only then, like her ancestors who had roamed the oceans for more than four hundred million years, did Sophie back off to resume her solitary trek north.

~

On an afternoon a month later, Kyle Kelley stood beside his father at the toe of the dune on a Nantucket Sound beach. They watched the heavy equipment operator tie one end of a thick rope to Sophie's caudal peduncle and the other to the excavator bucket. With the short rope now taut, the operator slowly raised the bucket, lifting her near-death body two, then four, and finally six feet off the ground.

"Where you want me to lay this huge girl?" The brawny operator shouted to Kyle's father over the roar of the machinery. The rope sprang and bounced as the tagged shark awkwardly wriggled and swayed while suspended in the air.

"On that trailer." Gris pointed to the flatbed trailer parked on the asphalt behind the dune.

The operator eyed the long, open flatbed through the dune cut and nodded. He pressed the joystick forward and steadily swung the body over the trailer, then lowered it on its belly, nose facing the truck cab. Kyle studied the shark's tail flex as soon as the rope went slack. Its third eyelid, a protective translucent membrane, was now drawn partially across its black eyes.

"Why's her dorsal fin cut off?" Kyle asked.

"Hmmm. I'd like to know the same thing. The New Jersey crew tagged her about three weeks ago off the New York Bight in 4,000 feet of water," his father explained "Al's crew named her Sophie and said she was one of the biggest girls he's tagged yet, but he never mentioned a sliced off dorsal fin. We're lucky whatever sliced it didn't take the tag."

"Could a predator take a swipe at her and slice her fin like that?" Kyle asked.

"I guess, but that's unlikely, and there are no clear teeth marks. I've never seen one like this one, cut down almost to the body. It could be due to a propeller collision, but there is no typical prop pattern that I can see. Last year we tagged a large male with a sliced off tip. Named him Buzz Cut. But this is no cut off tip. It looks more like someone has a taste for shark fin soup but didn't cut the fin very well."

"But finning's illegal, right?"

"Yeah, it is, but that's never stopped the industry or consumers, just slowed them down."

"Think she's dying because her first dorsal fin was removed?" Kyle asked.

"Not likely. Though, she probably had some trouble swimming. It looks fresh. She's got some heavy scarring on her head," Gris noted.

"Look at that," Kyle pointed. "It looks like the letter V at the based of the fin."

"Or an upside down letter A," his father added.

"Is that part of her fingerprint?" Kyle asked.

His father stopped to think about his son's question. "To identify her? I'd say so. Doesn't really look like a scar."

"Humph. What'd the New Jersey crew call her?"

"Sonic Sophie. The crew said she reached sprinting speeds up to 20 knots to elude the harpoon boat when they moved in on her to set the tag. Took them four tries to finally stick her," Gris reported. "But later they shortened it to Sophie."

Early on when the tagging program was initiated, Gris had found the ordinary "people names" given to the tagged sharks silly. Big Betty, Buzz Cut, Finner, even Elvis were some of the names bestowed to the tagged white sharks. But later when Gris learned it was program managers who usually selected names for the tagged sharks in recognition of regionally significant people or program benefactors, he could see how some would understand the value. Despite the reasoning, he still thought it amateurish and preferred scientific database labeling for the tagged sharks. If asked he would recommend the program use CCT-001, CCT-002, CCT-003, short hand for *Carcharodon carcharias*, the scientific name for white shark with its tag number in lieu of the anthropomorphic names that sounded more like those you'd find for members on a seniors dive team. But no one ever sought his opinion, so he kept his thoughts to himself.

"So how old do you think she is?" Kyle asked.

"Hard to say without sectioning her vertebrae for an accurate age estimate. But probably 40 to 50 years old," his father speculated.

"That's old," Kyle blew out with amazement. He cocked his head to the side to examine the shark's rows of nearly 3,000 razor-sharp teeth when he heard footsteps approaching.

"Heard they can slice through a man like butter," a man interrupted as he walked through the dune cut from the parking lot.

"Those mighty jaws can cut a giant tuna in half with a single strike," the man continued.

"Name's Tom Cutler." He extended a hand to Kyle who slowly reached forward to shake it. The man's name was familiar, but he couldn't place it.

Cutler kept talking. "Nothing but trouble for my brother and me, not to mention the commercial fleet."

Gris joined Kyle on the same side of the trailer where the operator untied the rope. "Really, I heard great white sharks are a welcome sight for the fleet, since they take out so many horsehead seals. You know what they say, less horseheads means less catch consumed," Gris corrected.

"Yeah . . . well, for me, the sharks are an unwelcome sight and more a pain in my ass. All they do is scare the hell out of my customers. Hard to run a dive tour on a wreck with great white sharks circling," he added.

Kyle took in the man's comments as he studied the 16-foot, 2,200-pound female shark in front of him.

No dive captain would ever be able to convince him to swim with the fish, never mind *pay* to swim with the fish.

"Actually glad to see there'll be one less circling the wreck this weekend," Cutler said. "Beginning to think I was a fool to listen to my brother Bobby's great plan to head north with my dive boat from the Bahamas."

As the man blathered about his voyage to the Cape, Kyle began to put together his identity. He thought back to his first sighting of a white shark strung up on the dock and the boastful captain who had caught the legendary "Executioner."

This guy had to be the boastful captain's brother.

"Moved my dive boat north a couple years back after a lady got her arm bit off by a big Tiger diving the Shark Wall ten miles off New Providence, Bahamas from our dive boat. All I can say is 'Thank God for signed waivers!' After that, my lady and I moved our tours to Andros Island on the outer edge of the barrier reef there, a beauty that plunges 5,900 feet down the Andros Wall into a drop-off known as the Tongue of the Ocean. Sea life was plentiful for our divers, but so were the tigers, bulls and hammerheads. So that's when my brother Bobby convinced us to head north to Cape Cod."

That's it, Tom is Bobby's brother.

Kyle and Gris continued to listen while the operator moved his excavator.

"So we hauled our butts north. First two years were great. But then 'the men in grey suits,' as you all call them up here, showed up after not being around for decades. Beginning to feel like I'm some sort of enticing fish lure for these sharks. Everywhere I go they show up. Those White Pointers, they're nothing but trouble." He shook his head before continuing.

"So what're you doing with that dead shark? Going to chop it up for chum?" He directed the question to Gris.

"Not yet. We think the shark died unexpectedly, so we're conducting a necropsy back at the Marine Fish Lab. We'll likely dump it at sea when it's completed," Gris said.

"A what?"

"Necropsy. You know, an autopsy for an animal."

"Why would you want to do that? It's just a shark. Isn't a fish allowed to just die?"

"White sharks are considered vulnerable and under protection with both the federal and state government. We've had a couple die recently, so we are running some tests to see what may have caused its death." Gris answered patiently while Kyle listened and watched.

"Sounds like a waste of money," Cutler said. "Can't we all just let a fish die without going overboard with inspecting it?"

"Sure and that happens all the time at sea. But when a fish which never approaches land beaches itself, then we usually conduct a necropsy to rule out any issues," Gris explained.

"Like illegal?"

"Yes, that's one. But more likely connected to fishing-related issues. Or maybe changes in the ecosystem like pollution that could affect their diet and health."

"Seems like a waste of time and money to me. But I guess nobody asked me...." Without even a wave, the man plodded across asphalt and climbed into his Suburban, which was wrapped in a colorful undersea image with his company's name painted over the doors in aqua-marine lettering.

"Not sure how you do this all summer, Dad."

"What's that?"

"Constantly answer questions about these fish."

"Yeah, I know. But when sharks from the tagging program start washing ashore, handling questions from the public is the least of my worries." Gris rubbed a hand across his brow.

The shark was called into police by a late afternoon jogger when he spotted her rolling in the surf at 6:00. The man said he found the huge fish writhing in the lapping waves, flexing its gills open and closed. With its magnificent jaws apart, it appeared to be gasping, but alive.

Offering to give his father a helping hand, Kyle and Dr. Kelley arrived 20 minutes after the shark had been called in to find the fish in fact alive, though moribund. Gris estimated it would pass on within the half hour. He was anxious to collect fresh samples before post-mortem effects set in.

This was the second white shark they had found in this near-death condition in last four days. The other, Gris had learned about the Friday evening of Big Betty's sighting and Larry's shark bite to the girl.

Kyle climbed onto the trailer flatbed and knelt to collect the blood vials his father was lining-up on a clean cloth. His father pushed another new vial onto the blood collection needle. He pushed at the tissue around the entry site to increase blood flow into the vial.

Over the next three minutes Kyle collected the vials one by one from his father, then zipped them into a plastic bag and placed the 15 vials into the bottom of an ice cooler. He would later spin the whole blood in a centrifuge to separate red blood cells from plasma back at the Marine Fish Laboratory. The clear, yellowish-colored plasma would be drawn from the vials and frozen in an ultra-low freezer and later analyzed for proteins, hormones, immune system cells, natural toxins, contaminants, and clinical information about the general health of the shark.

Kyle placed the small cooler containing the blood vials on the front seat of the truck and rejoined his father. Gris was collecting fresh muscle tissue samples near the base of the shark's first dorsal fin with a biopsy punch. Once finished, Gris slid down to the end of the trailer near the shark's caudal fin. He drew out a serrated filet knife to collect red muscle samples from the fish's powerful tail section.

Next, Gris ran a wider filet blade along the shark's soft abdomen. Kyle tore open two boxes; one contained gallon glass jars and plastic sample bags, and the other contained jugs of fixative. Gris intended to remove internal tissue and organs to check for reproductive maturity, stomach contents, all for contaminant testing and identification of potential lesions or disease.

Kyle worked quickly to keep pace with his father as he watched him easily segment off sections of fresh organs and deposit them into the jars and plastic bags. After another 90 minutes, Kyle and his father loaded the samples into the rear truck bed in several larger ice coolers. Then Kyle lashed the carcass to the trailer with ratchet belts. They planned to haul the huge carcass to the Marine Fish Laboratory for a full necropsy and approval from the National Marine Fisheries Service for disposal.

Gris was eager to uncover the cause of death.

EIGHT

Life's a Train Wreck

Kyle's head was pounding. It was Friday; two weeks had passed since Larry's shark bite and a week since Kyle and Lucy's high school graduation. Kyle was searching for something to soothe the ache and fill his stomach before he faced the world.

The young surfer Kyle had rescued from Larry's shark bite was released from the hospital after two operations, one lasting nearly seven hours. Though much of her right thigh muscle was torn in the attack, doctors were able to save her leg. She would be in a cast for the remainder of the summer, then onto physical therapy to regain strength.

Kyle knew the moment he stepped into the kitchen he'd run face to face with his father's line of questions on his summer employment plans. He also knew this questioning would only worsen his headache.

It wasn't the first time his father raised the subject. In fact, he'd mentioned it three other times during the final weeks of school. Each time, Kyle assured him he was working on it.

But Kyle wasn't working on it. For him, landing the perfect, most challenging, responsible summer job was not a priority. Spending time with Lucy, surfing, hanging with Brodie and other friends topped his list.

Rifling through a kitchen drawer, Kyle at last found a bottle of pain reliever and swallowed three without a drink as he braced for his father's questions.

Gris sighed with aggravation, and Kyle wondered if his mother had called. His parents had only talked face to face at his graduation when the family sat together and the day they had argued. She'd returned later that afternoon, only to find Gris gone. She left a note saying she'd be at her college roommate's for a break while the start of white shark season commenced. That was two weeks ago. With each day she was gone, his father had grown more agitated.

Finally, Gris mumbled something about delays as he read over a piece of mail. Kyle watched him run one hand through his hair and let out a soft moan.

"Bad news, Dad?" Kyle raised his eyebrows, then dropped them just a quickly when the pain returned to his temples.

"No . . . well, yes . . . but it's none of your concern, son." He tucked the folded letter back into the envelope. "Just having one of those days."

Kyle rarely saw his father in a dark mood. If it wasn't about his mother, he wondered if someone may have passed away or worse, he'd received a letter from the IRS.

"Want to talk about it?" Kyle offered, now feeling like he was the parent, as he reached for the letter.

Gris paused to consider whether he should share with Kyle the benefits the new tag promised to offer marine scientists despite its high price tag.

"About two months ago, I got the green light from the agency to order a new high-tech product known on the shark tag market as the VSAT or a Video Satellite Archival Tag. Developed by a small technology firm known as Smart Fish Acoustics, it hit the market at the end of last year," he said.

He had Kyle's full attention.

"A high technology tag like this one had never been purchased by the Marine Fish Laboratory, mostly due to its high price but also because the state usually waits a while for products to be field tested. They don't like being used as guinea pigs.

"So after six months of field testing, the studies not only confirmed it was a high-end automated tag, but it performed better than expected in the field."

"What's so great about this new tag?" Kyle asked.

"The biggest difference from any other is that it captures video of the underwater world when attached to the shark."

"That's cool, but doesn't video eat up all the storage on the tag's drive and burn the battery out fast?"

"That's another difference. It uses a rechargeable battery onboard that recharges when the circular propeller mounted on the end of the tag body whirls around as the tag drags through water."

"Now that's really cool, like ingenious cool!"

"Right, it enables marine scientists to ride along with the sharks in their underwater world from both forward facing and aft facing cameras. It's pretty amazing." Kyle watched his father's eyes light up with enthusiasm.

Kyle's eyes narrowed as he visualized the camera perspective. "Bet you feel like you're on a roller coaster at times when viewing the video. Anyone lost their lunch watching videos?"

His father let out a soft chuckle and shook his head. "Up until now we've only had PSATs or pop-off satellite archival tags to track sharks. Don't get me wrong. The PSATs have been a great workhorse for our shark-tagging program. But from a biologist's perspective they are limited. Most scientists see them as data loggers. They track the fish's movement, estimate its depth, record the water temperature and from a mapping perspective, show tracked patterns of the fish within its home range and the many habitats that includes.

"Now, the VSAT does all this, plus it records video. With video we get so much more information. We get a firsthand observation of the shark's food choices, mating habits, preferred travel routes, interactions with other fish species or other sharks and even where and how they deliver their pups. Most of these activities have never been documented.

"So you're saying with a video camera on board, the knowledge gained could be endless?" Kyle asked.

"Maybe not endless; though it has a light with the video camera, for the most part it only provides solid data during daylight hours and where the water visibility is decent. But it's a tool that will help us begin to fill in our major gaps in knowledge about where they mate, when they mate, where they deliver and if they travel or feed in groups. Come to think of it, I guess the knowledge gain could be endless," Gris finally agreed.

"This tag must be huge with a video camera on board," Kyle said.

"Actually it's only slightly larger than the PSAT model and instead of looking like a submarine-torpedo tag, it looks more like a miniature version of a remotely operated vehicle. But it's still tethered to the fish by a toggle barb that enters the shark's flesh near the base of the dorsal fin like the PSAT tag. You know, like an arrow locking it in place."

"So after a few months does the new model simply break off the fish from corrosion? Like the PSAT, so it can dump its stored data via satellite?" Kyle asked.

"No, it stays on the fish indefinitely because it has a rechargeable battery and can simply dump data anytime the fish nears the surface. So it doesn't need an actively corroding release section that pops off and floats to the surface after four to five months when it finally transmits its data."

"But you still have to wait for the shark to break the ocean's surface with its fin before any data can be uploaded by satellite to your computer, right?" Kyle asked.

"Actually it can transmit data every time the shark swims 3-5 feet below the surface, like when approaching surface prey. At that depth the long antenna whip can reach the surface and transmit the stored data."

"How much did this amazing tool set you back?" Kyle asked.

"That's the major reason why I waited. These tags are triple the cost of the PSATs and cost $9000 each."

"Whoo," Kyle bellowed at his father's answer. "That's an expensive toy, Dad."

Gris frowned at his son's choice of words. "It is. But it does so much more than any others. So I figured its scientific benefits far outweigh its cost."

Gris drummed his fingers on the kitchen table, his thoughts far away.

Kyle read the letter his father received. It relayed that the manufacturing company for the VSAT was reorganizing, and the order would be delayed. Kyle knew his father was theorizing how the delay would impact his summer shark research schedule.

Gris leaned back in his chair and balanced on two legs when his cell phone vibrated across the table. The caller ID read MARINE FISH LAB. He let the chair fall back to four legs, took the letter from Kyle, and then answered his phone.

"Kelley here."

"This is Special Agent Justin Sharpe with NOAA's Office of Law Enforcement. I'm here in town from the Northeast Division in Gloucester."

"Yes." Gris' eyes widened.

"My colleague, Agent Zimmerman from the state Fish & Game office and I were dispatched to come down to your lab this morning to get your input to help determine if there has been any criminal activity regarding some unusual activity concerning great white sharks in your area. Are you available to meet with us now?"

"Right now?" Gris checked his watch.

"Yes, sir. We can wait here at your lab or meet at your current location. Your choice."

"You mean today? Like right now, today?"

"Yes, sir. Like right now, today!" The agent didn't hide his irritation.

Gris moved the phone away from his ear and let out a soft groan. He rubbed his left temple. "Can I call you right back? I need to check on a few things," he stalled.

"No, sir. But I will hold while you verify your business."

Gris shook his head. He knew this guy had to be retired military by his use of the word *verify*. He also knew the man didn't plan on leaving town until he got what he came for and that was to speak with him.

"Agent Sharpe, it's almost 11:00 now. Can I meet you and your colleague for lunch at a local pub in an hour?"

"Yes, sir," Sharpe affirmed instantly.

"Have you been here before? I mean, are you familiar with the town?"

"No."

"The pub is called Hoolihan's. It's in the center of

town, about six miles from your location at the lab on Main Street, three blocks from the water. Can't miss it. I can meet you there a little past noon. Just give them my name, and they'll seat you at a quiet booth so we can talk. If I'm not there on time, go ahead and order, and I'll be right along. I just need to finish some business first."

"At noon. Dr. Kelley. Please bring any information you may have regarding the recent shark 'interactions,' as we've heard you refer to them."

"Right." Gris snapped his cell off. Elbows on the table, he pressed his palms against his eye sockets and let out a long sigh. When he opened his eyes, he saw the envelope from Smart Fish Acoustics on the table. He contemplated the recent call and considered how to proceed with the letter.

"Who was that?" Kyle asked.

Gris had almost forgotten Kyle was there.

"Everything okay?"

"You know . . . for all the careful planning I do, my life sure is a train wreck right now." Gris was half talking to himself, half answering Kyle.

He raised his head and looked at his son, then stood up, walked across the kitchen to grab the pot of coffee. He picked it up, searching for his mug, put the pot back on the burner, and returned to the table where he'd left the mug. *What in blazes was he doing?*

"Okay, so let's consider your options." Kyle broke the silence and redirected the conversation back to the letter. He was assuming the role of counseling his father. The role reversal made him uncomfortable.

"That was NOAA's Office of Law Enforcement calling."

"What?" Kyle was stunned. "Why?"

"One of the agents is in town with a state marine

fisheries law enforcement officer. They want to talk about the recent interactions."

"Seriously?

"Seriously. They want me to meet them for lunch at Hooligan's. I'd take you with me, but after your mother's last protest about you answering questions from the press about the rescue, I think I'll do this on my own. I'm already in hot water with her."

Gris continued pacing, clearly still processing the phone conversation with the agent.

"So Dad?" Kyle said. Gris stopped and focused on his son.

"When will the new tags be in?"

"Good question. They're not sure."

"Okay, so what are your options."

"Options? You mean for the tags?"

The news could not have come at a worse time. Now the second week in June, he had heard from a tagging program colleague that seven of the 44 currently tagged white sharks, including all the newly tagged fish from this summer, were lighting up his computer screen with green location dots. The fish were on a steady course north into Gris's territory, likely in search of prey. Gris estimated their arrival in a week or less.

"There are no options, Kyle. My hands are tied. It's too late to switch equipment. We've already seen Big Betty and Larry, had Sophie wash ashore and heard from herring fishermen about the death of another white shark at sea. More sharks will be heading here this week."

"How did your biologist friend in New Jersey get his new tags so quickly?"

"You mean Al Yates?"

Kyle nodded.

"His were delivered in late April just after the

company was purchased and was rehiring. But only because he told them some sharks had been spotted in his region as early as April last year. They told him the dozen tags he'd get were only good for field-testing and may have a few glitches because the full-production manufacturing hadn't really begun. I guess none of his tags were ever run through a quality control check. Two of the twelve he received arrived not calibrated, so he was going to return them. He said he only has two left."

Kyle considered the situation. His father was right; he was stuck. Smart Fish Acoustics was the only company that manufactured the VSAT tags, and its design was proprietary. It was also the principal tool for his father's summer research. With the tags on backorder, all his father could do was wait and use inventory of the older PSAT tags from last summer.

The initial 18 months of startup for the underwater acoustic telemetry company, Smart Fish Acoustics, were solid. The new high-tech company specialized in ultrasonic receivers designed for tracking aquatic animals from boats or shore-based laboratories. They had been basking in the success of record-breaking results, with investors ecstatic about the overnight success of the company, until the firm decided to launch another new product.

After the introduction of the company's VSAT, however, the business began seeing losses. The tags were expensive to manufacture and the technology complex. Some said the company was rolling out new products too rapidly. Others blamed mismanagement of funds within the firm. Some even hinted at embezzlement.

Whatever the case, by the fourth quarter of its second year, earnings slowed, and by the first quarter of its third year, earnings crumbled. The 80-person company, composed mostly of engineers, technicians, and a few sales staff, tumbled quickly from comfortable earnings in the black to crisis losses in the red. Notification letters were sent to all buyers stating their orders were on hold while the company reorganized.

Laying off all but three of its employees during the same week, the CFO now operated with a skeletal staff to keep the company buoyant. He began reaching out to his business colleagues, past contacts and previous employers to seek advice on how to end the company's financial hemorrhage and launch a plan to get it back on track. Though optimistic that the business could move toward stabilization, the CFO could not be sure. So he quietly hatched a rumor that the company intended to file bankruptcy by the end of March.

By late March, the CFO's plan had worked. He was fielding two calls from prospective buyers interested in taking over the fledging acoustics group prior to entering receivership. By the middle of the month, the new ownership went to the highest bidder, one of the largest chemical and pharmaceutical conglomerates in the U.S. The takeover was swift and keenly orchestrated by the conglomerate's stable of attorneys to close the deal.

Initially, under the new ownership, all sales account managers were instructed to accompany each new order for delivery as a show of the group's good faith. It was an opportunity to quell any concerns about product quality and assure customers the company's financial troubles had ended. All orders would be filled no later than the third week in June. As an incentive to retain its customers, the group even provided a 25 percent discount voucher to all current orders and any reorders within the next three months.

The good news was that Smart Fish Acoustics was

back in business and ready to distribute its hot new product.

NINE

Lunch to go

Gris was running late for his meeting with the two agents. He walked briskly to the back room past the booths to a corner table where two men in crisp white button down shirts and ties were seated. As he approached the table, the two special agents stood.

"Dr. Griswold Kelley?"

"Yes."

"I'm Special Agent Sharpe from NOAA's Office of Law Enforcement." The man shook Gris's hand firmly.

"Call me Gris."

Sharpe nodded. "This is Agent Tom Zimmerman from the Boston office of the state's Fish & Game."

Gris extended his hand again. He noticed both men's handshakes delivered a firm grip. They were also awkwardly slow on the shake, forcing Gris to meet their eyes and slow down his hurried movements. He knew this was on purpose. It forced Gris to focus and give them his full attention.

"Our query is not yet part of an official investigation, but we would like to ask you about the recent shark interactions." Sharpe's voice was a monotone.

Gris ran his hand slowly through his disheveled hair and noticed how meticulously combed Sharpe's was.

Standing behind two seats Gris waited for the men to sit back down.

"Please have a seat." Sharpe gestured to both empty chairs in front of him.

As Gris settled, he remained quiet. He was meeting them at their request. He would wait for them to start.

"Thanks for coming. We only ordered drinks." Sharpe waved over a waitress. "We can order now."

All three ordered the lunch special, and when the waitress left, Sharpe resumed speaking.

"We were briefed by the director at the state's Fish & Game office," Sharpe said. "It is our understanding you are in charge of the great white shark tagging program here."

"I'm not in charge of the program." Gris set the record straight. "I work with a team of biologists and pathologists throughout the Northeast. I merely order the tags and coordinate the offshore component with harpoon captains to tag the sharks since the fish come here to feed on-horseheads."

"Horseheads?" Sharpes asked.

"*Halichoerus grypus* is its Latin name, more commonly known as the gray seal. Though the Latin translates to "hook-nosed pig of the sea," most locals think the seal's head looks like the shape of a horse's head, especially a full-grown adult."

"Never heard that before," Sharpe cocked his head then cleared his throat and resumed his questioning. "What can you tell us about the great white shark tagging that has occurred this summer so far?"

"We haven't conducted any," Gris answered.

"What about the interactions that have occurred? These were tagged great white sharks, are they not?" Sharpe pressed.

"Yes, they are part of groups of sharks tagged on the Atlantic coast. But none were tagged here. Our work has yet to begin because our order for the newer

VSAT tags was delayed, through no fault of our own."

"If you think there are no links between the shark deaths and the great white shark interactions occurring in your waters so far this summer, then what is your opinion?" Sharpe drummed the table with the fingers of his right hand.

"White shark," Gris corrected.

Sharpe stared at him before tilting his head, "Pardon?"

"Their common name is simply white shark. People commonly refer to them as *great* white sharks because of their size and daunting appearance. But the shark's name is white shark," Gris explained as if to a child.

Sharpe leaned back in his chair and folded his arms across his chest.

Gris could tell the man didn't appreciate the correction. "There have been three interactions this summer with white sharks in our waters. Though none were tagged by our boat crew, all the sharks involved in the interactions were either tagged during previous summers or were recently tagged by the biologists out of our sister lab in New Jersey. To my knowledge none of the sharks tagged in Florida this last spring have been spotted in our region yet."

"So they were tagged in New Jersey, but are now here? Or were here at the time of their deaths?" Sharpe was still struggling to get the story right.

"Correct. They were tagged in waters off New York and New Jersey and have since traveled north into our waters." Gris spoke with forced patience.

"How many shark deaths?" Zimmerman asked.

"Two that stranded ashore on which we conducted necropsies. One other died at sea, presumed dead but not confirmed."

Sharpe started to open his mouth then closed it when Gris continued.

"The first was a 16-footer that washed ashore on

one of the Nantucket Sound beaches with significant head scarring, a cut off dorsal fin, and moribund upon arrival. She has been identified as Sophie, tagged in May by the New Jersey crew. I just received video clips from the days leading up to her stranding.

"The second shark, a 12-footer named Finner, was reported to us by a herring captain who encountered him on Georges Bank while he was trawling. The captain said Finner exhibited abnormal behavior," Gris continued.

"Abnormal?" Zimmerman interrupted.

"He breached near the herring boat, swam on his back for a long distance, and rammed the side of a trawl net at 20 knots, tearing it open. Though he became entangled in the net, he was released alive. One of the crew snapped a few photos of Finner. I was able to view them to confirm the fish was in fact released alive. The white shark had heavy scarring on its head and torso and a severed dorsal fin. The day after Finner was first spotted, another herring boat captain called the same fish in to the Coast Guard when he saw it near the outer edge of Georges Banks floating belly up, bloated with the releases of gases after apparently dying. A few hours later, the same fisherman saw it again, this time two miles away where it sank out of sight, apparently dying."

The waitress approached the table with three plates of food balanced in the curve of one arm. Leaning forward, she doled out each plate to the men and waited for any other orders when Sharpe waved her away.

"Apparently dying?" Sharpe asked.

"Yes, apparently," Gris repeated.

"So its death is unconfirmed?" Sharpe ignored the hot food in front of him as he cross-examined Gris.

Gris unraveled utensils from his napkin. "The captain could only infer it was dead. He found the shark belly-up, bloated and sinking."

"Was it moving in the water?" Sharpe asked.

"He didn't say."

"Did he conclude it was dead because it was belly up?"

"Likely and maybe the odor. But I really can't guess at what the fisherman was thinking."

"Because I've seen researchers hold sharks on their backs for a few minutes, then flip them, and the sharks seem fine and swim away," Sharpe said.

Gris eyed the man and thought about asking if those instances included fish which were bloated and malodorous, too, but refrained from scrutinizing Sharpe's facts further.

"Not white sharks. These sharks can't remain belly up for very long. They need to be moving water across their gills or they will asphyxiate."

Sharpe and Zimmerman both nodded at Gris' answer.

After a long draw on his soda, Gris continued. "The last interaction was a shark bite at an ocean beach. A 10-foot white shark identified as Larry bit a girl who was surfing at sunrise. A person who witnessed the interaction said the fish had scrapes on its head and was swimming erratically."

Sharpe pushed his plate aside and wrote quickly in his notepad.

"First Larry pushed the girl off her board, then he swam on his back for 40 yards belly up and then came back to attack the girl while she tried to swim ashore," Gris finished and drew in a deep breath.

"I read about that one in the paper," Zimmerman said.

"Is that fish dead, too?" Sharpe asked, holding his pen still.

"It's unknown, but Larry hasn't shown up on our shores or been spotted since the interaction."

"Were all these fish tagged this summer?" Zimmerman asked.

"All except Big Betty,"

"Who?" Sharpe asked.

"Big Betty. Our crew tagged her two summers ago. Shortly after her tagging, she disappeared. About four months later she lit up our computer screens as she moved down the coast around the Florida peninsula into Gulf of Mexico waters off Texas. With her ambling route, she had traveled almost 13,000 miles. This is Betty's third summer in our waters."

Sharpe flipped a page on his pad. "I don't have a Big Betty. Was she a fourth interaction?" He lifted his eyes from the page to Gris.

"No, but she was spotted directly in the vicinity near Larry during his interaction with the young girl surfer," Gris answered, focusing on his plate.

"Did Big Betty also atta...I mean interact with the girl?" Sharpe corrected himself.

"No."

Zimmerman interjected, "So all of these sharks were tagged this summer in New Jersey, right?"

Gris nodded. "Yeah, Al Yates's crew was the only one who got the new VSAT tags. Like I mentioned, we're still waiting for our delivery."

"And all of these fish had scarring on their heads and torsos, right?"

Gris nodded.

"And all of these fish exhibited what you call abnormal behavior?" Zimmerman continued.

"Not all," Gris stopped Zimmerman questioning. "Not Betty or Sophie. That's confirmed from the video footage of Betty, but we haven't seen the footage from the New Jersey lab on Sophie."

"Okay, but Sophie had scars on her head and torso, right?" Zimmerman repeated.

Gris nodded again. "Yes, most whites have scarring or marks on their bodies to some degree, but these were numerous and appeared to be fresh."

"How about the sliced off dorsal fins? How many

had sliced fins?"

"Three. Finner, Larry and Sophie. Betty had no fin damage."

"The sliced fins concern me. Finning is a federal offense. White shark dorsal fins are worth a lot of money on the black market. Do you think those dorsal fins were sliced off intentionally?"

"Hard to say," Gris said. "We've seen sharks in the past with tips sliced off from propeller collisions. It's well known that whites and many other shark species can be attracted to the electric field emitted by an outboard motor and have been seriously injured when they approach a motor with the propeller in gear. But these—"

"These what?" Sharpe asked.

"Well, the slices don't look like the markings of propeller collisions. And it's unclear if the cuts were deliberate—like fin removals. There are some rough edges and what may be infections, but it's just difficult to tell."

"Is that your scientific opinion? That the dorsal fins on these sharks were purposely removed and didn't occur by accident from say a propeller hit?"

"No. I mean there is no way to be sure. I don't know why anyone would go to the massive effort to catch a white and only take the first dorsal anyway. Someone selling fins would take all the fins, or at least the quads, not just the first dorsal. It's just that—"

"Just what?" Sharpe didn't let up.

"The fin cuts are deep and jagged and close to the shark's body, not high up on the tip. In some cases they almost looked seared, like the tissue was burned or cauterized. Or at least it appears that way. From all my years working these animals, I've never come across anything like it," Gris finished.

Sharpe leaned over and whispered something to Zimmerman while Gris waited.

"Dr. Kelley, the information you shared has been

enlightening, particularly the fin removals. We have an undercover team examining finning in our region. Because finning is an international practice, the FBI is also involved. I'm sure all would be interested in your findings."

"Okay." Gris nodded slowly at the mention of the FBI.

"Would you be willing to speak to the FBI about your findings?" Sharpe asked.

"I . . . I don't have any findings," Gris corrected.

"But you are willing to speak with the FBI, right?"

Gris thought hard. "I don't think it's necessary to speak with the FBI at this date. Especially when I don't have any definitive answers about the condition of the shark fins."

"Dr. Kelley, I don't see it that way. Working alongside and knowing these agents at the FBI, I can tell you they won't see it that way either."

Gris's eyes widened.

Sharpe continued. "My director is a man who doesn't like to make waves unless he has to. He appreciates his men working alongside other federal agents when there is the potential for an international infraction, like finning."

Gris wiped sweaty palms against his jeans and swallowed his churning stomach into place at Sharpe's subtle threat.

"Now, can I tell my director that you are willing to provide information to the FBI agents working on the undercover finning operation? Or is there something you are trying to hide?"

The agent's threat drew a glare from Gris. If only he could travel back in time to take back the comments about fins!

Sharpe was on a manhunt. By sharing a peculiar observation, Gris had somehow become Sharpe's target, a vehicle to uncover and arrest the FBI's finning suspect. Never mind the fact that Sharpe's plan could destroy Gris' professional reputation, or worse, put Gris' life in jeopardy.

TEN

It's Company Policy

The next morning came early with a call from harpoon boat captain Vinnie Mancini, who told Gris and Kyle to meet him at the town fish docks within the hour. Mancini's crew had good news from the video satellite tagging company. The company's financial woes had been settled, and the high-tech tags would be hand-delivered by a company salesman at 5:30 that morning.

Mancini's boat crew was scheduled to work all day with a spotter plane to find white sharks and guide the boat to the fish. They were running behind schedule since the first sighting of Big Betty nearly two weeks ago. It was time to burn the daylight hours and tag as many white sharks as possible over the next two months while the big fish feasted on seals in local near-shore waters.

Though surprised, Gris was pleased by the early wake up call. Just a few weeks earlier, he'd received a troubling letter from Smart Fish Acoustics' CFO explaining their company's troubling financial matters. The letter was followed by a sales call two days later reiterating the new VSAT tag order would be delayed. A subsequent call assured Gris the order was back on track, but a date of delivery was still pending. So this news from Mancini raised Gris' spirits. Even better, it pulled him away from the empty house where his mind was consumed by

111

thoughts of Audrey.

Knowing his son had no plans for a summer job, two day after graduation, Gris had offered Kyle a summer job as a deckhand and lab tech processing white shark blood and tissue samples. He would also assist with tagging. Kyle's first thought was of how he would reek of fish all summer. His second thought was the low pay. His last thought was the long hours. It would pull him away from Lucy, and he'd never get time to hang with Brodie.

Assuring his father he'd secure a good job, Kyle declined. The truth was, he was aiming for a more carefree, less responsible summer position. Kyle remembered how his father bit his lower lip to control his urge to lecture Kyle about responsibility. But it was the change in his father's tack that caught Kyle by surprise. Gris acknowledged the long hours and informed him of the high hourly wage. It was more than Kyle expected and it enticed him. After a few minutes Kyle rescinded his original answer and took the job.

With the early wakeup call from the boat captain, Kyle rolled over when his father woke him at 5:00 am to meet the boat by 5:30. He was now rethinking the hours and the job. The only lure was the money. Was he really going to take a job just for the money? *Yes.*

By midafternoon Gris was still aboard the harpoon boat. He'd be late for the town's executive council closed-door meeting. He usually called Audrey on the radio to be a messenger when he was at sea or running late. Tonight, the mayor, who had requested his presence, would have to improvise until he arrived.

Random thoughts of Audrey bounced in and out of Gris's mind throughout the day. She'd been so angry the day she walked out. Once a celebrated season, she now despised the frenzy that summers brought into their lives. She called the invasion of the press a 'three-ring-circus,' a jumbled mess that interrupted their once peaceful, balanced life. She's been even more than angry when the press had come to their home after Kyle had rescued Annie. Gris couldn't get the image of Audrey alarmed face out of his mind—the moment she realized that perhaps her greatest fear had occurred: Gris had chosen his occupation over her.

Now gone 15 days, Audrey's presence in the house was everywhere. He could barely sleep; her scent lingering on their bed sheets was driving him crazy.

Married 26 years, Audrey had met Gris their first year of college. The two got off to a rocky start. At eighteen, Gris was exceptionally striking with a slim build, broad shoulders, and blue, piercing eyes. One look at Gris and Audrey's heart raced and her skin tingled. But she downplayed her interest and kept their conversation to classwork and campus happenings while she tried to determine if he was a player. He certainly had enough girls fawning over him.

Despite being ogled constantly by female classmates, Gris appeared disinterested. Instead, he was determined to engage Audrey, striking up any conversation to pique her interest.

Audrey had a difficult time ignoring the persistent gazes and head turns from girls each time he came around. The whispers and giggles drove her mad. Some girls even followed him around campus. Unable to cope with the borderline stalking, Audrey decided it was best to maintain an arms-length relationship with Gris.

Until one snowy afternoon in early spring.

Audrey had ducked into a restaurant doorway to avoid being sprayed by a passing snowplow. She heard her name called and turned to see Gris waving at her in the back of the almost deserted place that was more pub than restaurant.

Gris was holed up in a corner booth, his notebooks open and papers splayed across the table.

He'd watched Audrey cross the quiet pub dining room, still bundled in her heavy coat, scarf and mittens. He'd smiled and commented on her reddened nose, then insisted she stay for a cup of cocoa before returning to brave the cold.

He'd explained he was cramming for midterms because back at his apartment, his roommates were involved in watching a rowdy game of football on television. He'd told Audrey that he needed a quiet place to focus on his studies.

Without the distractions from others buzzing around, Audrey had found Gris funny, smart and extremely interested in her. That was it for her. Within weeks, they were inseparable, studying together, eating together, and walking everywhere together. Their courtship lasted through graduate school and first jobs.

One day an old flame reappeared in Audrey's life. Gris was introduced and immediately read the guy's intentions. Gris remembered how frantic he'd been over the idea of losing Audrey to another man. He proposed, and they were married three months later.

Audrey had always feared that Gris' obsession with his job would drive a wedge between them. So here he was, proving her right. Audrey was gone, and he'd just spent his entire day on a boat searching for white sharks.

A radio call came in from the spotter plane around four o'clock with coordinates for a shark about two miles south of their current location.

Captain Mancini pushed both twin engines levers down, planing off the heavy harpoon boat in less than a minute and steaming forward to meet the aircraft that hovered over a 14-foot female white shark.

Spotting it from the boat's tuna tower, Mancini called to his first mate that he needed to prep the harpoon on approach to the huge fish. Nimbly climbing the tower and taking over the twin engines, the first mate throttled back the heavy boat. It settled back down in the water as the engines lost their scream, revving down from thirteen to three knots. Instantly the boat's impressive rooster tail disappeared, replaced by a tame wake of whitewater churning out slosh that resembled a boiling pot of water.

Now positioned on the bow, Kyle pointed to the triangular dorsal fin ahead. He watched as the white shark shimmered a foot below the surface just beyond the bow wake. Her wide girth was profiled by the afternoon sun as she repeated an s-curve at four knots along a tidal rip formed a day earlier by wind shear. Preoccupied by her appetite, she hunted her next meal along the rip.

The wind had died down in the late afternoon, leaving the captain near-perfect conditions to maneuver his boat's 20-foot pulpit overtop the fish. It would give Mancini, the harpooner, a clean shot to stick the video tag barb into the base of her dorsal fin.

Gris had met Vinnie as a young man working aboard the Kelley commercial fleet when Mancini had first acquired his own sword fishing boat 21 years earlier. Even as a child, Kyle had enjoyed the burly sword fisherman's rogue humor.

Gris was on board to oversee all research operations, including tagging and collection of blood and tissue samples from any shark caught by hook and line.

Gris had yet to meet the shark tag salesman onboard, but he'd caught a glimpse of him. He looked vaguely familiar. After delivering the box of new tags to the dock, the salesman insisted he come along for the first few trips as a symbol of his company's commitment to the product and the program. Since Mancini had room aboard, the captain allowed it.

When Gris got wind of a salesman escorting the tagging trip, he became wary. Not only did Gris find the man's assertions odd but also irksome. Kyle read his father's face and could see he was miffed.

"So tell me—Mr. Kane, is it?" Gris extended his hand to the salesman. "Tell me about this proprietary technology."

"What about it?"

"This is the first I've heard of the proprietary technology and need for any company reps to come aboard. Is it necessary?"

Kane nodded. "I am aboard at the request of our CEO. He wants to assure our buyers of the company's commitment to our products. He asked that staff who have completed the acoustical engineering graduate course be available to answer any questions," Kane said, obviously intent on proving his expertise.

"Can you tell me why the toggle barb is florescent orange? I don't remember it being that color when ordering."

"The toggle is painted with an anti-corrosion coating that carries a new lifetime warranty."

Gris nodded then turned on his heel. "Sounds like bullshit to me," he murmured to Kyle. "When I ordered these VSAT tags, there was never any mention of a proprietary technology or anti-corrosive coatings." Gris continued in a deliberately low voice edged with irritation. He hated corporate or government waste, despised redundancy and had little patience for the misuse of time or money.

"Let it go, Dad. So he's aboard for a few trips. I bet the CEO drops the condition halfway through the summer when they see sales drop because all the salesmen are out on boats fishing. We'll probably see him two or three more times, and then poof, we never see him again."

Kyle watched Mancini grip the tag from Kane's hand and walk onto the pulpit where the 12-foot fiberglass harpoon pole was lashed to the rail.

The captain waved his mate forward, and he responded with a slight push on the throttle for both engines and a higher pitch roar of the engine. The white shark was now on the starboard side.

Tag in hand, Mancini walked and few more steps out onto the 20-foot pulpit. He unlashed the two ties holding the long harpoon pole from the pulpit rail. Laying the hollow flexible pole along the inside rail, he walked to the end of the pulpit in preparation of loading the tag holder into the pole tip.

First he slipped two tight rubber bands over the pole about two feet from the hollow end. Moving back to the open end he slid the sharp shark tag tip holder into the open pole end and threaded the shark tag securely into place. Then he rolled the rubber bands over the tag body away from the sharp tip that would pierce the shark's skin and allow the barb to implant.

Once the tag was set into the skin, he would yank a rope attached about halfway up the pole away from the shark. With the yank, both rubber bands would snap open, allowing the fish to swim away with the tag securely attached.

Now mounted and ready, Mancini focused his full attention on the large female shark 30 feet directly in front of the pulpit but too far for him to throw the harpoon with any accuracy.

Mancini waved to his first mate up on the fly bridge to slowly throttle forward. He then climbed onto the angled foot rest at the end of the pulpit. The box allowed him to catch the rail at his hip and hang outward three feet beyond the boat to see the fish below.

It wasn't the most secure or comfortable position. If attempted without years of training, most fishermen would find themselves overboard. But for Mancini, it was a customary position for throwing the long stick forward into the base of the dorsal.

The boat slowly bobbed forward at two knots. Startled by the boat's approaching shadow, the shark darted right. Keeping his eyes on the fish, Mancini held the pole in one hand and signaled to his mate to move right. He pointed to the fish with the sharp end of the pole.

The boat slowly rotated 90 degrees to the right. Mancini continued pointing. The boat crept at a slow pace and rocked from side to side when it crossed over its own wake.

Mancini lifted the harpoon stick out over the fish. She was within range to throw the harpoon. The boat bobbed closer, now ten feet. Closer still, six feet. Finally over top, Mancini leaned out as far as he could.

Kyle watched him tip back and forth on the rail with his feet lifting off the step. He was sure the captain would be in the water soon, eye to eye with a 14-foot angry white shark.

Kyle's jaw hurt, and he realized he was clenching it as he focused on Mancini.

The shark swam to the right, her movement taking her 10 feet away. Mancini pointed the end of the pole to the fish and the first mate ground the portside twin engine forward while the starboard side remained idle.

Mancini lifted his head up, tipped it sideways, signaling his mate. He then raised a hand to stop all engines. The boat coasted to a stop directly over the fish. Mancini adjusted his grip, pulled back the harpoon as if he was throwing a javelin and threw the pole straight into the shark's back. A perfect hit!

Mancini rocked back onto the step and yanked on the fastened rope attached to the fiberglass pole to retrieve the harpoon stick and snap the rubber bands free from the tag.

Kyle leaned over the bow rail and watched as the fish waggled from side to side then darted ahead of the boat. Like a pro, Mancini had set in the best location, about two inches away from the dorsal fin base.

They knew she would flee the area to shake off the assault and return to feed in a week when her stomach rumbled.

"She's tag #47. Got a name for the old girl?" Mancini asked Gris.

"No, I didn't get any list of names from the program staff, so I guess we're on our own. Did you see any unusual markings on her?" Gris asked.

"Nothing unusual. Didn't see any slash marks on her head or cuts to her fins. For that matter, I didn't see any significant marks. As the first of the season, I would say she's a real beauty," Mancini said.

"If we have to use names and can't just refer to these fish with numbers, I think it only appropriate we call her Audrey Marie, after my patient wife," Gris pronounced.

Mancini let out a hearty laugh while Kyle smirked.

"You sure it won't stir any trouble for you when she hears you named a large white shark after her?" Mancini asked.

"Well, when you put it that way, she could. But I'll stick with tradition. It's known to bring good luck to name your fishing vessels after your woman. So I think it appropriate I name the first shark of the season after my Audrey. What'd you think, Kyle?" Gris glanced to Kyle who quickly wiped the smirk from his face.

"Oh, no, you don't. You're not dragging me into this. You picked her name. You own it. If she doesn't like it, then it's your butt. Not mine." He waved to his father and walked toward the wet lab.

Gris chuckled at his son. "Then Audrey Marie she is."

Mancini climbed down from the pulpit and walked to the ship's lab, where Kyle was waiting for the satellite signal's green blip to appear on the laptop.

Gris slapped his son on the back when the green blink glowed.

The VSAT tag recorded location via a satellite-tracking chip, showing the shark's current longitude-latitude coordinates within 800 feet when the shark finned at the surface. The video would come on line once the battery charged.

Gris reached out to shake Mancini's calloused hand and praise his friend who was accompanied by the salesman.

"Gris, this is Jon Kane of Smart Fish Acoustics," Mancini offered.

"Yes, we've met. I received a full briefing on the new VSAT tag and its proprietary technology." Gris thought about the salesman's name. It didn't ring a bell, but he was sure he knew the face.

"Have we met before? I mean before today?"

"Not a chance. I'm new in town," Kane said in a low voice.

"Well, then you must have a twin living nearby. I never forget a face." Gris laughed.

The salesman looked away.

"Mr. Kane, will you be joining us for future trips?" Mancini asked.

Kane looked toward Mancini, "Yes, all trips that will employ our new VSAT video tag."

"All trips. Does your company have the time for you to be aboard on all trips? I mean, we have a heavy season this summer with many early morning departures."

"The choice is not mine. Our new tags utilize a proprietary technology that protect against corrosion. Since this coating is proprietary, company officials want either an acoustical engineer or a salesman aboard to answer any questions." Kane sounded as if he were reciting a corporate edict.

"Are you a salesman or acoustical engineer? Mancini asked.

Gris listened for his response.

"Both. Many of our sales reps have advanced training in acoustical mechanics and engineering, including myself. The company's new owners require all sales managers to be knowledgeable about our products and insist on the completion of a graduate-level course prior to representing our products."

Gris considered his answer and pondered the costs of graduate course training. No wonder the company was in financial trouble.

The salesman took advantage of the interruption and moved away, pulling his cell phone from his pocket.

Gris stood next to Kyle and surreptitiously eyed Kane. He watched him dial and respond to someone on the other end.

Gris checked his own cell phone. No bars. How it was even possible for Kane to get cell coverage this far from shore since most cell towers only provided a half-mile reach? And why did he look so darned familiar?

ELEVEN

Brief Exchange

After a hectic day aboard the harpoon boat that started at sunrise on the fish docks and ended after sunset, Gris was running late. He'd promised the mayor he'd attend an important meeting, but first he needed to stop by the house two blocks from the fish docks to call his fin industry contact. He wanted to know if any of the three sliced fins had been reported and if he could forward photos to him. The more he thought about the dead sharks, the more he pondered whether the fin removals played any role in their deaths.

Kyle voted down his father's plan. After a fifteen-hour day, Kyle knew Gris needed food to continue functioning. So he let his father walk home while he took the truck into town to the pub where Lucy worked. He'd grab some hot sandwiches before picking up his father to head to the meeting. He had missed Lucy all day and needed to connect with her.

Kyle parked the truck along the street near the bar entrance and spotted Lucy through the front windows working the bar area overflowing with patrons willing to eat their dinner on barstools. He walked in and waved to her. She nodded to her customers as she passed out menus then strode toward Kyle. He grabbed her hand, kissed it and walked to the back wall to order food.

"Can you put in for a couple sandwiches while I watch you work?"

"Anything for you," she smiled then wrote down his order. As she walked away, he grabbed her hand again and twirled her back for a small kiss but didn't let go of her hand. Placing both hands on his chest, she indulged him, giving him the extra moment to linger.

"You smell like the ocean, and you look sunburned." She ran her fingers through his unruly hair. "You been surfing?"

"I wish. Been on a harpoon boat all day looking for fish."

"Find any?"

"Yeah," he nodded. She gave him another minute to rub her hands before interrupting.

"Kyle, I've got customers and need to put in your order. Especially if you're in a hurry."

"I'm in no hurry. It's Dad who's in the hurry."

"Ah, right." She raised her eyebrows and glided out of his reach. "Between you and Brodie stopping by, I'm having a tough time getting any work in today," she complained while flipping through her orders.

"Brodie stopped in?"

"Yeah, with Alicia for a late breakfast or early lunch."

Kyle cocked his head to one side. "Didn't you see him last night?"

"Yeah, he was in here with Chloe."

"Dating two girls at one time. That guy's headed for nothing but trouble."

"You think he cares? I mean, it's not like he has any trouble reeling in the women. One flash of that megawatt smile, and girls go weak in the knees." Lucy caught the beginning of a frown on Kyle's brow. "Not me, of course. I'm just saying, I've seen girls get all dewy-eyed and blush when he shows off those teeth.

124

I've even seen some fan themselves when he walks by."

Kyle's lips turned downward.

"Not me, of course," she added.

"Of course." Kyle grabbed Lucy and planted his lips on hers for a possessive kiss. "Now, who were we talking about?"

"I don't remember." Lucy smiled, touching her lips, then with obvious reluctance, pulled away. "Darn, I have to get back to work."

Satisfied with her reaction, Kyle flashed her his smile and walked toward the bar out of the worn paths of the servers and leaned against the wall. He crossed his ankles and watched Lucy move from customer to customer, offering a reassuring nod and wide white smile. *No wonder she makes so much in tips. Who could resist that sweet smile and those dimples? Damn.*

He dropped his gaze toward the floor to rub his neck when he heard a familiar voice. "Mister Kelle . . . we meet again." Jon Kane sat at the bar where a beer and two whiskey shots lined up in front of him. Kyle gave him a chin lift and decided against any small talk. He looked away to watch Lucy move through her tables.

"Know her?" Kane persisted.

Kyle shrugged. Kane accepted his response and fixed his eyes on Lucy. Kyle didn't appreciate his gawking. In fact, it was infuriating to watch. Then Kyle reminded himself that Kane might be doing it to get a rise out of him.

After a few minutes, Kyle's phone vibrated. It was Lucy. His food was ready. He told her he'd meet her near the kitchen.

When he got there he took the packed food bag from her and tugged her elbow. "Meet me in the Ladies' Room."

"What? Kyle, I'm *super* busy. Can we do this

another time?"

"Meet me there," he repeated in a more demanding tone. "It will only take a minute," he gritted out, his mouth pressed to her ear. Kyle stepped back to allow her to pass down the hall then slipped into the restroom behind her.

"Kyle, you're acting odd. So what's this all about?"

"I want you to watch your back tonight."

"What? Why?"

"I want you to watch yourself when you leave work tonight."

She rolled her eyes. "Watch myself?"

"Yeah, like when you leave, go with a group of people so they can keep an eye on you."

"I can take care of myself."

"Ah . . . right. . ." He thought about her answer and decided not to run through the litany of examples to remind her exactly how oblivious and innocent she had been another time.

Lucy studied Kyle's face.

"I didn't want to scare you, but you aren't listening."

She tucked her food list into her apron and crossed her arms over her chest. She had customers waiting and didn't have time to challenge his opinions.

"Look, there's a guy at the bar. You'll see him when you get back to your tables. He has greasy black, medium length hair, pock marks on his cheeks and jaw, and narrow, cagey green eyes."

Her eyes widened at his description. "Sounds attractive," she muttered. "Kyle, why are you telling me this?"

"He's the salesman who sold Dad the shark tags. He was with me on the harpoon boat today and is seriously a weird dude. Not weird, more like creepy." He now had Lucy's full attention. "Anyway, while I was at the bar waiting for my order, I noticed him watching you. He also asked if I knew you, but I didn't answer."

"Kyle, you're freaking me out. Why are you telling me this?" she repeated again.

"I don't trust him." He paused.

"I'm sure he's just bored hanging at the bar with no one to talk to. Lots of people hang at the bar and people watch," Lucy offered. Kyle raised his eyebrows at her attempt to discount his concern and give Kane the benefit of the doubt.

"Just do me a favor and have one of the bar bouncers walk you to your car tonight, okay?"

"Okay, okay. Now can I get back to work or is there more?"

"Yeah. Pick you up later at your house?" He leaned in to kiss her and got her cheek when she turned away. She was irritated with him, but he ignored it and pulled her back to meet his face. "You're probably right. Just because I got bad vibes from him on the boat today, doesn't mean he's a bad guy. Most likely he just thinks you're nice to look at, which you are, and he's just taking in the view like so many other guys."

Lucy's mouth popped open. "Kyle, I do not have guys watching me. I would know it if I did."

"Luce, you do. I have seen them for years."

She pressed her lips together and turned away. She was not only irritated with him but also freaked out by his observations.

"Okay, so never mind what I said. Just do me that favor and have someone walk you to your car. Okay?"

She nodded in solemn agreement. He pulled her toward him and wrapped his arms around her. "Luce, you're safe. You're with me," he murmured into her hair. "Just text me when you're done, yeah? I'll head over after you clean up. Yeah?"

"'Kay," she whispered. He squeezed her again then lifted her chin and kissed her gently.

The short order cook pushed open the door and hollered Lucy's number, "Order's up, Number 5."

"See you later." She spoke into his lips, then broke from his embrace and rushed to the kitchen.

~

As Gris walked up the hill from the fish docks he thought about how much he wanted to mend the rift with Audrey and hoped she had returned home early. But when he arrived at the house, he found no sign of her. What he did find was the same note she'd left earlier in the week saying she'd return to town tomorrow evening.

The sound of Kyle's truck pulling into the driveway diverted his thoughts. He heard his son take the rear steps two at a time and push the door open.

"You're here," Kyle said, catching his breath.

"Wanted to see if your Mom stopped by. Only thing here is her note saying she'll be back in town tomorrow evening."

Kyle dropped the bag of hot sandwiches on the counter and turned to meet his father's solemn face.

"She doesn't seem to be budging," Gris said, running a hand through his hair.

"Yeah, well, can't blame her," Kyle blurted out, then realized how harsh his comment was.

"What'd you mean, you can't blame her? I never intended to hurt her. You boys know that."

"Yeah, but Dad, the last couple years your work tagging these fish has sort of taken over." Kyle softened his tone.

"Taken over? What, our lives?' Gris paused. "Has it been that bad?"

"Not if you like living with a rock star." Kyle pulled the sandwiches out of the bag, the scent of hot roast beef escaping.

His father's eyes widened.

"Yeah, it's great for the rocker, the groupies and concert goers, but miserable for the rest, like the families on the road or at home." Kyle threw his father a quick glance. "I guess you don't get it, do you?"

"When you put it that way, I do," Gris admitted then swiftly changed the subject. He needed to think about his son's observations. If they were true, then he needed to hear it from Audrey.

"So, I need to drop off these blood samples at the Marine Fish Laboratory headquarters," Gris said.

"Dad, if I take it over tomorrow morning, will you do all of us all a favor?"

His father looked at his son and waited.

"Will you stop looking for a place to hide your head in the sand? Take an hour and bring some lunch over to the place where Mom's staying. Talk to her."

Gris stared at Kyle for a long moment. "I'll think about it." He didn't sound convinced.

"Seriously," Kyle's voice was louder. "You need a plan."

"I have a plan," Gris snapped. He didn't want to discuss this any further until he spoke to his wife.

"Well, then you need a better plan. Having you live here and Mom live there, is not a plan."

"Okay, okay I get you. I'll work on it." Gris pressed his palms together and rubbed them as if he was caressing the sides of a genie bottle, wishing for answers.

After devouring the sandwiches from the pub, Gris called his industry contact. There was no answer so he left a detailed message and headed out with his son.

Now late for the mayor's meeting, they silently passed through the Town Hall's side entrance and slipped into the back row of the closed-door meeting.

The mayor had asked Gris to attend in case questions arose on the white shark population.

Gris nodded as the mayor eyed him from the

elevated platform. Individually engraved gold nameplates in mounted walnut frames identified each council member sitting behind the dais. Still dressed in business attire with loosened ties and top buttons, the council members shuffled through pages distributed by one of the town's businessman, Joseph Bigelow.

Gris wasn't surprised to see the short, balding man who had arrived in town two years earlier after retiring as a CFO for a large biotechnology company. He had invested his millions in the purchase of a renowned five-star resort known as a secret jewel among the rich and famous where they hid on vacation without being ogled by the press.

Shortly after news broke of his purchase, rumors whirled that Bigelow had more ties to the area than previously thought. Spreading like wildfire, the rumor was that Bigelow was linked to one of only two survivors on a pirate ship that had run aground just 20 miles to the north of the town.

Bigelow was purported to be the long lost great grandson who had come to town to stake his claim to the gold on the sunken Spanish galleon. Others claimed a more far-fetched rumor that he wasn't just after gold, but that he was here to carry out a vendetta against the great whites that had killed all the men aboard, all but his own great granddaddy.

To this day, Bigelow, an attention hog, had yet to confirm or deny the rumors.

Now Bigelow was on a rant. For the second consecutive year, he had gathered town councilmen to voice concerns about the shark bite incident and demand a course of action from town leaders to minimize negative impacts on tourism.

Kyle found the proceedings absurd and stifled a yawn as he took a seat. With his phone only at 15 percent charge, he sent a quick text to Lucy.

Kyle: Done with work yet?

Lucy: Almost.
Kyle: Meet me at the town hall in 20?
Lucy: I need to shower and clean up.
Kyle: How 'bout 30?
Lucy: OK. Brodie said there was a beach party at Spinnaker's Landing tonight.
Kyle: We'll talk about it when you get here.

Kyle shoved his phone in his pocket and looked to his father. "It's nine now. How long you think this'll last?"

"Hours. But you go anytime. I told the mayor I'd stay for questions."

Bigelow's monotone voice droned on. Gris recognized the information as identical to a presentation provided the previous summer when two other shark attacks had occurred in neighboring towns.

Now on his soapbox, Bigelow raged, "The recent attack will positively decimate any summer profits for local businesses and rentals." His tone was all doom and gloom. "No local business could possibly show any decent earnings over the next ten weeks with such a gruesome attack." He dragged out the last word for affect, but began coughing when he tried to recover his breath, his round belly bouncing up and down with each cough.

Kyle rolled his eyes. "I thought business profits increased last year with the return of the great whites."

"They did," Gris nodded.

Regaining his composure, Bigelow continued, "Last Friday's attack unleashed the worst-case scenario for any seasonal business trying to bounce back after last summer's attacks. How is any business to survive with these monsters roaming our waters?" His thick fist slammed down on the table for emphasis.

Bigelow spoke of two shark attacks from the

previous summer.

The first incident had occurred when a small, juvenile, five-foot white shark pup bit a man after he caught it with rod and reel a mile from shore and tried to pull it aboard his 42-foot sport-cruiser through the transom door. The fisherman said the crazed fish gripped his hand and wrist that was sheathed in a Kevlar fishing gloves and would not release it.

After two minutes of excruciating pressure, his first mate radioed the Coast Guard for help. Once aboard, the Coast Guard medics skillfully released the fisherman's hand and tended his puncture wounds. Then the officers placed him under arrest for illegally trying to land a white shark. When he was told the maximum penalty was a $250,000 fine and up to six months in prison for landing the protected shark, the man protested, claiming he thought it was a Mako shark.

After Coast Guardsmen safely released the shark pup alive to sea, they took the man into custody and impounded the fisherman's sport-cruiser, all its gear and his vehicle ashore for evidence.

The other incident occurred when a swimmer riding waves into a sandbar suffered bites to his ankles from a seven-foot juvenile white shark in late August at a beach town near where the renowned pirate ship had gone down. The man fully recovered.

Kyle glanced to his side when he heard the exit door creak open. He nudged his father in the ribs when he saw Jon Kane, the salesman from the afternoon, stride in. Kane's eyes locked on Bigelow, and he took no notice of others in the room. Bigelow nodded to him as he stood nearby, refusing a chair.

Gris whispered under his breath, "I wonder what brings Mr. Kane to this closed-door meeting?" A minute later, Bigelow broke from his rant and requested a five-minute recess. The mayor allowed it.

Bigelow and Kane exited the room through the

same side door.

Gris nonchalantly rose from his seat to stretch and adjust his baseball cap. He watched the pair move beyond the door's glass pane from the foyer to the rear hallway. He started to follow when Kyle put up his hand and stopped him.

"Where you going?" he asked.

"Just curious what brings Mr. Kane to our fine town meeting," his father answered. "And what business does he have with Bigelow?"

"Let me check it out. It will look less conspicuous to the mayor and his cronies," Kyle suggested.

"Good idea." Gris held out some loose change. "Bring me a soda, will you?" He raised his voice so that others could hear. The vending machine was located in the back hallway, probably where the men were headed.

Kyle began to move when his father tugged at his elbow. He turned back to see his father holding out his phone. "Take this with you. Push this button to record any dialogue if you hear anything suspicious."

"You want me to take off my shirt so you can put a wire on me?" Kyle teased.

"Just do it," Gris said.

Kyle walked briskly through the side entrance and tracked the men's voices. Sure enough, they were huddled in an empty office adjacent to the vending machines. The door was ajar.

Kyle stepped out of the line of sight. Their voices were low but audible. When he heard the words "shark tag," he pushed the record button on the phone. The red light flashed, indicating it was recording. Kyle shifted closer while he eyed the soda choices.

"Any problems on the batch sent to New Jersey a few weeks ago?" Bigelow asked in a low voice.

"None," the salesman's voice was equally low but clipped.

"Any issues with fitting them with toggles?"

"None," Kane replied.

Kyle stood frozen as he eavesdropped. The red light on the phone was still flashing.

"How many of the new tags at each location?" Bigelow asked.

"All twelve in a box," Kane said.

"How many tagged so far?"

"Seven over the last three weeks in New Jersey. One here."

"How long before any effects?" Bigelow asked.

"Twenty four to 72 hours, depending on size."

"None drop until they head south this fall though, right?

"Right," Kane confirmed.

"Anything else?"

"No." The salesman's voice was garbled, as if he was chewing something.

"Stay here. I don't want anyone thinking we're acquainted," Bigelow instructed.

Kane snorted his disbelief. "We left the boardroom together."

Kyle heard Bigelow wiggle the door handle.

Quickly, Kyle slid the phone into his front pocket and fed quarters into the vending machine. Clink, clink, clink, clink, clink.

Bigelow stepped out and Kyle could feel the man's stare heat the back of his neck.

The blinking red letters scrolled, *MAKE A SELECTION*. Kyle heard Bigelow shift, then move past him. He pressed the buttons for a Mountain Dew. The can clunked out of the machine as Kyle watched the balding man stalk toward the boardroom.

Kyle bent to scoop the can out of the machine. When he straightened, he backed directly into a man's chest. Kyle knew it was Kane.

"Heard that stuff can be harmful to your health." Kane spoke softly to Kyle's ear. "Too many and I've heard they're lethal."

Kane was so close that Kyle smelled pungent chaw on his breath and heard his saliva snap along his gum line. Kyle turned to step past him when Kane blocked his path.

His face cast a threatening glare as his eyes narrowed. Kyle tried to hold his stare, but the man was not the same person he'd met on the boat that morning. He was more than creepy, even sinister. When he'd answered Bigelow, Kane had acted as a subordinate. As soon as the billionaire left the room, his entire demeanor changed.

Kyle spoke candidly as he stepped back from the soda machine. "She's all yours."

Outside the boardroom, Kyle leaned against a large square column. When he heard Kane's footsteps approach, Kyle nodded politely.

Kane's lips curled into a wicked smile, and he let out a small chuckle. Kyle felt like he was one of two male dogs squaring off for territory.

Kane walked past him, exiting the front door where he headed toward the parking lot.

Gris saw Kyle through the glass panel and joined him.

"Anything happen?"

"Bigelow and Kane talked. It was a cryptic exchange and hard to follow. Bigelow asked if Kane encountered any issues with the new tags. Something about toggles. I recorded it."

"Issues?" His father spoke softly. "Was production delayed due to issues or flaws?"

"Bigelow asked Kane about effects. Not sure what it all means. But you can listen to the whole conversation later." Kyle handed the phone to his father. Looking through the large glass panels across the Town Hall's front foyer, Kyle pointed at Kane who was climbing into a restored, forest green Jaguar E-Series roadster.

"That Kane?" Gris asked.

"Yup."

"Read the plate number to me, would you?" Gris waited to punch it into his cell phone. He read it back to Kyle.

"You got it, " Kyle affirmed. "So what's up with taking his plate number?"

"I have a friend who's a police detective at the sheriff's office. Think I'll ask him to run the plate for me. There's something about Kane that looks familiar. I just can't place him."

"A terrible thing, getting old, huh?" Kyle chuckled.

His father pulled off his baseball cap and smacked Kyle over the head playfully as Kyle ducked away.

Five minutes later, Lucy peeked through the door glass and smiled when her eyes found Kyle.

"There's my date."

"You taking the truck?"

"No, Lucy came to pick me up in her car," Kyle answered. "So you got this, Dad?"

Gris nodded, "Have fun, but not too late. Good weather forecasted for tomorrow, so we'll have a full day."

Kyle waved and headed toward Lucy. Her dimples deepen with every step he took.

TWELVE

Decoding Dialogue

"You were in my head all day." Kyle spoke into Lucy's hair as he curled her into his shoulder. The parking lot contained only a few cars, but no people. Lucy's smile widened.

At her car door, she reached to lift the handle. Kyle pinned the door shut with his knee and turned her to face him. He leaned in to kiss her forehead and wrap his arms around her. After a few tight squeezes, he lifted her chin to give her a long kiss. When he released her, she drew in a ragged breath. He smiled at her need for air and nuzzled her neck. She squirmed with an embarrassed laugh.

He pulled away to see her and drew in a deep breath. She smelled like spearmint gum and lavender shampoo. One corner of her lips curled up, deepening the dimples in her cheeks.

His body tightened, and he groaned softly.

"I guess I was."

"Yeah, these days make me feel like I've been away for half a week," Kyle whispered into her ear.

"Well, you haven't. Didn't I just see you at the pub?"

He didn't answer.

"And last night on my parent's roof?"

No answer again. "I think Dad knew we were out there, but he played quiet this morning," she finished.

Lucy's father was headed out of town on business and needed to run through their usual routine of how her mother would check-in and spend the night.

Though Lucy's parents were divorced, they lived only a couple blocks apart. Her father had wanted it that way. Thomas Wharton still loved her mother, so when their divorce was final, he bought her a home just ten houses away from his with a breathtaking view and state-of-the-art baths and kitchen.

To Lucy's surprise, her mother accepted the gift. Lucy's parents had a non-traditional relationship that was constantly on again, off again every few weeks. By now she was used to the pattern. When her mother had men call on her, Lucy's parents bickered and slung hateful words at one another.

She didn't know why her father took part in the battles. As far as Lucy was concerned, no man had yet measured up to her father. Lucy knew this, and she knew her mother knew it, too.

So for now the arrangement worked for their family. Despite their hurtful exchanges, Lucy knew they both loved her. And every time her father traveled, her mother seemed to look forward to being with Lucy and frequently stayed with her at her Dad's place. Her mother would call it "a girl's sleepover." While Lucy thought the term odd, she accepted it and knew it was the closest she'd get to mother-daughter time.

Kyle still had his eyes on Lucy. He was thinking.

"That was fun last night on the roof. Felt like I could just reach out and touch those stars." She continued the small talk. Kyle squeezed her again and propped his chin on her head.

"Not sure if I'm cut out for this line of work," he pensively reflected. "Nice day on the water, and we tagged one shark, but too many idle stretches."

"Want to tell me about it?" she asked.

Kyle thought about telling her about the odd

salesman who was creepy, the banter between the first mate and captain or the cryptic conversation between Bigelow and Kane. But decided against it.

"Nope." His eyes were now locked on hers. With one finger beneath her chin, he lifted her head and stole a light kiss, then deepened it when she slid her hands around his neck and pressed into him. His fingers slid across the softness of her jaw, touching her face. Their eyes met again, and she smiled, giving him a glimpse of one dimple.

Releasing her, he stepped back to pull open her door. She slid in and he closed the door for her before rounding to his side.

"So the day had some tedious stretches? Other than that, don't you like working with your Dad?" Lucy made conversation while she drove.

"With Dad? Um . . . yeah, he's good. Was cool to see him work with the crew, especially one guy, Vinnie, your typical offshore commercial guy. Nothing scares him. He's the guy who leans way out over the fish on the end of a 20-foot pulpit to harpoon it with a long stick. He's so far out there you just know he's going to fall in. I mean, he's out there, arms fully extended and just when you think the shark's going to dive, he jams the stick into its dorsal. Total pro. Dad said he's only missed three out of the twenty-four they've tagged here."

"Oh, yeah, that sounds like one tedious day. Wish my days were that tedious." She quirked one brow upward.

"Yeah . . . well, I guess it *was* pretty cool. Those are some bad ass fish for sure," Kyle smirked.

"Sounds like your Dad's doing something that he thinks will make a difference."

"Maybe. Sometimes he comes off as a little over the top on his quest to gather research. He forgets that not everyone grew up under the spell of Jacques Cousteau. And even if some had, not all have converted to save the planet." Kyle took a deep breath.

Lucy looked at him with curiosity, waiting for him to finish.

"I mean, his intentions are in the right place. He's convinced the more information available about these white sharks the better. Dad says people are scared of what they don't understand," Kyle finished.

"Sounds like you get him."

"Yeah. Sat through enough dinner spiels to have memorized his argument: take out the great white shark and you throw the whole food web out of whack."

"Bet he loves having you work with him."

"Probably. Think it takes his mind off Mom gone." His mother had been more exasperated than angry was when she stormed out of the house.

"She'll be back," Lucy assured him in a softer voice. "I can't image those two apart for long."

"This time was different." He turned to Lucy, "Like a line was crossed. Mom looked pretty hurt. He's got some serious groveling ahead of him."

"We heading to the beach party to join Brodie and his flavor of the week?" Lucy asked.

"That's mean. Girls can be so catty." Kyle shook his head with a chuckle.

"Well, are we?"

"I guess. As long as you let me keep my hand on your waist...or shoulder...or..."

Lucy cut him off. "When have I not let you?" She smiled at him. She saw his eyes melt at her smile.

"You know I can never say no to those dimples."

~

The next morning, Kyle watched his father toss a couple ibuprofen to the back of his throat, then chase it with a gulp of warm, black coffee. He swallowed again to push the pills further down his throat.

Kyle recalled being in the same position the previous morning. Only his headache wasn't from relationship troubles.

The coffee was now lukewarm. The automatic drip coffee maker had clicked off more than an hour ago. It was no longer piping hot, like his father preferred. Kyle took the cup from his father and slid it into the microwave. He pressed the button and the machine sang to life. In his head, Kyle ran through the dialogue he had overhead the night before as the plate turned.

His father sat at the kitchen table transcribing the recorded conversation onto a legal pad. He wanted to study it. Kyle knew his father's path to wrapping his head around complicated circumstances. He had a habit of writing ideas in a picture format. Visually seeing the information on paper aided his understanding.

"You headed off to the Marine Fish Laboratory this morning with blood samples?" Gris asked.

"Yup. You need anything else dropped off?"

"Maybe. I'm going back over the conversation and now wondering if . . . . Well, what do you think about getting one of those new, high-end tags analyzed by the Lab chemist?" Gris asked.

"Yah, sure. I mean why not? You come up with any conclusions on the exchange?" Kyle asked.

"If you're asking whether I solved the 64 thousand dollar question, no. But it seems logical Bigelow would consult a satellite tag salesman if he's buying that type of device. What I don't understand is why Bigelow would be buying one?"

Kyle pulled up a chair by his father.

"Here's what I got so far," Gris said. "Bigelow starts out asking Kane about a batch delivered to New Jersey. He's likely speaking of tags Al and his crew received. He asks Kane about fitting the tags with toggles. That question baffles me."

"Maybe they're using a newer toggle barb on the

VSATs?" Kyle asked.

"You could be right. But the original sales rep never mentioned any new toggle fasteners. I know because I asked about the length of life and any anti-corrosion features. It was a red flag for me, too. So just to be sure, I called Al. He told me he wasn't aware of new toggles. He did mention the order that was delivered had the fluorescent orange toggles with a lifetime guarantee for corrosion."

"Is that such a bad thing?" Kyle asked.

"Not at all. It's a good thing. But when I dissected those two sharks that washed ashore, there was no sign of any fluorescent orange coating on the toggles. In fact there wasn't even any visible residue. They were clean stainless. Whatever coating had been there was gone."

"That's weird." Kyle scratched his head. The conversation was intense for early morning. He needed more coffee.

"Bigelow also asked 'how long before any effects.' Then later stated that none will 'drop 'til they head south.' Have any clue what that means?"

Kyle didn't answer.

"Sounds almost like he's asking how soon the sharks will have side effects or die. What'd you think?"

Kyle was quiet. He didn't want to answer. He didn't want to agree with his father. If he agreed with that theory then it meant Bigelow and others were trying to take out the species his father had worked for so many years to protect. If he agreed with his father, he would be confirming his father's greatest nightmare. Furthermore, he would be acknowledging that his father was being used as a pawn. Used by people who wanted kill off the white sharks with the scientific tool of his own tagging program. *Was that even possible?* His father was a man who was doing what he thought was right, what he thought was his duty.

"Kyle, I asked you a question," Gris spoke forcefully.

"Yeah, I heard you. What'd you say we run this by the police, the state agents or maybe the federal agents?" Kyle suggested as he considered the implications of his father's theory.

"I've already talked to them. They are more interested in the sliced dorsal fins. I prefer it that way, at least until I get a better handle on cause of death. If someone told me this story, I'd call him crazy. We need more information."

Kyle pulled the slip of paper from his wallet with the plate number. He passed it to his father. "You were going to call your police detective friend."

Gris broke away from his diagram of notes and dialed his cell. Detective Mark Ellis, a Barnstable County Sheriff's detective took down the plate number and said he'd get back to Gris with results in the next half hour.

Gris rose to stretch his arms and clear his head. He looked over at the sink and thought of Audrey humming to herself each morning as she dressed for her day. She'd return to town tomorrow evening. He thought about seeing her again, what he would say. He stomach fluttered at the thought.

Not but five minutes passed when Kyle heard his father's phone vibrate, followed by a booming voice say, "Plate's registered to a Jon Stevens."

He watched his father scratch his head and repeat the name aloud. "Jon Stevens? Okay, so Kane must have borrowed a friend's car," he told Detective Ellis.

"No. He's Jon Stevens," the detective corrected.

"Yes, I heard you."

"No, Gris, the man driving was Jon Kane and Jon Stevens."

"Come again?"

"Jon Stevens is his real name, Kane is one of his aliases," the detective explained.

"Aliases? Why use an alias?" Gris asked and thought about how ridiculous his question was. "Don't answer that...either he's a criminal or evading taxes, right, yeah?"

"You're catching on," Detective Ellis teased. "May even want to consider changing your line of work." Ellis chuckled.

"What's he messing with that requires aliases?" Gris finally asked.

"Mostly small time stuff, nothing aggravated. Jon Stevens started stealing cars with a couple teens from the neighborhood when he was 14. When he turned 16, the chop shop he worked for was busted. At 17 he was charged with money laundering, was convicted and served a short time in juvenile detention. He somehow came away from the experience with the drive to get his GED. He then started working at a bank as a teller, and because he was bright, was trusted to keep track of several of the long-time bank clients. Later he was charged with embezzlement three different times for large amounts of cash missing. But all charges were dropped for lack of evidence.

"From what I can see, after he left his teller job, he acquired his first alias. After that he moved from bank to bank. His juvenile record was expunged, and he's remained clean the last five years. So either he's cleaned up or become smarter and more savvy."

Gris thought about his conversation with Kane on the boat the previous day. He'd found him intelligent, able to keep pace, even stay ahead of most questioning but easily irritated.

Detective Ellis continued, "Former addresses include Savin Hill in Dorchester and before that, Massachusetts Avenue in South Boston, then it jumps back seventeen years to a very affluent community on the South Shore," the detective continued.

"That's quite a mix of residences, like opposites,"

Gris commented.

"And he's no stranger to our area either. Looks like his father's parents have a summer home here where he visited as a boy."

Though Kyle had never been to either inner Boston location, he knew their reputations from his junior high school years. Both were very dicey and plagued with crime and drugs. When he was in seventh grade, he'd heard Savin Hill called Stabbin' Hill and Dorchester dubbed Deathchester.

"Here? In town? How old is he?" Gris asked.

"Thirty-eight."

"A few years younger than Audrey and I. But there's a chance we still could have crossed paths. Jon Stevens. Hmmm." Gris went quiet for a moment. "I knew a girl when I was about Kyle's age. Her name was Samantha Stevens. Met her my summer before college. We dated a few times. She was pretty, very pretty. But she was a wild child, except when around her grandparents. With them she played the angel. Only met them once, at a summer baseball game on Chase Field under the lights. They climbed the hill to ask if she needed a ride home. She declined, said she'd be along any minute, but not to wait up. About four hours later I dropped her off. After that I only saw her couple other times.

"Think he's any relation to her?" the detective asked.

"She never mentioned a brother," Gris added.

"I'll run her stats in a moment." the detective said.

"His grandparents still own the place?" Gris asked Ellis.

"The property is listed as Life Estate of Kane, George F. and Kane, Margaret E. on the tax record."

"So it's still in their names. What's that address?"

Detective Ellis paused, "9 Goose Neck Road. Samantha Stevens married Grayson Pratt of Boston when she was age 22. She is an administrative

145

assistant in a law firm in Boston where he is a partner."

"Thanks. Anything else?" Gris asked.

"Not from here,"

I appreciate it. I'll be in touch," Gris added before hanging up and turning to Kyle.

"Looks like our Mr. Kane is formerly Jon Stevens," Gris explained.

"Yeah, I heard your conversation. Hard not to with the detective's booming voice."

"Looks like he left that life of crime five years ago. No criminal record or charges since then, and he's moved on to high tech engineering work to earn an honest paycheck," Gris added.

"Doesn't sound like that to me from the conversation I overheard," Kyle disagreed.

Gris was swallowing a gulp of coffee when his phone vibrated across the table, so Kyle answered it. It was Vinnie Mancini calling with the day's departure time.

Gris held up 10 fingers, followed by five. Kyle nodded and told Mancini they'd be at the fish docks in 15 minutes. He stayed on another minute for Mancini to finish his instructions as he shoved the second piece of toast into his mouth.

"Is it always this busy? I mean working on the water one day after another?" Kyle asked as he put the phone down.

"Pretty much in summer. It's a short season. So if it's not blowing snot or the wave height is not so high that your kidneys will turn to sausage or the glare on the water doesn't obstruct spotting, then we head out." Gris put his coffee mug on the counter.

"So in order for me to ever see Lucy again or surf again, I need to pray for bad weather?" Kyle raised his brows.

"A very smart scientist once said, 'If you want to be a scientist, you got to get out of the laboratory.'"

"Do we have to live that motto every day?" Kyle grumbled.

Gris chuckled. "Okay, okay. I get you. Write down what days you need off or whatever days Lucy has open on her schedule, and I'll try to get you the same days. That work?"

"Thanks, Boss."

"Now go into my office and grab the box of old satellite tags. We'll use those today instead of the newfangled tags onboard until we get some results from Dr. Chang. We'll drop off one of the new tags to Marine Fish Laboratory for chemical testing on the way to the boat," Gris added.

"Oh, by the way, Captain Mancini said we'd be working on the 57-foot sword fishing boat moored in the town harbor. Says we need it because it's larger, more stable and equipped with a lowering cradle along the starboard side for you to take samples from smaller sharks if needed," Kyle explained.

"Spotter plane underway?" Gris asked.

"Already on the prowl."

THIRTEEN

Fluorescent Orange Toggle

At the dock, Kyle and his father loaded equipment over the vessel's rail to store in the wet lab. While fueling, Mancini talked through two radio calls from the spotter plane. They had coordinates for two whites a couple miles off shore. They needed to make tracks.

"Mr. Mancini," yelled a voice from the fuel dock.

Mancini ducked his head out from the aluminum bars of the tuna tower. It was Kane.

"Come aboard, Mr. Kane," he issued permission.

Gris leaned out of the wet lab door to see Kane climb aboard. When their eyes met, Kane stopped mid-step.

"We meet again, Mr. Kane," Gris offered his hand to assist him over the rail.

Kane tipped his chin and grabbed Gris' hand. His palm was sweaty and his grip weak.

"Joining us for another very complicated trip to explain the proprietary features on our newly acquired tags, Mr. Kane?" Gris mocked.

"Company policy," Kane spit out.

"Uh huh," Gris nodded.

Kyle walked up behind his father and nodded in Kane's direction. Kane didn't return the gesture, but instead offered a creepy glare.

"The CEO of our parent company requires salesman to be available to answer any questions about all of the tag's new features. Proprietary technology coating on the toggles is just one aspect. The new video technology alone is extremely complex, and we want to make sure it is functional on every tag during this initial trial period. Company policy." Kane's answer was well rehearsed.

"Yes, yes, I heard that your company was obtained by a biotech or is it a drug corporate giant?" Gris inquired.

"A well-established biotech," he elaborated.

Gris nodded as he tucked his head back into the wet lab to finish prepping the work area. He took all the new VSAT tags out of the packing box and moved them into a 2-gallon plastic tub, then snapped the lid shut and handed it to Kyle.

"Do we even need Kane aboard today if we're not using VSATs?" Kyle asked.

Gris considered the question. "Not sure he needs to know we are testing his product. He could get protective about the proprietary angle."

Kyle nodded and then stored the new tags below the counter in the equipment storage locker out of sight. Next, he unpacked the old tags and loaded them into the empty VSAT box. The old PSAT tags looked very different from the new ones.

Despite the growing swell, the two-hour trip offshore passed quickly due to the extra prep Kyle and his father did to ready the wet lab for sampling and the rigging of the cradle over the starboard rail.

The boat's engine cut back to half throttle, a signal the captain had zeroed in on the spotter plane's coordinates for the first shark. Kyle stepped out into the damp air. They had crossed over the edge of a weather front.

Over the port rail, a seven-foot immature male white shark swam in an s-curve at the surface. He dove when the boat neared, only to resurface 50 yards ahead. The pattern repeated another three times before Mancini was able to maneuver over top of the young shark.

"But Kane will know we are using the old PSAT tag instead of the new one when he hands off the tag to Mancini," Kyle said.

"Right. That's why I'm going to have you hand Kane your video camera while I pass the PSAT to Vinnie," Gris explained.

Distracting Kane would be a challenge. Kyle grabbed his video recording equipment while Gris picked up the PSAT tag. Together, they walked toward the forward deck.

"Mr. Kane, would you mind helping me here?" Kyle stepped in front of the salesman. "I need some help with this video camera equipment and was hoping you could hold it on the shark as we approach."

Kane passed the camera to Kane who had no choice but to take it. The distraction allowed Gris to pass behind his son toward the pulpit. Kane lifted the camera to focus the viewfinder on the shark.

Captain Mancini shuffled back off the pulpit to grab the toggle end of the tag from Gris.

At that moment, Kane slid his eyes away from the viewfinder window and did a double take as Gris handed off the tag to Vinnie. He shoved the video recording camera into Kyle's ribcage and strode toward Gris.

"What the hell is this?" he shouted at Gris.

"Beg your pardon?" Gris was all innocence.

"What's this?" Kane held up another of last year's PSAT tag. "This isn't one of the new tags with a lifetime warranty. Get one of the new VSAT tags for me," he demanded.

"We'll use the PSAT for now," Gris said, standing his ground. "I left the box of new tags at the Marine Fish Laboratory." He did not like to lie, but the end justified the means.

"It doesn't have a coating on the toggle." Kane spoke to Gris as if he were a grade-schooler. "We should use what was ordered for this year."

"Just send Gris up with the tag in his hand!" Mancini yelled to Kane. "This shark isn't going to stay in place for long!"

Throwing the PSAT tag on the deck, Kane ignored the captain. "I have a few in my bag we can use." He strode to his gear and pulled out a fully rigged VSAT tag. "Got it," he said, turning his back on Gris to quickly step onto the upper deck about five feet from Mancini.

Kane unraveled the tag apparatus with his right hand, holding the video camera of the rig in the left hand.

"Any chance you could hurry that along before this shark takes off and we lose him?"

Kane let out an expletive when he noticed the whip wire needed to be untangled.

"Losing time here, Mr. Kane. Would you like me to untangle it?" Mancini asked.

"Right. I mean no. I got it." Kane tucked the long VSAT body under his arm with the whip now extending out in front of him. The toggle end dangled behind his back.

Mancini shuffled from one foot to the other as Kane fumbled with the tag cords.

"Okay, I've waited long enough. Kane, hand over the tag now." Vinnie held out his hand.

"Okay. It's ready. It's ready." Kane stepped forward with the tag still tucked under his arm.

Spooked by the shadowy movement on the pulpit, the young shark swerved and bumped into the port side bow. The sudden shift of the vessel knocked Kane off balance. As he stumbled sideways, then backward, the long vinyl coated wire attached to the toggle wrapped itself around the cleat behind him, jerking him to a sudden halt.

Completely off balance, Kane went down with a thud onto his backside, his left elbow colliding with the cleat. He tried to roll to his right side.

"Argh!" Kane screamed.

"What the hell?" Mancini cussed.

Kane twisted to see what was pinching his arm. At the sight of the long thin coated cable cord extending out from his armpit, his eyes widened. He tugged at the whip.

"Argh," he screamed again. "Damn it! Pull it out!" Kane shrieked, looking to Vinnie for help.

The captain was busy sliding the harpoon shell into a holster along the pulpit. By the time Kane screamed the second time, Vinnie was by his side. "I'm not sure how you did this. Somehow you've wrapped the toggle end around the main deck cleat and fallen back on it."

"What the hell? What's pinching?" Kane practically screamed again.

Vinnie bent down to take a look. "Quit squirming. It's the toggle. The tagging rig became so entangled that when you lost your balance and slammed down on the cleat you also slammed down onto the toggle. It looks like it made a tiny cut into your bicep."

Shaking his head, Kane pushed himself up on his right arm, but quickly collapsed on it. His eyes closed, and his lips turned into a thin bloodless line. He sat up again, clutching his elbow and lower bicep with his right hand to stifle the pain. He slid it farther left when he felt the toggle protruding out of his skin.

"Damn you. That's no tiny cut!"

"You're right there. Tagged a lot of sharks in my day, but never seen a person tag themselves," Mancini said with a small chuckle as he tried to unravel the wrapped coated wire connected to the toggle. Then he offered Kane a hand.

Kane folded his knees in and stood facing Mancini. "Help me!" he demanded.

"Hold still, lad. I want to take a quick look. See how deep it's gone in. Probably be able to just slide it out and reuse it." Mancini moved toward Kane, who began to sway. "Hey, hey, man, this isn't a fatal wound. Hell, it's no more than a mosquito bite."

Kane's eyes glazed over and rolled back into his head. Mancini wrapped his muscular forearm around the salesman's back to cushion his fall as he dropped backward onto the deck, less than a few inches from the cleat.

"Kyle!" Mancini called out, "help me stretch him out. The man's a wuss, fainting at the sight of no blood!" He then called to his first mate to spin the vessel to starboard to drop shade onto the forward deck where the salesman lay trembling in a cold sweat.

Kyle leaned over Kane and dabbed a wet cloth across his forehead and down his neck.

Kane's eyes fluttered to life. He fingered the wound to find the toggle still jammed into the back of his arm just above the elbow. "I thought I imagined it," he said, his voice starting at a whisper, then rising to a squeal. "Get it out of me! You've got to get it out of me!"

"Calm down, young man," the captain said with full authority. "If you hold still, I can yank her out in nothin' flat." He examined the wound. "Lucky for you, I can tell that the toggle isn't in a locking position. It's going to slide out easily."

"What's the orange stuff?" Kyle asked.

Gris leaned in to study the wound. "Looks like traces of fluorescent orange coating. That's not supposed to happen.

"Get it out, get it out fast!" If possible, Kane's voice rose even higher, resembling the sound of a mortally wounded jungle animal.

"Okay, okay," Mancini said, not bothering to hide his irritation. "It's going to hurt, but it's only pain. It's not going to kill you."

"That's what you think!" Kane blurted out.

"What do you mean by that?" Gris asked from a kneeling position opposite the captain. Kyle hovered over Gris.

Kane's eyes cleared then narrowed. "I mean, I mean, uh, I'm allergic to, uh, the coating, the orange stuff."

"Do you have an Epi-Pen on you?" Gris asked.

"Uh, no. I never thought I'd get shot with the thing."

"You weren't shot, you fell on it all by yourself," Mancini corrected him in a terse voice.

"Okay, okay, I fell on it. Just get it out of me!" Kane's face was as white as a seagull's wing.

"I need a pair of long-nosed pliers," the captain said.

"I'll get them." Kyle disappeared for a long moment, then returned with the requested tool.

"Thanks, son. Now, Mr. Kane, I'm going to get hold of the barb and twist it so I can pull it out without ripping off a piece of your bicep. Ready?"

"Hurry!"

"It's not very far in," Mancini assured him. "Kyle, get some sterile wipes and a clean towel in case he starts bleeding. I've yanked out a fish gaff from my calf that was deeper than that with the barb locked in."

"Get me to a hospital," Kane demanded. "Call the Coast Guard. They can helicopter me to the nearest trauma center."

A couple of the crew laughed at the absurdity of the demand, and the captain had to force back a guffaw of his own. "That won't be necessary. This is a simple flesh wound, and I don't see any swelling that comes with an allergic reaction. Some antibiotic cream, a Band-Aid and you're good to go."

"I'm telling you, I have to get to a hospital, you

dolt!"

"Now, now, you don't have to get nasty," Vinnie said in a calm steady voice. In the next second, he jerked the barb out.

While Kane screamed, Kyle reached in to dab at the tiny trickle of blood.

"If you don't get me to a hospital, I will personally make your life miserable," Kane said through gritted teeth.

"I knew he was going to be a pain in the ass as soon as I set eyes on him," Vinnie said to Gris.

"If I go into anaphylactic shock, you and your crew will be up shit's creek without a paddle!" Kane's eyes turned wild and spittle formed at the corners of his mouth. "I'm cold, so cold!" His shaking limbs proved his point.

"Geez, man," the first mate said, "the captain just got a fish hook out of your arm, and you're threatening to sue him. What kind of thanks is that?"

"Never mind, Cam, get on the radio and find the nearest boat heading for harbor. I want to get rid of this pain in the ass more than he wants to see the last of me. Find a boat that will pick him up. I'll call for an ambulance to be waiting at the dock."

Kane's head dropped back in abject relief at Vinnie's words.

Gris examined the barb. "So much for a lifetime guarantee on the coating for these new tags," he mumbled. "Kane, didn't you say the toggles were dipped with a special orange coating that guaranteed anti-corrosion? Kane?"

"He's out, Dad," Kyle said.

"Good," Vinnie said. "I hope help gets here before he wakes up again, or I might just throw him to the sharks."

An hour later, Kane was transferred to a vessel going into harbor, and Captain Mancini happily turned his boat back to sea.

"Come on, we've got some sharks to tag," he said with obvious relief.

FOURTEEN

It's a Floater

The delicious aroma of American chop suey with linguica and Portuguese sweet rolls filled the air of the galley. The varnished wood and dark brown vinyl cushions exuded an aged, masculine look. Kyle filled his plate and slid onto the bench at the gimbaled table fastened to the vessel's center beam. He listened to the raucous talk while he waited for his father.

As Gris joined him, Kyle heard a strange noise behind him. He looked and then tapped his father's shoulder, "You hear that?" Kyle could barely hear his own voice over the crews' laughter.

"Hear what?" his father yelled back.

Kyle stood and pulled his father's arm closer to the side of the boat hull. A repetitive slap, slap, slap, boom, boom, boom sound reverberated along the side of the hull.

"That," Kyle answered in a quieter voice.

"It's probably just some floating debris. The crew is heading back up. They'll handle it. Now eat some chow. I'd like to get to the next set of coordinates so we can get back at a reasonable hour today."

Kyle forked a few more pieces of pasta. He heard the scuffing of feet and loud commotion topside as the boat began to list to one side.

"Gris, you better get up here, quick," Mancini yelled down the main cabin hatch to the galley. Kyle had a bad feeling of what they might find on deck.

Taking two rungs at a time, Gris and Kyle scrambled up the ladder to the deck. Deckhands congregated along the vessel's port side. Whatever the object was, it continued to slap along the vessel's hull with a repetitive whap, whap, whap. The floating object was still concealed from Kyle's sight.

"Step aside. Clear the way," Mancini ordered his mates aside.

Now with a clear path, Gris and Kyle saw a large mass on the surface. It looked like a bloated whale. But once Kyle reached the rail, he recognized the repulsive odor. It was the body of a 15-foot white shark, belly side up.

"It's a floater," Mancini shouted, handing a long gaff with a rubber tube on its pointed end and a telescoping boat hook to his crewmen. He ordered them to roll the shark away from the boat.

When the men moved the hooks toward the shark, it flicked its tail and sank below the surface. Still upside down, the shark began to move on its own with another swish of its tail. It wasn't dead, at least not yet. But like the others that beached themselves, it was moribund. From the stench and its condition, Gris estimated it would die soon.

"Hold up," Mancini shouted.

The crewmen backed off the rail with the gaff and boat hook and waited for the fish to resurface.

"Any chance you can use those hooks to roll the girl over so I can see if she's tagged?" Gris asked.

Mancini gave a nod to his men, and they dipped the hooks under its pectoral fin, mid torso. Together the men pulled up on the fin to roll her over. But instead, the fish slid away and sank six feet below the surface under the vessel's hull. Kyle heard the thud of its tail as it frantically moved below the hull.

"Cam, start up the port side engine. Put her in reverse and slowly back her off the shark," Mancini directed his first mate on the tuna tower. Kyle thought back to how delirious Kane had been during the stabbing event. He then reflected on the conversation between Kane and Bigelow. His father was right; he needed to more information on these new tags.

Breaking from his thoughts, the shark reemerged and floated back to the surface along the port side, again with its belly side up. It was swishing its tail, moving the fish ever so slightly forward, then sideways, then forward in an uncoordinated path. Cam drew the boat alongside the fish. Kyle could see its nose covered by scar marks, jaws agape, and black eyes now covered over with its third lens. Oddly, like the other, this shark had the top half of its dorsal fin hacked off.

He saw his father's eyes widen when he saw the dorsal fin, then he shook his head.

"Grab a line and loop it around the shark's gills. Cinch it tight. Then we'll see if we can roll it," Mancini ordered to his second mate.

Kyle stepped back. He suddenly felt queasy as replayed his childhood flashback. He flashed back to his brother's voice as they confronted the catch together.

"Kyle, come here! Isn't it the coolest thing you've ever seen? Dad works on some pretty bad fish, but this one—this one is BADASS. Look at its teeth. How'd you like to go nose to nose with him in a wave?

Kyle took two paces back from the rail and swallowed the bile building in the back of his throat. He walked toward the starboard side of the boat, but the choking odor that wafted across the beam was so harsh it seared his nostrils.

"Kyle, can you give me a hand with this?" his father called.

But Kyle didn't hear him. He was still trying to shake away the memory of that first grotesque shark. One more breath and he bolted to the side, hurling his lunch over the rail into the lapping waves.

Mancini handed off the end of the rope and lunged to grip Kyle's elbow as he hung over the rail. The weathered captain steadied Kyle, a boy he'd watched grow up. He wrapped his large muscular forearm around Kyle's waist and pulled him back from the edge.

"Happens to all of us, son," his words were soothing and coaxed Kyle out of his trance.

"Feel better? Or you got more?" He gently rubbed Kyle's taught six-pack where he caught him on the rail and chuckled.

Kyle shook his head slowly. The top of his head felt like it was splitting in two.

"How 'bout you take five—away from the stream of stench coming off that fish while my crew flips this ogre over?"

Mancini steadied the boy and then moved him to a spot against the cabin. He turned back when he reached the main hatch and shouted to his second mate for soda crackers and a Gatorade for Kyle.

"Got it."

"Captain, she's rolled and tagged," Cam yelled over his shoulder as he held the line taught.

Gris knelt on the port side deck and leaned into the water to read the tag number. "She's too far to reach. Any chance you can drag her around and into the cradle on the starboard side?" Gris asked Cam.

Kyle walked to the forward deck in time to hear his father speaking. "It'll let me get a closer look to record her tag and get blood and tissue samples."

"Aren't you going to bring her in, Gris?" Mancini asked.

"If it's not too difficult to haul her to port. But the blood samples can't wait. They have to be drawn at sea, while she's still alive, before post-mortem effects set in. I'll slide them into a small Dewar flask we brought. It's not cryogenic cold, but it's ultra-cold compared to a regular ice cooler," Gris added.

Cam nodded slowly, then stopped and shook his head, "I'm fairly sure you're not talking about Scotch whisky. Though I wish you were."

Gris chuckled. "You're right about that, Cam."

"You looking for the Dewars?" Kyle asked. His father nodded.

"I always told you he'd turn into a smart kid someday, eh?" Mancini pointed his finger at Gris in the shape of a gun and flicked his thumb like a trigger.

Cam called back to the second mate and explained his plan to move the shark. Over the next 20 minutes, Gris and Kyle watched as the men expertly guided the fish into the starboard side cradle.

"A bit easier when the 1,800 pound shark's not flailing against the side of the hull trying to swim away. She's pretty docile for a great white," Cam noted.

"I'm afraid she isn't long for this world. But before she exits and body starts to decompose, I need to get these blood and tissue samples.

Gris leaned over the rail and pulled the tag to read the shark's tag number. "She's Number 44, Giant Greta, tagged by the New Jersey crew about three weeks ago."

"Did your friends in New Jersey mention she was sick or malnourished when she was tagged?" Mancini asked, looking the shark over.

"We don't tag sickly sharks. I read the notes on all those tagged by the New Jersey crew. She was in good health. Don't think they would name her Giant Greta if she was malnourished or sick." Gris contemplated Greta's condition as he slung his leg over the cradle and stepped onto the shark's back.

"Whoa, whoa, whoa. Hang on there, Ms. Greta," Gris whispered. "Just need to take some fresh biopsy punch samples."

The shark bucked like an unbroken horse. "You

getting some training for when the rodeo comes to town, Dad?" Kyle laughed.

Hearing the commotion, Mancini came back to the side rail.

"Got $100 riding on you, Gris, that says you can break her, get her ready for that new saddle," the captain said.

The shark lurched forward, nearly catapulting Gris into the water.

"Okay, enough of that, Kelley. Don't need another accident today. Do me a favor—just in case this little filly decides to buck you off, throw this on." Mancini tossed a body harness to Gris, who strapped himself in. The captain then clipped his end to a secure line on the deck.

"You'll see. She'll calm in a few minutes when she's use to my weight," Gris said.

"Or when she is exhausted," Kyle added.

"Glad to see you all have my back."

Slowly, Gris straddled the shark and pushed the punch sampler into her muscle tissue. Her tail wriggled. Then she went uncharacteristically still.

Kyle watched her from the rail and studied her scarring. What looked like a Letter L was scribed at the base of the dorsal fin, but he didn't mention it to his father.

Over the next 20 minutes, Gris punched 20 fresh tissue samples and 25 sealed blood vials.

"This rodeo's over. Time to move her," Gris said, hoisting himself over the rail off the shark.

Mancini helped Gris aboard and loaded the vials into the ultra-cold cooler. Opening the deep freeze box, Mancini handed a vial at the time to Gris to slide into each slot. When they reached the last slot, Gris realized he still had five vials remaining.

"Got any other extreme-cold freezers aboard?"

Mancini nodded and carefully placed the remaining five vials into a small Styrofoam box. He walked away from the group to store the five vials below decks.

By the time Gris got back to the wet lab, Mancini was already at the bridge on the ship to shore radio with the Coast Guard. He was explaining how his crew had come upon a floating white shark carcass, that they had a special permit on board and were seeking to land the protected species. He asked for permission to tow the carcass to shore at the town docks for a necropsy.

Mancini waited for a response. Five minutes later, the officer initiated the process to issue clearance. First, the officer requested the permit number and the name of the individual listed. Mancini read the numbers slowly into the hand piece.

Next the Coast Guard officer requested his vessel's coordinates. Mancini read them into the hand set.

Finally the officer asked Mancini for his direction of travel and at which port they would land the protected fish. Mancini gave the final information to the officer. In a tone of authenticity, the officer granted a temporary clearance to proceed and warned Mancini that the 42-foot Coast Guard Safe Boat was now underway and would meet them within the next hour for an escort into the harbor.

Mancini headed back on deck. He caught Gris's arm and whispered, "Remind me that the ampoules are below when we get back to port. The last thing I want is for an officer to board my vessel to come across five unaccounted blood vials."

It was now 2:00 and the sun was high in the sky. Oddly, the shark was still alive. With the samples in cold storage, Mancini gathered his crew. He explained that they needed to release the 15-foot shark from the cradle and move it to the stern with a harness for towing.

The crew knew the drill. Cam shouted instructions

for the safest way to move the fish without losing her to the depth of the sea. Over the next half hour, the second mate, Cam and Kyle worked together to secure her body.

With a steady onshore current and light breeze, Cam calculated the boat had drifted half a mile toward shore. At 3:00 the boat began its slow steam back to port. It would take them six hours to return to port with an estimated time of arrival at 9:00 pm.

"That shark has a letter on its dorsal fin, just like the others." Kyle said while the first mate checked the tow harness. His father nodded.

"Probably just a deep scratch mark."

"I know you think it's a coincidence. But what if it isn't. Those letters mean something?" Kyle asked.

"White sharks have all kinds of marks on their bodies. Marks on their dorsal and bodies have been used to identify white sharks like fingerprints for people. But I'm not sure it really means anything."

"Maybe, but there's been a letter mark on every one we've found stranded," Kyle reminded.

"You kept track?"

"Yeah. Well, not the actual letters. But I know we've seen them. They'd be documented in the photos we took for your records. I'm sure I'd recognize them. Maybe we have repeats. Maybe those with the same shapes all came from the same area of the world. Or maybe they are from the same mother, just different litters. Maybe they are genetically connected." Kyle jumped from one thought to the next while his father listened and Cam stood by.

Cam's eyes widened as he stepped away. Gris caught his eyes.

"What the hell do you feed this kid? I mean what kid thinks of that stuff?" Cam shook his head.

Kyle dismissed the comments and considered Mancini's estimated time of arrival. It was better that they arrive under the veil of night. The carcass would not make it to the necropsy lab until after midnight, but at least their chances of running into the press would be minimal.

FIFTEEN

The Unaccounted Five

Kyle woke from his deep sleep with the gentle shake of his father's callused hand.

"At the mouth of the harbor, Kyle. Time to wake up," his father's voice was gravelly but soothing.

Kyle stood up and stretched. His body fatigued from the long steam in, he glanced off the stern to see the mammoth white shark attached to the stern by a bridled harness. He squinted to see the movement of something in the water behind the fish. Assuming it was a gray seal, he thought how ironic the scene was to have an ordinary prey nipping at the carcass of the great predator. But with a closer look, Kyle realized it was not a seal.

His father gestured with his chin and said, "It's an 8-foot white shark. He joined us about half way into the trip to feed. He's a healthy eater. Kept pace at nine to ten knots easily, all the while darting in to tear off one foot wide chunks from the carcass' sides behind the pectoral fins."

Kyle was riveted with the sight. The shark had no fear of the vessel or the people on board. He thought about the circumstances and wondered how his father was going to feel taking food away from a protected species in the name of science. Kyle shuddered at the thought as a seal rode the vessel's bow wake when the boat slowed speed once inside the inner harbor.

"You going to try to tag him before we dock?" Kyle asked his father.

"Would love to, but it's dark as pitch out here and we're towing a 2,000-pound fish. My gut's telling me I'd never convince Vinnie and Cam to chase it around the harbor in this darkness with a couple flashlights from the deck of a 16-foot workboat. So probably not tonight. "

Kyle laughed at the thought.

"Any news about Kane?" Kyle asked.

Gris shook his head. "Just that the ambulance met him at the dock and took him to the hospital."

Kyle startled when the engines roared into reverse on the captain's approach to the docks. The small shark darted to the right in pursuit of two taunting fat seals. He marveled at how well trained the seals had become, automatically heading toward the docks with the approaching sounds of an incoming vessel and the piercing whirl of the propellers underwater, even in the dark of night.

The captain spun the vessel into the dock, pinning his starboard gunwale against the dock decking. Cam stepped off the rail and wrapped a thick dock line onto a nearby cleat. The second mate tossed him the bowline and Cam secured it as well.

Kyle headed to the wet lab where he loaded his father's scientific gear into one oversized, plastic, fish-packing box. He placed the collected blood vials in a second oversized box. It would take him two trips.

He dug the truck keys from Gris' dry bag and took the box with the vials to edge of the dock. He'd move the vehicle closer and not have to carry things so far.

On the way back in the truck, a drunk staggered in front of the truck. Kyle slammed on the brakes and yelled out the window at the man who weaved back into the darkness of the night. In the flash of headlights, Kyle caught a brief glimpse of a second man darting behind a dumpster. The man's face reminded Kyle of Jon Kane, but that was impossible. Kane was either still at the hospital or at home sleeping at this ungodly hour.

Kyle was punchy from the long day on the water; it always tired him out and he was imagining things.

He pulled the truck as close as he could to the almost deserted dock which looked and sounded eerie in the middle of the night, lit by a few bright lights spaced every ten feet or so.

Cam was calling all hands on deck to guide the fish off the stern and pull it along the pier toward the shore. He planned to beach the fish and then hoist it up with a crane adjacent to the loading area. Because of the shark's length and weight, Gris would have to conduct the necropsy from the trailer before disposing of the carcass.

Kyle carried the second box to the truck. Sliding it into the bed, he halted. Something wasn't right. The box was lighter than he remembered. His heart constricted, his pulse speeded up and his stomach took a dive. The blood vial cooler was missing!

What was going on? He called to Gris who was directing the crane operator. "Did you take the blood cooler and some of the data sheets?"

His father shook his head. "I've been busy over here.

What the hell was going on? Kyle jumped back on board and ran to the wet lab. Perhaps in his exhaustion, he forgot which box he'd actually picked up.

In the lab, he examined the second box. No vials! He ran back on deck, hopped off the boat and headed toward the activity around the shark.

He raised his arms over his head, waving them to get the crew's attention."

"What's the problem, son?" Vinnie paused.

"Did anyone take the blood vials out of that box?"

A murmur of "no's" rose from the crew.

"No." Mancini's eyes were bloodshot, and his frown indicated he was impatient with the interruption.

"I loaded the cooler containing all our blood vials and our data sheets into that box!" Kyle pointed to the container on the dock.

Mancini settled his large hand on Kyle's shoulder. "You're tired, son. We all are. You probably misplaced the samples. They'll show up."

"No, Captain Vinnie, I didn't misplace them. They were lifted," Kyle's voice cracked.

"Lifted, like stolen?"

Kyle nodded.

"That's a pretty big assumption. You think the little cooler and sheets were stolen? Who on earth would want to steal blood samples and data sheets, eh?" Mancini shook his head.

Gris came over and placed a hand on his son's shoulder. He steered him to the box.

"Okay Kyle. Let's go over what happened." His father's voice was calm.

Kyle was beginning to think the lack of sleep was playing with his head. Maybe Mancini was right and he'd misplaced the little cooler and sheets. Maybe he never packed them, and all this was a figment of his imagination. His stomach churned and head ached.

"Let's check the truck," Gris said.

As Kyle followed his father to the vehicle, the fleeting image of a man resembling Jon Kane jumping behind a dumpster flashed through his mind.

Kyle had dismissed the idea that Kane was at the dock. He was probably still at the hospital, and if he'd been released, surely he'd be in bed sound asleep.

"Nothing here," Gris said after perusing the interior of the truck's cab.

The more Kyle thought about the transient image, the more he thought he wasn't imagining things. "I think I know who took the blood cooler and data sheets!"

"Who would do something like that?" Gris asked.

"Kane. I thought I imagined I saw him when I drove the truck up to the dock. But now I think it really was him."

Gris studied his son's tight features. "Let's assume you did see him," he said slowly. "What would an acoustical tag salesman want with blood samples and data sheets from dead sharks? It doesn't make sense."

"No, it doesn't, but I think that's what happened. There's something weird about the guy."

"I agree, but we have to give him the benefit of the doubt. He's probably under the gun from his boss. The company's gone through a lot and is relying on the new tag to restore their reputation."

"But Dad, we don't have any blood samples to show for a complete day's work! It was all for nothing. And it's all my fault." Kyle raised his arms, shoved his fingers through his disheveled hair and turned his back on Gris.

"Don't blame yourself, Kyle. These things happen. The good news it we still have blood vials."

"What are you talking about?" Kyle asked, whirling around to face his father.

"When Vinnie and I were loading the vial cooler, we discovered we took five more blood vials than we had room for in the cooler. I asked Mancini if he had a deep cold freezer on board where we could store them 'til we docked. They're below."

Kyle dropped his arms. "You mean we still have the live blood to run? You mean I didn't lose Greta's blood, and we can find out why she died?"

Gris nodded and threw his arms around his son for a quick hug. Kyle would normally be embarrassed at a display of affection but he was too relieved to care. He hugged his dad back.

Vinnie appeared at their side. "I hate to interrupt this little love fest, but it's getting late. Any chance we can get Kyle to back that trailer up to the platform so we can leave here before midnight?"

Gris chuckled, "Cute, real cute, Mancini."

Kyle pulled away from Gris. "I'm on it, Dad, Captain Vinnie. Just so you know, I'm gonna solve the mystery of the missing vials, just wait and see."

SIXTEEN

More Bad News

Jon Kane tossed his backpack across the bench seat of his car before sliding in. He was bone tired and a bit groggy from the mild tranquilizer the doctor had given him. He'd slept a bit in the emergency room while he waited for treatment, but he was not only physically exhausted but mentally strung out as well.

By the time he was seen by the intake nurse, he'd amended his story about an allergic reaction. He said he had panicked because he had sustained a similar injury when he was a teen, an injury that turned into an infection that almost killed him. The staff seemed to buy his story, and after cautioning him about high blood pressure, he was given a tetanus shot, a prescription for Xanax and released. With growing nausea, he went straight to the town fish docks where he dozed in his vehicle until he heard Mancini's boat arrive.

He couldn't believe his luck when the Kelley kid left the box unattended on the dock. He just hoped the kid hadn't recognized him as he'd passed by in the truck.

As he followed the curve in the road, he considered the last 24 hours in his head. *Complicated. This type of job is always complicated.* It had been eight hours since he'd stumbled backward on the boat, landed on the cleat and jammed a sharp toggle into his arm.

Kane waited behind a car at one of the stop signs in town and considered his options then dialed the number.

"Talk," the man answered.

Typical greeting. No phone etiquette. Let's rephrase—no etiquette, period.

"Talk," the man repeated more forcefully.

"Right, this is Kane . . . I mean Stevens," he mumbled into the receiver.

"I know that. Is there a reason for you bothering me in the middle of the night?"

"No," Kane answered and hung up. He then turned off his phone.

After arriving at his house, he lay down for 30 minutes then decided he was too antsy to sleep and took a shower, covering his arm with plastic wrap. He dressed, made a pot of coffee and waited for the sun to rise. Wired with caffeine, he climbed into the old pickup truck parked in the barn and headed to his office. He needed a plan to collect his commissions from Smart Fish Acoustics then exit as he'd originally planned.

When walked into the employee break room for a bottle of water, he spotted the television screen at the rear of the room. A reporter was standing in front of the 15-foot white shark corpse covered in ice on the trailer outside the Marine Fish Laboratory. The screen flashed to an interview with Gris Kelley, while a scroll bar ran along the bottom of the screen announcing a press conference at 2:00 to share results. He watched a brief video clip of the near-death white shark floating at sea near the harpoon vessel.

"Hey, you, turn that up?" Kane barked at a young woman sitting in a chair near the television. She slid the remote control across the table and returned to her novel.

The reporter was describing how fisheries

biologists in New Jersey had tagged the shark just two weeks earlier when the fish was in good health. Having found her near-death and floating at sea late yesterday, shark biologist Dr. Gris Kelley hauled her in to the Marine Fish Laboratory to conduct a full necropsy and process blood and muscle tissue samples for toxins.

"What the hell? Kane mumbled softly to himself.

"You say something?" the woman across the table asked.

Kane glared at her through narrowed his eyes. The woman shrugged her shoulders and returned to her book.

Shit . . . Kelley's conference was scheduled for 2:00. Kane headed to his office to print the last few release and payment forms for his sales commissions and walked the signed forms to the Smart Fish Acoustics accounting office for payment. He stood in front of the department's secretary desk and dropped the forms at the center of her desk. She stopped her typing and looked up.

"I need these processed. Today. Now."

"I'm sorry, Mr. Kane. Checks are cut weekly and that day was yesterday. You'll have to wait till next week," the finance secretary spoke in a soft controlled voice then offered him a forced smile.

"I'll be out of town the rest of the week through the weekend with members of the board of directors. In fact, Mr. Bigelow will be with me. I need you to cut it now."

The secretary's eyes widened at the mention of Bigelow's name.

"I understand. I can hold the check for you until you return," she offered.

"No!" Kane's response came out loudly. Another employee in a nearby cubicle turned around in her chair when she heard Kane's voice rise. "That won't work."

The woman from the cubicle rose and walked toward Mr. Kane. "Can I help you, sir?"

"I need these processed now. If you continue to resist me, we can call in Mr. Bigelow. Your call. But if either of you know him, then you know he doesn't like interruptions. So I'll explain again, I need these processed today."

The two women looked at one another then back at Kane.

"What'll it be, ladies?"

"Our finance director is at a lunch meeting and will not be back until 3:00. How about you come back then?" The other employee suggested.

"Yeah, you know that's not going to work," Kane pulled out his phone and in an audible whisper repeated the name Bigelow as he scrolled through his contacts. "Ah, there's the number. Shall we call Bigelow now?"

The two women looked at each other. Then one offered, "Let me call our assistant director to see if we can assist you, mister . . . mister?" she waited.

"Kane. Jon Kane. Working with Mr. Bigelow." The woman scurried back to the director's office. A moment later she returned stating it would be available in an hour.

"Make that 30 minutes, and I will wait," Kane stated and folded into the chair in front of her desk.

"Ah . . . right," she looked at him seated just three feet away and knew he wasn't moving until the check was cut. She rose and briskly walked to the back office.

While Kane waited, he thought about his next move. He would collect his payment and move on to the next step. He broke away from his thoughts when the secretary returned within a few minutes with a single check.

"I think you'll find all the commissions combined in this one check, Mr. Kane." She handed him the envelope containing the check.

He tore open the envelope in front of her and read the check. The secretary held her breath while she waited for his response.

Without a word he turned and left. He had business across town.

SEVENTEEN

Don't Be Ridiculous

With the shark loaded and partially packed in ice from the town fish dock, Kyle and his father drove the 1,800-pound fish to the Marine Fish Laboratory at the edge of town, arriving as the sun peeked over the horizon. Though the roads were nearly deserted, Gris hoped they didn't run into anyone.

Once there, he backed the long trailer into a reconstructed circa 1790 English frame-scribed hay barn, which housed his office, necropsy lab and an open bay for vehicles and storage. Unlike the Laboratory's main field office building at the entrance to the property, the hay barn was located at the crest of a sloping field at the rear. The three-story post and beam hay barn was converted to an open floor plan after Gris had the structure moved from a working cranberry farm dating back to the early 1900s. It had housed draft horses used to pull drag lines during the fall cranberry harvests.

Gris centered the trailer over a floor drain to catch any fluids that dripped. He and Kyle shoveled mounds of ice from the enormous ice machine onto the fish. Gris pressed a remote control to crank open all four skylights just enough to keep out the light drizzle that moved in after the left the dock. He punched on all three 10-foot industrial venting fans while Kyle continued to shovel ice to slow decomposition.

Neither planned to return to complete the necropsy until they gained showers, food and sleep.

Driving home in the light rain, Gris stared straight ahead as thoughts swarmed his mind. He waffled between heading back to the Lab to complete the shark necropsy or seeking out Audrey to make amends. He considered the melting ice and rigor mortis settling in. The logical destination was the lab to process the fish.

But he wasn't thinking logically. He was thinking about Audrey and her question, *where does your pursuit to 'save the species' leave our family?* All this thinking on no sleep set his head to pounding.

He decided to delay any decision until after a shower, a few hours' sleep and a meal. Perhaps by then his thoughts would clear.

"Boy, am I glad that's behind us," Kyle said through a yawn.

Gris grunted with agreement as he pulled into the driveway. His brain was again awash with thoughts of Audrey.

Up until three years ago, he had always put his commitment to Audrey and the boys first. He had married his best friend and the most gorgeous woman he'd ever seen. He adored her and had trouble keeping his hands off her. They rarely argued and worked hard not to let tension from their jobs separate them. Until now.

Father and son headed to the kitchen, where Kyle downed a leftover sandwich.

"Later, Dad," he said and clomped up the stairs. He thought about a hot shower but decided it was too much effort. With sleep scratching at his eyes, he collapsed on top of his blankets when he heard his phone ping on the bedside table. It was Lucy.

Lucy: *Where r U? Everything OK? Working breakfast.*

Kyle: *Yes. Just docked. At home now. Need 2*

sleep. Text when up.
Lucy: *Was worried. Y didn't U txt?*
Kyle: *No bars.*
Lucy: *Worried me.*
Kyle: *Sorry. Night-Luce.*
Lucy: *It's morning. I'll txt later.*

Kyle set his phone on the bedside table and buried his head in a pillow. A few seconds later he was asleep.

Across the hall, Gris fished his keys, wallet and cell phone from his pocket and dropped them on the dresser top. His phone screen glowed with a voice mail message from Audrey. It had come in at 6:10 the night before. Her familiar voice tugged at his heart as she said she'd be at a friend's beach cottage.

Great, he'd missed his chance.

Once again, work had interfered and prevented him from getting back to her on time, something that would have sent a clear message that she's a priority in his life.

She added that she needed to stop by in the next few days to get her things.

What the hell did that mean? Giving her space was one thing, but this has gone on too long.

Gris jumped into his truck and sped toward the small cottage while he replayed Audrey's message on his phone. He wasn't completely familiar with the cottage location, but thought he had been near the address during his childhood. He turned down a road and hit a dead end after 200 feet. He backed the truck up into the roadway before continuing on.

"Where are the damn road signs?" He took another street, this time rolling slowly down the road. It wound around a large pond which looked vaguely familiar. His mind flashed to a memory of fresh water fishing on a pond with his father when he was a boy. Not much had changed, except the houses which now were rundown with untended yards. Broken beer bottles littered the edge of the road where kids had partied. The sight raised his blood pressure.

He parked his truck and walked toward the front door of a cottage with the same house number as Audrey had listed. Not knowing if he even had the correct road, he knocked. When no one answered, he knocked again, louder this time. Still no answer.

He turned away and began to retrace his steps to his truck when he heard the click of a lock, then the creak of hinges protesting

"Audrey?" he said, turning.

"Gris, what are you doing here?" Audrey peeked through a crack before opening the door.

"I knocked but there was no answer."

Gris drank in the sight of her. He hadn't seen her in weeks. An eternity. It was the longest time they had ever been apart. And by the way she was studying him, she had missed him, too. At least that's what he told himself.

"I'm careful about answering the door here. There aren't many neighbors."

Gris looked from one side of the yard to the other and nodded.

"When my friend offered the cottage I guess I had a different picture in my mind. But inside it's cute and quite comfortable."

Gris waited for her to invite him in. But she didn't. An awkward silence fell between them. He finally broke the silence. "Audrey, I want you to come home."

Audrey stared at her husband. "Is that it? I just come back, and we continue on as if nothing's changed?"

"No. I've made arrangements for the press never to come to our home. All information is already being released at the Lab."

"Anything else?" she asked.

"Tell me what else you want and I'll make it happen. Listen, Audrey," he said, his eyes darting around the neighborhood, "I don't think you should be staying here, and I want you home." His voice turned hard. She had her space and oh, how he wanted her to come home! He was finished with their little tiff, and he knew if she were honest with herself, she was, too.

"What if I'm not ready?" she asked.

"You would rather be here . . ." He peered beyond Audrey into the dark knotty pine cottage with its original 1960s furniture, "than with me?"

"What do you think?" She threw the question back at him. Did she even have a plan for a future without him? He didn't want an answer to that question because the thought of her not being with him scared the hell out of him.

"I think you are not thinking straight. I know you're mad with me, but for Christ's sake, Audrey!" Gris didn't know what else to say for fear it would be the wrong thing. He was a master at dishing out scientific data, but when it came to something as personal as what was in his heart, he was at a loss for words. Especially the right words and even more so when he was angry. Truth be told, he was terrified he'd say something he'd regret.

"So you're convinced I'm not thinking straight?" Audrey glared at him.

There! He'd already said the wrong thing. He took a deep breath. "Listen, Audrey, I was head into the office to tie up some things for a client. Have an early lunch with me now."

"Ah . . . well. Actually, I have plans."

"Plans? With whom?

"Just plans."

She was stalling. Lying. She was an awful liar. "Okay, then a drink later this evening?" He wasn't going to let her go. Even more he wasn't comfortable with her accommodations. If he had to, he'd return this evening and sleep on the couch.

"I can't," she answered.

"Then breakfast. You always eat breakfast. So I'll swing by about 8:00 for breakfast tomorrow."

"There you go, making decisions without me, running our lives without my input. But I'll give you points for persistence."

Gris did not have time to process her revelation, so he latched on to her observation about his dogged resolve and leaned into the door jamb to indicate to her than he wasn't going to take no for an answer.

"Okay, okay. Dinner tomorrow night. But I'm warning you, Griswold Kelley, if there is a reporter within two miles of us, I'll be out of there so fast your head will spin." She crossed her arms over her chest, her mouth tightening into a thin line and held his gaze.

Gris suppressed the urge to smile. "Have it your way." He made a move as if to leave, then stepped closer. "But just so you know, I'm coming back tonight to sleep on the couch."

Audrey's mouth dropped open. "Oh, no you're not." She glared at him and shook her head.

"Listen, Audrey, this 'cottage' is unsafe. I'm coming back tonight."

"Don't be ridiculous. I'm not 12 years old."

"I know," he said. "Listen. I gotta go."

He really did have work to do, a client to contact, but he hurried to the truck before he said anything to make her cancel their dinner date. He didn't get what he came for. She wasn't coming home. Not yet.

He started the truck and with a wave and a lingering look headed out of the neighborhood. A surge of satisfaction cleared his head. At least they were talking and would have dinner together. When he returned later, he'd be the perfect guest by giving her space. And he'd stay on the couch despite the yearning desire to take her in his arms and kiss her senseless, or at least until she would agree to come home with him.

It was hard to leave her at that place, but he vowed he'd depart early in the morning. Tomorrow night at dinner he would convince her to come home.

Gris turned onto the main road and dialed Kyle.

"Dad? Where are you?"

"Damn, Kyle, your mother is a stubborn woman. And getting more so as she gets older. But you're right, I can't blame her. I've got to get my act together." He plowed on, ignoring his son's question, expressing his thoughts aloud. "I just get so caught up with my job, especially in the summer, that I forget I'm part of a marriage. You know, son, your mom is really special. Some women would concede defeat and let a situation roll on. Not Audrey. Not the mother of three willful boys."

"That's right, Dad, blame us kids!"

Gris was glad to hear Kyle laugh about the situation with his parents. Audrey's absence was hard on Kyle, too, although in a different way.

"You know, Dad," Kyle continued. "I've been thinking about me and Lucy. She's mostly flexible, always spending time with me, doing what I usually want to do."

"Makes you think, doesn't it?" Gris said.

"Yeah. So, did you apologize? Are you back together?"

"We were never apart," Gris almost growled. "But if we're to stay together, then I need to flex as well, starting this morning."

"How?"

"By getting a better grip on my work and its impact on you and mother. I'm heading to the lab right now. I'm going to notify the press that a shark was found floating at sea. I'll hold a press conference at 2:00 today at the Marine Fish Laboratory. I'll be heading over there in the next 30 minutes to start up on the necropsy."

"Okay. So when do you want me to drop off the

blood and muscle samples?"

"Right now."

"Hey, who's being stubborn now? Mind if I eat breakfast first?

Gris laughed. "I don't mind, just don't make it a brunch. I want those results as soon as possible."

"You're a slave driver," Kyle groused but with a playful edge to the words.

"Nothing I haven't heard before."

~

Kyle grabbed a breakfast bar and a cold soda and headed to the Marine Fish Laboratory to drop off blood and muscle samples. He was reassured that the results would be ready by 5:00. After relaying that information to Gris, he decided to take a detour into town to surprise Lucy at Hooligan's before heading in to help his father with the necropsy.

As Kyle's eyes adjusted to the dim light inside the pub, he caught sight of Lucy tapping her lunch orders onto the computer screen above the cash register. She sidestepped right to the drink counter to fill her glasses. She was busy sliding in one cup after another when Kyle snuck up behind her and kissed her neck. She twirled around hastily with an angry expression that melted into a smile when she recognized him.

"Can't stay long, but wanted to see if you want to hit the bonfire tonight at Shark's Cove," he whispered in her ear.

"Sure. What time will you pick me up?"

"About eight. We can grab a bite on the way."

"Can you stay a few minutes? For a drink?" Lucy turned to fill a large plastic cup with Kyle's favorite soda but Kyle stopped her.

"I've got one in the truck. I'll be helping Dad with a necropsy today."

A familiar laugh from across the room caught his

attention. His mother was talking with animation to three friends at a corner table.

Kyle made a move in her direction, but Lucy grabbed his hand.

"Kyle, wait. Before you walk over there and create a scene, I'll tell you she just walked in about 15 minutes ago and asked to be seated in my section. Let her finish her salad, huh?"

He looked from Lucy to his mother.

"Whatever you do, please don't make a scene," she pleaded. "Let her talk with your father. Yeah?"

"Thanks for the advice, Luce. But Dad went to her house today."

"You mean they're on the mend? All patched up? She's home?"

"Not exactly, but they're grabbing dinner together tomorrow night. Dad said he may even sleep at her house tonight."

Lucy gasped. "That's a good sign, isn't it? She wiggled her eyebrows and grinned. One dimple pierced deeply into her cheek.

"I know what you're thinking. And I hate to put a damper on your thoughts. Dad told her he planned to head over because he doesn't think the place she's staying is safe. She didn't agree. I guess that's when he told her flat out that he'd be back tonight to sleep on her couch. Then he left before she could stop him."

Lucy's face went thoughtful. "Wow, this is getting juicy, huh? I mean, he's not taking no for an answer?"

"Geez, you women love this stuff, don't you?" Kyle said, searching her face.

"Kyle, I think it's sweet. I told you they wouldn't stay apart long.

"Yeah, yeah. Pretty proud of that, aren't you? But Luce, it's not a done deal yet. He's still got some groveling ahead of him," Kyle looked down at her now in his arms, her eyes level with his chin. She was still grinning.

Kyle shook his head and rolled his eyes back. "Right. Well, I gotta get back to the lab. Told Dad I would be there by noon. It's already past that. And on second thought, I'll take that." Kyle grabbed the cup of soda and kissed Lucy on her head.

"You going to say hello to your mum?"

"Nah, I'll see her later. I'm with you; she'll be home sooner than she thinks. Besides I don't want to break up her time."

Lucy cocked her head in surprise.

"What?"

"I thought you were more of a doubter?" she said.

"Oh, I have no doubt they'll be back together...and soon. I know they can't stay apart much longer without both of them going crazy. Life is miserable at home with Dad. She got back yesterday from her sister's, and he was at her place early this morning when he probably should have been sleeping. But he can't sleep, at least not with her gone."

"Number 5! Lucy Wharton," a booming voice called from the kitchen, "Food's up and getting cold."

"Right. You parked out back behind the kitchen?" Lucy asked.

"Yeah, near the back door."

Another waitress stepped up to the station. "You go ahead, Lucy, I'll get your order."

"Thanks." Lucy threaded her fingers into Kyle's hand as she followed him out to his truck where he pinned her against the door. He leaned in to brush her lips with his before he tucked a strand of loose hair behind her ear. She exhaled, and he kissed her jaw.

"Text me if you are running late," he whispered moving back to her ear. He wrapped his arms around her back and lifted her up to kiss her.

It was just a light kiss, but it brought their bodies together. Kyle had the shape of her memorized. He finally set her free, loosening his grip with reluctance, allowing her to slide down his chest until her feet touched the ground.

She sighed and said, "Kay."

Kyle released her and opened his door, then climbed in. The window was down. He backed up the truck and watched her, first through the window, then with a wave, through the rear view mirror. She blew him a kiss.

Lucy lingered even after Kyle was out of sight, despite the fact that she had customers waiting. She simply wanted to savor the memory of their embrace while she was still alone. Finally, deep in thoughts and the reverie that she was in love, she walked around the side of the building, heading to the side entrance.

Reaching for the door handle, she paused, sensing someone behind her. Before she could react, a strong arm came around her collar bone from the left. A hand from the right sealed her mouth shut with a piece of tape. Her first impulse was to see who was playing a trick on her, but a black cloth bag dropped over her head, cutting off her sight. A rope closed tightly around her neck, and her arms were twisted behind her. Sheer terror turned her into a statue.

EIGHTEEN

I've Got Your Girlfriend

"Stand up, damn you!"

No way was Lucy going to cooperate. She tried to scream, but with her mouth taped shut, the sound came from deep inside her throat, no more than a low growl.

Her captor twisted her arms more and dragged her across the gravel parking lot.

Lucy winced as she was thrown against the side of a vehicle where her arms were trussed behind her back.

Her attacker shoved her to the ground where she slumped to one side. She heard the creak of a car door opening.

Advice from the past popped into her head. Her father had tried to drill it into her: *Never, never let an attacker put you into a vehicle.*

Gathering her scattered thoughts, she rolled onto her stomach and tried to draw her feet under her with the intent to standing and running. But her attacker grabbed her by the shoulder and turned her around, this time shoving his knee to her chest.

Lucy kicked out her feet, but her feet made no contact with her assailant. She whipped her head around trying to confuse and stall the attacker.

Please, please, God, let someone see me from the parking lot.

She continued to flail on the ground in an attempt to get to her feet, but when she raised her shoulders and head, she hit the edge of the open car door with her ear. Now her ear throbbed along with her head. A warm trickle of blood slid down her jaw.

Weighing about 110 pounds, Lucy was easy prey for her attacker who easily yanked her to her feet. She again tried to scream, but the sound was muffled against the tape. She whipped her shoulders from side to side, but a hard shove had her landing chest first onto a wide bench seat.

"Oomph," she cried out as she landed face down.

Determined not to give up, she rocked from side to side in an effort to wriggle herself backward out of the vehicle.

Never, never let an attacker put you into a vehicle! The sound of a heavy vehicle door slamming shut was like a death knell.

The engine started. *No, no, no, this can't be happening!*

She tried to scream again and again. But her cries behind the tape were futile, and soon she grew dizzy from hyperventilating.

A sudden blast from the radio jolted through her, and she started to cry. The vehicle lurched forward, gravel crunching beneath the wheels. The driver stopped for a moment, then hit the accelerator hard. The wheels spun on the dusty rubble lot, then smoothed out as it bumped onto even pavement.

Lucy's shoulders jerked as she sobbed. *This couldn't be real! Maybe this was all a practical joke.* No one had ever been kidnapped from this well-heeled, quaint summer town that nearly got by on property taxes alone from its wealthy summer residents on holiday in inherited mansions.

It had happened so quickly! She prayed that someone had seen her bagged and pushed into the vehicle and was at this very moment calling the police to come to her rescue.

~

Kyle sat in his truck waiting for a break in the traffic when he heard someone call his name. He turned one way to see his mother walking toward her sedan away from him. In the other direction, Detective Ellis who had run the license plate for his father, darted up to Kyle's window. They both turned at the sound of gravel flying. A white pickup truck raced out the side entrance of the lot.

"Guess that guy's happy his shift's ended," Kyle said with a chuckle.

The detective pulled out his phone and, mumbling the vehicle's plate, typed it into his cell along with its color, make and model, before turning his attention back to Kyle.

"Ran a comprehensive background check on Jon Stevens or rather Jon Kane. Came up with some other information your father'll likely be interested in."

"You want him to call you?" he asked the cop. A glimpse in his rearview mirror caught sight of Audrey turning his way. His mother had recognized his truck and was walking across the lot.

"That'll work.

"Okay. I'll be at the lab this afternoon."

As Ellis turned to leave, Kyle pulled onto the shoulder and shifted into PARK

"Hey, Mom." Kyle stepped out of the truck to give her a bear hug. "Sure have missed you around the house. Saw you in Lucy's section having lunch, but promised Luce I'd let you hang with your friends."

"I saw you, too, as you and Lucy walked out the back door. When I saw your truck, I was sure she was still with you." Audrey peered into the cab.

"No, she said she needed to get back to tend her tables."

"That's funny. We waited for our check, but when Lucy never came back in, another waitress delivered it. Told us Lucy was still in the parking lot."

"She wasn't with me for more than a few minutes," Kyle said. "Maybe she hit the restroom on her way in."

"I don't know. I left as the cook was still calling her number. Almost came to get her when I heard her name for a fourth time. The other waitresses where checking around for her, too." Audrey's eyes squinted more from worry than the sunlight.

"That's not like Luce," Kyle said, fear stabbing at his chest.

"I know."

"If you don't mind, I'll go check on her. See you soon, Mom?"

"I can't promise anything, Kyle. But I'll call you. Now go ahead. Check on Lucy."

Kyle sprinted toward the pub's back entrance, his eyes scanning the parking lot as he ran. Inside, he checked the restroom, the kitchen, the bar, and finally Lucy's section. She was nowhere in sight.

He turned back toward her tables when her friend called out, "Kyle, isn't Lucy with you? She never came back into the pub."

"I'll check her car," he said and ran to the parking lot where she always left her car. It was locked. He could see her baggy purse on the floor under the front seat where she always stashed it.

Kyle ran toward his truck, still parked on the shoulder next to the pub's exit. His mother was talking to Ellis who was holding takeout.

"Your mother just gave me the story. Is Lucy in there?"

"No. No. She's gone," Kyle said, breathless. "Her purse is still in her car, which is locked. Something is terribly wrong."

"Son, let me go back in and clear the premises,

then we'll move on from there," Ellis assured him.

Kyle didn't answer. His mind was racing. He needed to keep moving. He needed to find Lucy.

~

As the abductor drove swiftly to his destination, Lucy struggled to rotate her torso so that she was no longer face down on the seat. The overpowering scent of fish boots left to bake in the sun on the stern of a boat invaded her nostrils with each breath she drew.

As she pushed herself back, she realized she was sitting on the floor of the passenger's side of a pickup truck. A large hump in the middle of the floor divided her from her assailant. When she tried to straighten, she felt her cell phone press against her buttock and she froze. Not wanting to alert her abductor, she carefully twisted her hands tied behind her to check if she could remove it.

Suddenly the truck dropped down a couple inches as it turned off the smooth pavement onto a bumpy dirt lane. She listened to the crackle of branches under the tires and decided to use the louder conditions to remove her phone. Once she grabbed it, she swiped it on. First she made sure it was on "silent," then pushed the upper button and held it in her captor's direction. Not even knowing if she was pointing the phone in the right direction, she tapped it repeatedly as she moved the phone to different angles. She felt the truck decelerate and took the cue to slide her phone back into her shorts.

A jarring bump, a change in the sound of the tires and the lower temperature told her that the truck was inside a building. She remained totally still as the man turned off the engine and adjusted the squeaky rearview mirror. *What was he doing? Smoothing down his hair?* His movements suggested he was also adjusting his clothes. What kind of kidnapper checks the mirror to see that every hair was in place before proceeding with a crime?

Another movement suggested he pulled something out from under the seat.

"Don't move," he growled.

He was agitated, a feeling Lucy shared, for different reasons. She slid two fingers over the top seam of the pocket to confirm that her phone was concealed. It was.

"Okay, Miss Lucy, I'm going to text your boyfriend now. But don't get your hopes up; the message will go through with my identity blocked. You see, I've done this before."

She heard him tap on the phone.

"Not that I always like it. But you're very easy on the eyes, so no matter that this is a complicated job with too many people involved, I'm not minding it too much." His laugh was wicked. "And you don't have to worry that I'll get caught—I never leave any proof behind. I'll erase all evidence that a call was placed," he bragged.

"Here we go," he said after a long moment of silence. "Me. *I've got your girlfriend,*" he read out loud. "And send!"

Lucy heard him open the door, his footsteps rounding the front to the passenger's side door. When it opened, she smelled fresh hay.

"Get out," he growled, pulling Lucy by her legs. She kicked at him but missed her mark.

"Do it again and you die," he warned.

Lucy froze.

The abductor reached in again, and this time she let him pull her out of the vehicle and onto her feet. The ground was soft beneath her shoes.

He pushed her forward from behind and she stumbled onto the soft dirt floor near a wall.

"Stand up!" He grabbed her belt and lifted her to her feet.

She leaned against the wall and heard a phone ping. It wasn't hers.

"Don't move," he ordered, pinning her against the wall with one hand to her throat, the other reaching for what she assumed was his phone. "It's your boyfriend. Listen to what he wrote back: *I don't believe you*. Goddamn amateurs. Hate 'em.'"

He backed away from Lucy, and in the next instant, she heard the click and saw a faint flash of light through the bag over her head.

She could tell that he followed a fastidious routine before attaching the photo in a return message to Kyle.

"See if he believes me now," he chuckled.

~

Kyle received the initial message from Lucy's abductor while he was driving to the Marine Fish Laboratory to meet his father. He pulled off the road thinking the text was a trick when he typed back his reply. The next text hit his phone almost immediately.

Kyle sat back and stared at his girlfriend's image with disbelief. Things like this didn't happen to ordinary people like him. He recognized Lucy's shirt, shorts and tied apron. When he saw a small scrape on her right arm she had gotten the other night when they climbed out her window onto the roof to stargaze, he drew in a ragged breath against the surge in his pulse. If something happened to Lucy, he'd kill the man responsible.

~

"Stand up," Lucy's captor said, pulling her up by one arm. "Start walking." He pushed her forward and she stumbled in an effort to get her footing.

"Move!"

Disoriented, Lucy hooked her foot on something and stumbled. A strong arm wrapped around her chest just below her bra strap to catch her

"You're a clumsy one, aren't you?" he muttered.

As he shifted, Lucy moved her head downward and tried to bite him but all she got was a mouthful of cloth. He let go of her and as she landed butt first on the ground.

"Stupid bitch! I was going to take the bag off your head, but now it stays on, Princess."

He picked her up by her belt and pushed her forward into a room with a concrete floor and a stronger smell of hay. She figured she was in a barn, most likely a stall.

He turned her around and pushed her backward into a chair.

"Stay there," he barked.

Lucy shifted and rotated her head back to stretch her neck.

"Bag stays on. So does the tape." Lucy's shoulders visibly shuddered at his loud voice, and she quietly whimpered to herself.

She heard his footsteps and a chair scraping across the concrete. By the sounds, she assumed it was a metal folding chair. She heard him drop onto the flimsy seat.

"You're one pretty catch," he said with satisfaction. "I don't need to see your face, you know. I've been watching you. Besides, I'd rather look at those legs in those tiny shorts any day."

He laughed as Lucy visibly cringed.

"Yeah. Watched you the other night with that kid. He couldn't keep his hands off you. If he doesn't do what I tell him, I won't either." When Lucy squirmed at his words, he gave a sinister chuckle.

Lucy's mind raced at his threat. She thought again about her father's warning: *Never let an attacker get you into a vehicle.*

Why had she let him drag her into his truck? He was crazy. Then she remembered Kyle's warning of the creepy salesman watching her from the bar the other night. Though she'd seen him, she'd never heard his voice. *Was he her kidnapper? Was he crazy enough to abduct her? Why would he take her? What did he want?*

The ping of a cell phone interrupted her thoughts. "This kid asks too many questions," the man growled then read the text.

Kyle: *What do you want?*

Smart boy. Finally we're getting somewhere. Time for some ground rules. Though he was forced to switch plans, he was glad he grabbed the girl. He liked looking at her body quiver with fear. At least this plan was falling into place.

Again, the man stood silently as he went through his two-step routine and responded to Kyle's query.

Captor: *Tell anyone and you'll get her back in tiny pieces.*

He sent the text and sat back down in the chair opposite Lucy. She turned her head as she heard him sit. His silence made her skin crawl. She thought about asking him why she was there. She thought it might anger him. He'd already told her that the tape stays on, so she waited for his next order.

He didn't have one. Not yet anyway. She knew he was watching her, waiting.

She heard him push his feet forward and lean back further in the chair as if he was more relaxed. But then she heard him shift forward with arms on his knees and she knew he was examining her.

She was attractive, very attractive. Her hands and arms were small and slender, even delicate, her waist quite narrow, making her chest appears large for a petite person. He wanted to see her face but hadn't decided if he should remove the cover. Keeping her tied up in darkness definitely made her apprehensive and skittish and he decided he liked her that way.

Kyle: *What do you want?*

Another text sounded on the abductor's phone. Kyle was in his truck on the side of the road when he sent the text. He waited for a response. He waited there 30 minutes feeling like he would lose his mind before a sudden ping jolted his thoughts.

Captor: *Want her to live, stop giving the press shark updates.*

He was rereading the abductor's instructions when his father's ringtone broke the silence.

"Hey, where the hell have you been?" his father asked as Kyle answered. He didn't respond immediately.

"Kyle, you there?"

"Yeah, yes, yes—I'm here," Kyle answered reluctantly.

"You on your way?" his father asked. "We got a press conference in 30 minutes."

A feeling of panic washed over Kyle as he thought of the abductor's last text—*want her to live, stop giving the press shark updates.*

"Cripes," he breathed out. How was he going to stop his father from holding a press conference?

NINETEEN

No More Updates

Easier said than done . . . , Kyle thought as he sucked in a breath and ran his shaking hands through his hair.

He was glad he'd pulled over or he might have run off the road into a telephone pole after reading the text. He couldn't wrap his head around the fact that his girlfriend had just been kidnapped, and if he ever wanted to see her again, he had to convince his father to stop talking to the press.

If Mom can't get him to stop, how will I ever convince him?

What he *could* tell his father was to cancel the 2:00 press conference. His father might cancel if he felt he was doing something wrong or reporting misinformation. Gris was all about relating facts.

Kyle decided on this angle when he started on his father. "You sure we need to hold a press conference? I mean don't you think it's premature?"

"What . . . what do you mean?" Gris asked.

"Wouldn't it be better to postpone it until we have the cause of death from headquarters? I mean, what if you give the press some misinformation about the sharks?" Kyle gave it his best shot.

How could Lucy be kidnapped? He was just with her an hour ago! He again considered talking to someone. But her captor had made it clear Kyle would never see her again. That was too gruesome an image to consider.

"How 'bout we talk about it when you get here?" Gris interrupted Kyle's thoughts.

Kyle arrived at the Marine Fish Laboratory 15 minutes later. Pulling in, he found a frenzy of television crews clogging the driveway. He backed up and parked his Bronco on the side of the road, then slipped through a side door to the building where his father was conducting the necropsy.

A waft of the dead shark hit him, his stomach recoiling in protest. He covered his nose.

"Where you been?" Gris asked.

"Got tied up in town."

"You okay, son?" Gris leaned forward.

His father always seemed to know when something was wrong, so Kyle diverted his eyes. "Uh . . . huh."

"Come with me. I have something to show you." Gris raised his voice to be heard over the fans and handed Kyle a paper facemask.

With the shark splayed open on the trailer behind them, Gris led Kyle across the room to his laptop. "I edited and clipped a few minutes of Greta's behavior from the last few days before her death." He clicked on the arrow to play the silent video.

"The first clip shows Greta chasing a seal. She bites it and even flips it in the air. But then she leaves it. This is strange because she never consumes it," Gris noted. "The next clip shows her spy-hopping off the coast of a crowded beach. She's in Big Betty's territory. You know, where you saved that girl?"

"I didn't save her, Dad. Just got her to safety sooner than later," Kyle corrected.

"Okay," Gris said, raising his eyebrows at Kyle's edgy tone then moved on.

"On this clip, Greta moves in for a pass along the beach. See here, you can see a swimmer's feet kicking and here you see a surfboard fin slice through another wave overhead. But Greta never engages."

"Is it unusual for a shark to mill around and watch swimmers and surfers?"

"Very. These are predators always on the lookout for food. They aren't sightseers. Sharks are very curious and will definitely check out their surroundings before attacking. But they don't usually get this close without even a test-bite." Gris forwarded the video. "The final scene is very disturbing. It shows Greta ramming into the side of a freighter. She swims away, but her movements from here on are jerky, and she is frequently seen swimming sideways and upside down from here until the end."

Kyle winced when he saw the impact to the shark's body.

"More than likely this collision led to brain damage. We'll know more when the brain samples are processed."

Kyle looked away from the laptop to the shark's open body cavity. Except for some organ entrails, the space appeared nearly hollow.

"See how emaciated this shark is? I found nothing in its stomach, except several parasites on the organs. Greta was tagged 20 days before she died. Looks as if she hadn't eaten since being tagged."

"Is that normal for them to go without eating for three to four weeks?"

"Sharks will fast for a few days when they feel sick, but not three weeks. Fasting saves on energy and lets the shark redirect the energy spent on digestion toward eliminating toxins and healing. The only other time feeding stops is when a pregnant female delivers her pups. But for Greta, her fasting went on too long. If she didn't die from brain damage, she likely died from starvation or toxins."

Gris pointed to a cooler loaded with ice and various labeled samples he had removed from the shark. "The blood, muscle, liver and brain samples will reveal the story of her demise. I want you to drop this off to Dr. Chang at the Marine Fish Laboratory when you pick up the results this afternoon."

"Kyle?" his father said.

Kyle was no longer listening. He had moved on to figure out how to find Lucy.

"Kyle?" his father repeated.

"Son," Gris reached out and touched Kyle's arm. He startled at his father's touch to his shoulder.

"You okay, son? You don't look like you are in this world."

"No, I wish you would consider not holding that press conference," he murmured.

"What's that?" his father asked.

"Don't hold that live press conference," Kyle repeated, his voice rising.

Gris took a step back. "You're beginning to sound like your mother."

"When you report information to the press that is not definite, isn't it like telling them a lie, or at the very least, leading them on?" Kyle was desperate.

Gris stopped and thought for a moment. "Well, I guess you could think of it that way. But I usually explain that we are awaiting results."

"Then why hold the conference at all? Why not just wait for the results?" He tried to keep panic at bay, but his voice betrayed him.

"Kyle, are you feeling all right? I've never heard you this concerned about a press conference."

"Yeah, well, I just think we should wait," he said with a stubborn tilt to his chin.

Gris studied Kyle's face for a long moment. "If it means that much to you, we'll wait until tomorrow or even the next day when the results are back from the Laboratory. I'll look them over together and then release a statement."

Kyle let out a ragged breath. "You mean it?

Thanks, Dad. Really, thanks!"

Gris' cell phone vibrated as Kyle stooped down to pick the cooler off the floor.

"That was Vinnie," Gris said, tapping his phone off. "Spotter plane found another floater at sea and has coordinates for two other sharks nearby. We need to meet them at the boat in 20 minutes."

Kyle shook his head. "I can't go, Dad. With the long hours last night, I promised Lucy I'd do something with her." He prayed his father would not see the lie in his eyes.

"I understand. It's short notice on four hours of sleep. I got this. Tell Lucy I said hello."

Kyle didn't reply as his father held open the side door to the barn. As soon the door swung open, cameras bulbs began flashing.

Kyle stared at his father with a look of dread mixed with panic. "Not sure how you put up with these clowns, Dad."

"Kyle, you just deliver those samples. Let me handle the press. I'll let them know we're awaiting results and it'll be a couple days before we hold another press conference." Gris walked toward the microphones.

Kyle headed to his Bronco, setting the loaded cooler onto the floor of his truck, then lashed it down with a bungee cord. He waited to start his engine and listened to his father relay the bad news that he still lacked information and the press conference would be rescheduled.

Kyle let out a heavy sigh. One disaster averted and any number ahead before he got his Lucy back.

207

TWENTY

Tell No One Or Else

Kyle sat in his truck at the town docks parking lot and reread the text messages from Lucy's abductor. He considered who would want to squash the broadcast of the recent shark deaths and who would be concerned about the newest floater spotted offshore.

He grabbed a notepad wedged under the seat and made two columns: *Pro shark / Anti-shark.* He listed any person or group who would gain from either perspective.

Pro-shark
Commercial fishermen (eat seals who commercial catch)
Environmental activists (save species)
Scientists (gain knowledge)
Federal and state agents (legally bound to protect)
Tourists (curiosity seekers)
Recreational fisherman (chance for observing
Sharks in the wild, hook on line)
Tag or equipment companies (benefit from sales)
Finning industry buyers (more fins available, more $$)
Elected officials (boasts local economy)

Anti-shark
Commercial fishermen (eat fish, damage gear)
Business owners (scare away tourists, loss of income)

Lifeguards (job hazard)
Surfers (risk of injury or death)
Tourists (closed beaches, no swimming)
Elected officials (scares away tourists)
Dive boat owners (scares and eats divers)

3 groups anti great white sharks:
Business owners, lifeguards, surfers

After he compiled the lists, he reread them and wrote in reasons, then compared the two lists. Only three groups stood out as gaining no benefits from the arrival of white sharks: business owners, lifeguards and surfers.

Odd how the lists confirmed what he already knew. As a surfer, he knew sharks were unwelcome visitors. After all, they posed a threat to survival. For lifeguards, the reasons were nearly identical to surfers. Sharks posed a hazard at work, sometimes preventing them from doing their job and a very real threat to life. But for business owners, the reasons were clearly different. It wasn't about a threat to human life. Their reasons related to a loss of income.

People depended on these twelve glorious summer weeks to capture revenues more than any other weeks of the year. Many business owners, though not as vocal, agreed with Bigelow. The sharks affected the town like a double-edged sword. On the one hand, they generated great interest for visitors who stayed over to walk the town's beaches and coves just to see if they could glimpse the great white sharks. Then before departing, they frequented the town's shops for souvenirs to commemorate their stay. On the other hand, a sudden attack frequently scared off visitors, who then canceled their reservations or their daytrips, like ants fleeing a rainstorm.

The most vocal critic of white sharks Kyle knew

was billionaire and resort owner, Joseph Bigelow.

Kyle checked his watch. He still had a couple hours to burn before meeting Lab Chemist Dr. Chang at the Marine Fish Laboratory. He reached into his pocket to check his cell phone when the detective's business card dropped into his lap. He'd forgotten to tell his father about the detective's message. He'd forgotten a lot of things since Lucy had gone missing. He flipped the card over and texted his father Ellis's number and asked him to call him ASAP.

He cranked over his engine and reread the number to himself as he drove the half-mile home. He wondered how risky it would it be to speak with him on his personal cell phone about the texts he'd received.

By the time he reached the driveway, Kyle decided the risk was too great. He wouldn't call Ellis. But maybe he'd call his best friend Brodie. Over the last two years, Kyle had acted as a vault for information Brodie wanted to keep secret. Surely Brodie would return the favor.

He parked his truck in the driveway and dialed Brodie's cell. It went directly to voice mail. He decided not to leave a message and hung up. He leaned an arm over the top of the steering wheel and let his forehead rest against it as he contemplated his next move.

He dialed his friend again and this time left a message. "Lucy has been kidnapped. I think I'll look for her out on Goose Neck Road. Don't tell anyone or she's dead. Call me when you get this message."

He walked up the path to the kitchen door when he heard his mother speaking on the phone. She was hanging up when he walked through the screen door. He wondered if Dad knew she was at the house. Last update, his father said he'd seen her that morning and she was not yielding.

"Mom?"

"Ah, Kyle!" She wrapped her arms around her son

and kissed his temple. "Twice in one day, I love it. They find Lucy at work?"

Kyle shook his head.

"Oh, Honey. You must be worried."

Kyle considered telling his mother. She already knew Lucy was missing, so she already had partial knowledge of the day's events.

"Did you tell your father?"

Kyle shook his head. "He's headed back out on the harpoon boat, they spotted three sharks."

Audrey raised her eyebrows. "Three in one day. You all have been busy. So are you meeting up with Ellis to try to locate her?"

"No, he can't file a missing person report for 24 hours. But I got—" He stopped, then diverted his eyes from hers.

"What? Kyle what did you get?"

"Nothing. It's nothing," he quickly answered and headed to the fridge for the carton of orange juice.

He could feel his mother's eyes at the back of his neck studying him. He hated when his mother studied him. She knew he meant to say more, and Kyle knew she'd pry it out of him.

"It's something. You wouldn't have said you got something if it was nothing." She confused him with her logic, but not enough for him to bend.

She waited. She wasn't going to let the subject drop. "Kyle Kelley, tell me what you were going to say." Her voice was soft. She was using kind tactics to get the information from him. He looked into her warm eyes. She smiled at him and her smile lines pinched the edges of her eyes.

Whenever Kyle and Lucy had a disagreement and he had trouble reading Lucy's actions, he had confided in his mother. He always asked her to keep it to herself, and she'd always been a vault. Not once did she spill. Of all people, she was probably the best person to speak to about the texts and how he could find his girl.

He took a deep breath and pulled out a chair at the kitchen table, then motioned his mother to sit down. He pulled a second chair out for himself and rotated it so he could sit with his chest against the back and legs straddled. His mother waited patiently for him to begin.

He drew in another deep breath. "You've always kept information I told you to yourself and I appreciate that, Mom, I really do" He closed his eyes and tilted his head back before resuming his tale. "Today after I left the pub, I received some information on Lucy. Not just information but texts, threatening texts."

His mother adjusted her seat. He had her full attention.

"From the person who took her," Kyle added.

His mother covered her mouth with one hand. From her son's expression, she realized he needed her to be strong, like a rock. So she dropped her hand and gulped down her worry.

After Kyle hesitated, she finally asked "Would you like to share the texts with me?"

"I think so. But if I do and her abductor finds out, Lucy could be killed."

His mother froze at the thought. "But only if her abductor finds out you shared the texts, right?" She hoped she understood Kyle correctly because his statements were coming out in bits and pieces, and she didn't want to press him. She knew eventually he would share all the information, when he was ready.

"Right . . . only if he finds out," Kyle blew out a heavy breath. He pulled his phone from his back pocket and placed it on the table. He watched as his mother's eyes shifted to the screen.

"I don't want him to kill her. So I am trying not to tell anyone, because if I do, then he said he'd give her back to me in tiny pieces . . . but I need to help her and just . . . just . . . I don't know how to help her."

The anguish Audrey saw in her son's eyes was almost too much for her to bear. She wanted to hug him, tell him everything would be all right and that Lucy was strong and she'd be home soon. But she couldn't promise him that. Though she wanted to believe it, it may not be true. So she just waited for him to share his information.

"So here goes." Kyle tapped on his phone and right there in front of them were the abductor's messages and the photo of Lucy trussed and masked. Kyle stared at the texts for a few seconds before turning the phone around for his mother to read.

Audrey pulled the phone closer to reduce the glare and read the abductor's demands and Kyle's responses. She read them twice and lingered on Lucy's picture before pushing the phone back to her son. Her face was red with fury.

It wasn't the reaction Kyle was anticipating. He thought she'd be a fretful, emotional mess. Instead she was mad, so mad he thought steam would come out of her ears soon.

"I stopped Dad from holding the press conference today at the Lab. But he doesn't know about Lucy's abduction. I just convinced him to hold off on the press conference until we have all the lab results back. So after a long argument, he finally agreed."

Kyle was staring at his mother's flushed face when his phone pinged to life on the kitchen table.

"Hang on, Mom. Here comes more."

Audrey's eyes blinked wide open as he picked up the phone and read the text.

Captor: *Stay silent and she lives.*

Kyle quickly returned a text.

Kyle: *I have. We have.*

Captor: *Who're we?*

Kyle: *I have. No one else.*

He sent a panicked look Audrey's way as he again

waited for a response. A ping bounced back almost immediately.

Captor: *The press conference – later today?*

Kyle read the text, then typed his response quickly. *Canceled.*

There was a long pause. Kyle couldn't stand the silence, a roaring silence. The abductor got what he wanted. Now Kyle needed to get what he wanted. An answer.

Kyle: *When will she be free?*

A ping signaled an immediate reply.

Captor: *Patience.*

Kyle read the response, his face tightening with anger. He stomped his boots on the floor and let out a growl after he reread the single word three more times.

"*Patience? Patience?* Who the hell is this control freak?" He turned to Audrey. "Does he really think I can control the press? Does he really think I can have patience when he has Lucy? Goddamn him! If he does anything to hurt her, I'll . . . I swear I'll kill him."

"Okay, okay. Kyle. I get that you're mad. You have every reason to be," Audrey cautioned. "But mad isn't going to get Lucy home." She spoke in an even reasonable tone. "He obviously wants the information on the sharks to remain quiet. Do you know anyone who doesn't want anything about shark deaths or tags released to the press?"

Kyle shook his head. "Only people I know who don't want the sharks around are surfers, lifeguards, maybe a dive boat owner, and some of the town's business owners. Then again, it seems most of the business owners like them around because they're making a killing off shark souvenirs."

"This guy obviously wants the whole shark story to go away. So remind him that all information has been discontinued. End of story."

"Not sure he'll believe me."

"Well, maybe not. But I think your reassurance will at least buy us some time."

He picked up the phone.

"Wait. Who are you calling?" His mother placed a hand on his hand holding the phone.

"I'm going to send him that text, that there will be no more press conferences."

"Well—wait, Honey. I think we need more of a plan than zipping off text after text. Let's just think for a minute."

~

While Kyle headed over to the Marine Fish Laboratory to collect the lab results, Gris headed to the harbor to meet Mancini at the harpoon boat.

But first he had to call Detective Ellis. He pulled out his phone as the harpoon boat pulled away from the dock. The plan was to meet the spotter plane offshore to tag two great whites and investigate a floating shark nearby.

Ellis answered immediately.

"Was wondering if Kyle delivered my message." Ellis waited for Gris's response. "Then again, I can't blame him if he hadn't, with Lucy being such a distraction. She's a pretty girl, and they seem quite close. I just hope everything works out for them."

Gris was surprised by how direct and inappropriate his friend's comments were. As the boat plowed through the harbor channel, he decided to let them go.

"Kyle mentioned you have some further information on Jon Kane, I mean Stevens?" Gris asked.

"As you know, Jon Kane is Jon Stevens. His sister is Samantha Stevens, and they spent their childhood living here in town visiting their grandparents until Jon's father committed suicide when Jon was 12.

"His father's death forced Jon, his sister and mother into poverty. While his older sister was able to marry wealthy at age 20, Jon turned to crime. His crime of choice started with car theft at 15, but he quickly moved on to money embezzlement in his late teens through mid-twenties. The length of his rap sheet from his early adulthood surprised me. But in the past eight years, he has managed to stay under the radar.

"As you know he is currently a salesman at the acoustical tag company. I spoke with the company's CFO this morning. He told me Kane is under surveillance for possibly stealing sales commission from other associates and verbal threats to his so-workers, mostly women."

"Has he served any prison time?" Gris asked.

"Yes, convicted 21 years ago as a minor for money laundering. Sentenced to 12 months in a juvenile detention center, of which he served four and was released. The charges were later expunged from his police record, so essentially he is now clean. Since then he hasn't been back but does have four different aliases," the detective added.

"You mentioned the aliases. So he's not really dangerous, just driven by money, right?"

"Jon Stevens is a criminal, but not one that commits capital crimes like murder, rape, aggravated kidnapping and treason, at least not yet. His crime of choice is white-collar crime, like embezzlement. You hit the nail on the head. He's motivated by money. But even more, he is motivated to hurt those with the power to control money."

Gris shifted to his other leg as he listened. He thought about Kane and his weird behavior aboard the harpoon boat. Kyle was convinced that Kane had stolen the blood vials. Why Kane would steal them was still a baffling mystery, and what he planned to do with them even more unknown.

"Do you know where he's staying?"

"No. I haven't checked on that and haven't had a chance to drive by his grandparent's old place in the woods."

"Okay, anything else?"

Ellis paused for a moment, "Gris, I don't want you to think this guy isn't dangerous. He may know that he's under investigation at work. He may feel like he's getting backed into corners with limited options. When that happens to criminals, they react differently from you and me. They can act outwardly with extreme actions instead of thinking their options through calmly."

"So, what, this guy is a criminal who could lose control? Who may act without a clear plan? Who may be unpredictable, or even dangerous?"

"Yes, all of the above," Ellis confirmed.

"Great. That's just great. Well, hopefully from here on, we won't see much of him on the harpoon boat since his accident."

"What accident?"

"He had a small accident on the boat today when the barbed end of one of the tags stabbed his bicep. It was a simple mistake that happened when the coated tag cord tangled around a cleat, and he stumbled back as the boat shifted. He landed on it just right so that it stabbed the back of his bicep.

"With all his screaming you'd have thought he'd been stabbed with a six-inch hunting knife through his femoral artery. Sounded like a little kid." Gris took a breath then let it out. "Talk about dramatic. He definitely took home an Oscar for his performance today."

"Kyle says he gives him the creeps. Can't say I blame him. Okay, Gris, now you have his background. If I were you, I'd keep an eye on this guy."

"Right, got it," Gris let out another tired breath. He was exhausted, with only three hours of sleep earlier this morning. He heard a break in his phone line and checked the incoming caller ID. He didn't recognize the number.

"Heard a break in your words. You have an incoming call?" Ellis asked.

"Don't know the number, but I'd better take it."

"One last question. Can you give me Kyle's number? I just want to check in on him to see how he doing."

Gris called out the numbers then asked, "Everything okay?"

"Sure, just want to be sure he doesn't need any assistance. You know?" Gris didn't know, but he would ask his son when he got home.

"Right," Gris lied and thanked him for his help. Then he tapped off the connection and took the incoming call.

"Kelley here."

"Dr. Kelley, this is Agent Sharpe. We met for lunch a week or so ago."

"Yes. Yes, I remember."

"Agent Zimmerman and I have been on the periphery of the undercover finning investigation in our region. A colleague asked me about a shark finning report you filed last year from work you completed in China. My question for you is did you find a black market for fins in China?" Sharpe got straight to the point.

"The research I was involved with didn't examine any black market sales. In fact, it didn't look at sales at all."

"Yes, but from what I read in the report, sales are often determined right at the dock where you worked with the finning fishermen and likely saw them haggle over prices. I was thinking you might have come across tradesmen and buyers there?"

"My research was funded by a research organization investigating fin identity. Essentially I identified shark fins prior to processing, packing and trade, with a special focus on the three largest species out there, white, hammerhead and tiger because of their vulnerability and decrease in numbers."

"So you're telling me you never watched sales go down?" Sharpe pushed.

"Sure, I saw men buying fins and fishermen preparing boxes of fins for pickup. But I only interacted a few times with a couple traders. I don't know their names. And really, I would only know them if I saw them."

"Do you know who was buying for traders in China?"

"There is no formal list, but likely all the restaurants and resorts in China since restaurants are the main buyers of the fins."

"So you don't recall any trader names that we can contact?"

"Is this part of that undercover work you spoke of on illegal finning in our region or something else?

"Uh . . . um . . . well. I can't share that with you." Sharpe muddled his words.

"Can you tell me what your inquiry is about? I'm not sure I am the right person for you to speak to on this."

What Sharpe didn't know was that Gris didn't have any trader phone numbers. He didn't have names, except maybe first names or nicknames. In the finning trade, you didn't just email a couple contacts and have an investigation lead. Gris learned that you have to be on the ground where the landings taking place. To glean the information Sharpe was looking for he would have to walk the shorelines, docks and open markets to gain contacts.

Sharpe let out a weighty sigh. "When Zimmerman and I returned to headquarters last week after we met with you, we had a debriefing with my director. He asked that we look further into the three dorsal fin cuts you mentioned to us at lunch. He is concerned the whites in our region are being targeted because their dorsal fins are so large and draw a very high price per pound."

Gris thought about the meeting and how he and Kyle had considered the idea of finning when they first saw the sharks. He knew prices for shark fins depended on the length of the fins and the amount of fibers or needles. He had heard since larger sharks were becoming scarce and difficult to find, and the smaller shark fins were worth very little, the finning market had plummeted. He thought about the recent fin slices he found on the three dead sharks. Though notable, he didn't consider them the cause of death during the necropsies.

"Perhaps, but I didn't attribute the death of those sharks to the cutting of their dorsal fins."

"So you can see why I am trying to get a handle on who is grading the fins, who is dealing the fins, and who is buying the fins?" Sharpe asked.

"I still don't think my work in China will give much insight. In order to get the information you are seeking, you need to walk the shorelines, the docks and the markets in Hong Kong's Sai Yun Pun district, the center of global trade for shark fins," Gris finally elaborated.

There was a long pause from Sharpe before he said, "So when can you be ready to leave?"

"Oh, wait a minute. I want to help you out, honest. But we are at the height of white shark season here," Gris protested.

"How about next week?"

"Are you crazy? I can't just up and leave. In fact, I'm on a harpoon boat heading offshore as we speak."

"Okay, I'll give you 'til tomorrow to open up your schedule while I get clearance from our director."

"I'm not saying I can make this happen, Agent Sharpe. Our shark schedule is very erratic right now.

I'm not sure I can even reach this person," Gris warned.

"I'm sure you will, though," Sharpe asserted before he disconnected.

Gris tapped his cell off. Now was not the time for Gris to be running off to Hong Kong. In fact, now was likely the worst time to be planning a trip to leave Cape Cod.

~

"Got a lock on the first shark's location. Can you get the tag?" Mancini called out from the steering tower.

Gris poked his head out of the wet lab, "Mr. Kane aboard?"

Mancini shook his head. "Said he needs a couple days."

Mancini handed the wheel to Cam and scrambled down the ladder toward the pulpit. Gris was right behind him with a PSAT tag. He was committed to using the PSAT tags until he received a clean report from the chemist on the new high tech tags.

The boat slowed to two knots, and they hovered over the shark. It was six inches below the surface, acutely aware of the boat running alongside.

With one jab to the dorsal fin, Mancini planted the toggle firmly under skin. "Too bad that's not a video tag. This one looks pretty wile." After the sharp stick, the shark rolled energetically away from the boat and flicked its tail at the surface before diving deep into the depths.

"What's the tag number? Mancini called to Gris when he dropped his digital camera after capturing photos of the dorsal fin.

"Number 49."

"Number 49?" Mancini questioned.

Gris nodded.

"Call this one Wild Willie, Number 49 for his outstanding evasion tactics. Almost went in for the stab twice when he darted right."

Mancini stood at the pulpit and threaded the harpoon back into its holder when he heard the buzz of the spotter plan approaching. At nearly the same time he heard it, Cam yelled down the position of the first floater straight ahead. The shark they'd just tagged might have been tracking the scent of the dead shark for a meal.

Over the next two hours the group identified two male white sharks, an 8-footer and a 10-footer, floating belly up a quarter mile from each other. Only one was alive upon arrival, barely moving, upside down, and after Gris took blood and muscle samples, died. The New Jersey boat crew had tagged both during the last month. Much to Gris' anger, both were found with their dorsal fins sliced and mutilated.

Gris pulled dorsal fin photos from his file. Oddly, this time the cuts were closer to the tips, making him question whether boat propellers could be responsible. When he looked closer at the photos, he questioned whether some of the scratch marks on two sharks' upper dorsal fins resembled more letters. This time the 8-footer had the markings of a Letter B, while the 10-footers had a Letter C. He noted the letter markings to give to Kyle. But he'd let his son decide whether he'd include them in his version of *Wheel of Fortune*.

Gris spoke to the Coast Guard to request landing both sharks in port with his special permit. He gained clearance within 30 minutes, tail wrapped one to each side of the transom and began heading back to port at a slow speed, taking them well over an hour. As they approached the harbor inlet, Gris heard two voice messages from his funders at Marine Fish Laboratory headquarters. They'd heard the press conference had been canceled and asked that he reschedule one for later in the day to mollify public curiosity and concerns, and to stave off rumors despite pending results.

Gris groaned when he heard the messages. He quickly dialed his contact at the local newspaper, then another at the local television station leaving word that a conference would be held at the Marine Fish Laboratory at 6:30 tonight for a brief shark update.

Staring at his phone, Gris jumped when it vibrated in his fingers. He didn't recognize the number.

"Dr. Kelley here."

"Hey, Gris, it's Chang."

"Hey, Li. Had any luck on running those tests?"

"Actually I just handed Kyle a CD that included most, if not all of the results. I included a brief summary for you at the end on my interpretations. But it is in no way comprehensive. As a veterinary pathologist, my insight is limited."

"Any particular result point to a cause of death?"

"No. I mean the results show a mix of strange synthetic chemicals in the blood and muscle tissue. I'm not really the . . ."

Three beeps interrupted Chang's answer then stopped and returned to his voice.

"Wait, Li," Gris cut him off. "I didn't hear your last few words because a beep on the line broke in on your words."

"I said my training is limited and I'm not the right kind of pathologist to fully interpret these results. I'm thinking with your years of experience in examining fish findings, you'll have a greater understanding of how at least three peculiar chemicals got into the sharks' systems. If not, I'm not sure who would."

"I'll take a look at the results. Were the results really that unusual? You sound puzzled."

"Puzzled? Puzzled isn't really the word I would describe my thoughts when I discovered what chemicals tested positive in the samples."

"What'd you find that was so odd?"

Chang didn't answer right away.

"Seriously, Li, with all your years of experience, I'm not sure I've ever heard you sound this baffled."

"Ever hear of botulinum toxin?"

Gris let out a quick breath. "Damn, really?"

"That's just one of the chemicals I found on the short list of chemicals I found most prevalent in the samples you sent. Found that one in the livers."

"Damn it," Gris whispered.

"Yeah, well, I'll agree with you on that. I'm just not sure how it or the others got there. I'm counting on your experience to shed some light on finding the answers."

"Okay, okay. I'll look at the results as soon as Kyle walks through the door and I can get my hands on the CD."

"Yes, please call me. I'm curious to know what you come up with about what caused those sharks to die."

"Hey, we're docking. I have to go, but I'll ring you later."

The return to port landed them home by late afternoon, giving Gris ample time to clean up, eat dinner with Kyle, hold the press conference and keep his promise to Audrey that he'd sleep on her cottage couch if she didn't return home by dusk.

225

TWENTY ONE

Off The Deep End

Gris rubbed the towel vigorously through his hair inside the modern glass shower when he heard the screen door slap shut. He was tired from hauling the sharks from the boat to the Lab for necropsies. He'd placed a call for Kyle to meet him there to help, but he'd never picked up.

Gris walked to the head of the stairs with the towel now wrapped low on his narrow hips and waited to see who had entered. He hoped it was Kyle back with the Lab results on the blood, organ and muscle samples.

There was no movement, so he slipped on boxers, faded, soft jeans and a thin black t-shirt with a shark logo over his left peck. He walked to the head of the stairs to listen for movement, then softly padded down the stairs in his bare feet. He could only see his truck parked in the driveway.

"Kyle?" Gris called softly when he rounded the kitchen corner and saw Audrey leaning over the kitchen table reading mail. She spun around to the sound of his soft voice, her lips parted from startle.

"Hey . . . twice in one day. I thought you said you were busy tonight, so I didn't plan to head over to sleep on your couch until later," Gris reminded her of his previous response.

Audrey raised her eyebrows, then leaned against the kitchen bar and folded her arms across her chest. She wasn't impressed with his reminder.

She wore a low cut, cotton, sleeveless top tucked into faded cutoff shorts. Her top and shorts showed off her curves, but then, just about any clothing showed off her curves. He pushed those thoughts from his head so he could focus on speaking to her with a clear head.

A slender woman of medium height, Audrey continually ensnared Gris' attention, never mind the eyes of most men when she entered a room. Having started in college as friends, she and Gris essentially grew up together, providing one another room to mature. Their sons often teased Gris of acting like one of their teenage friends whenever Audrey came around. Her large chestnut eyes, dark lashes and long silken brown hair so easily captured his attention. They teased that when she entered a room, he couldn't resist. He needed her near, he needed to hear her voice and her movement in a room; he needed to touch her even if just with an elbow or knee. She was not only his fix but also his grounding rod.

Now she had dirt on her cheek and a pair of dirt stained gardening gloves on the counter. She must have been working on her flower gardens in the front yard when he first came home. Her car was most likely parked in their pole barn garage behind the house.

Gris pulled out a chair at the table. "Can I get you a cup of coffee?"

She followed him with her eyes. He was having trouble reading her mood. He braced and finally breathed out when she agreed. "Okay. Just came over to wash my laundry, but it's still drying."

This was good. She was talking and not visibly angry.

Gris shoveled a spoonful of sugar in and added a

little milk in her coffee, then handed it to her. He waited for her to take a sip before lifting his gaze. "Can I get you something to eat?"

She paused then shook her head. She contemplated telling him about Lucy, but remembered her promise to Kyle that she'd be his vault for sharing information. So she decided to use the time to express her thoughts.

"Beth thinks you've gone crazy," Audrey uttered. "Right off the deep end."

Startled by her bold remark, Gris almost spit out his entire sip of coffee.

He grabbed a paper towel and wiped his face. She was ready to talk. He put his coffee cup aside and gave her his full attention before speaking. "What do you think? I mean about Beth saying I'm crazy?".

"She says because you're turning 50 in another couple years that you're experiencing hormonal changes. That you're having a mid-life crisis. That's why you're so driven to save the sharks, or better yet, save the planet."

Gris tilted his head and searched his wife's face. "What do you think?" he repeated with a stronger tone this time.

Audrey didn't answer but instead sipped her coffee. She took her time responding, clearly considering her words.

Still waiting, Gris moved closer to his wife who casually leaned against the bar. He put six inches between them and placed his hand over hers. His touch forced her eyes to meet his.

"Audrey, I asked you a question."

Audrey held his eyes.

"What do you think?" he repeated more softly.

"I think . . . I think she's right . . . to a degree." She nodded once, still holding his stare.

Gris raised one eyebrow at her response.

"Do I appear to be 'crazy' right now?" he asked.

His voice was soft and smooth, the voice he used when he wanted her to cancel her plans and stay with him for the day or evening or weekend.

He pulled the cup out of her hand, placed it on the bar, then reached down and picked up her other hand. He held both against his chest.

She didn't resist. Instead, her eyes grew glassy. Her lips were partially open, and Gris considered kissing them.

Audrey shook her head as if shaking herself out of a trance. She had been thinking how handsome he was, with his really nice deep sapphire eyes. She'd been away two weeks and now remembered how beautiful they were to look at. She glanced away to gain her bearings and recapture her confident attitude.

"You think I can't see through this, Gris Kelley? I know what you're doing," she cautioned.

"What am I doing, Hon?" He let one of her hands go and brushed his knuckles across her cheek. He quietly breathed in the scent of her bath soap.

Audrey heard him draw in the calm breath and knew what he was doing. "You're . . . you're trying to distract me." She pushed him back, but his chest and abs tightened, making a dense, impassable wall. "Stop it . . . stop it, Gris," she said swatting his knuckles away.

"You're trying to move ahead like nothing happened here a week or so ago. Like you didn't break your promise, like you didn't just proceed with a decision without my input. Like all's normal...you know?" she asked, then continued without letting him answer. "I only wish all was normal," she muttered. "But it's not. Gris, it's not," she paused.

"No? Well, then tell me," his voice rumbled softly. He stepped closer to close the gap so there were only a couple inches between them.

She tried to pull her right hand from his, but Gris

tightened his grip. He would let her vent. Venting was fine, but he wasn't letting her run again. And she wasn't going back to her friend's cottage. Not if he had anything to say about it.

Not getting very far with her retreat from him, she reminded herself not to look at his eyes. He had compelling eyes, so she turned her head away, forcing her to maintain control and realized she was too late. She could feel herself getting heady. It was a nice feeling, a feeling she hadn't experienced in a while. But she still had a lot to say to him and was determined to tell him before . . . well, before she got sucked into the Gris Kelley trance.

"Oooooh, Gris. This isn't fair. You're trying to make moves, and I'm trying to tell you something. Please...can you give me some space and a moment here?" She pushed his hands away and tried to clear her head.

"Anything. You can have anything." He lingered a moment to stare into her eyes. He let her other hand go, gave her time but didn't give her any space.

Audrey looked at her husband, then turned her head away again to refocus.

"Our life isn't normal. It's not normal when you can't even go out to dinner with your husband of 25 years without being bombarded by five reporters while you walk across a parking lot." She took a step sideways, attempting to gather her thoughts. He stepped with her, determined to keep their connection.

She narrowed her eyes and continued. "And when you finally make it inside the restaurant to your romantic table for two and the wine steward serves you this magnificent bottle of wine, you're invaded, interrupted yet again from your delicious meal by some obnoxious reporter and his impatient photographer to answer just a few questions so he can finish off his story. Stupid jerk!" She took a breath and paused. "I know you don't understand this, but . . . ."

"I agree," Gris admitted.

"What?" She jerked her head and stared at him.

"I said I agree with you."

"What do you mean, you agree with me?

"I agree with what you're saying."

"Maybe Beth is right. You really have gone off the deep end . . ." She tried to raise her hands, but he held tight and grinned. He was holding off his responses to give her time to lay all her feeling out. She shifted her legs and paused.

"Look," Gris said, "they were wrong to intrude on our lives, and I was selfish not to stop them and put their needs before ours."

Audrey narrowed her eyes and wondered if she heard him correctly.

"I don't believe you. You're just selling me some line so life will get back to normal. Whatever that is." Working to maintain her snit, she squinted her eyes at him.

The argument was going his way. Though she was feisty, she was hearing him. Banter he could handle. Feistiness he could handle. It was her silence that was his poison. His lips twitched as he listened to her make her case. She was trying to hold onto her anger at him. He gave her time to finish then broke through her glare.

"Audrey, what you said is true. I have put my career ahead of you and our boys."

"So you're telling me what? That things will change? Everything will be different from today forward?" she quizzed. "Oh and by the way, it's the start of white shark season, you know," she mocked.

He ignored her reminder of the time of year and her sarcasm. "Yes, if that's what it'll take."

"What will take?" she continued to quiz.

"If that's what it will take for you to come back. Be here. Look, Babe, I can't look into a crystal ball and tell you that it won't ever happen again. Regardless of what you think, I'm not a psychic or a super hero. I can't read people's minds or control their actions." He could see she was fighting back a grin as she listened.

"But I can react differently to their demands, make our ground rules known and set boundaries to protect us and our boys."

He had Audrey's full attention, and he squeezed her hands. She paused and looked away.

When she looked back, his eyes were locked where she left them, a molten cobalt blue.

"You'll do that?" She was cautious, still testing.

"If that's what it takes to get you back, I'm in." He waited for her to speak. When she said nothing, he moved forward and quickly, before she could resist, scooped her into this arms. She tipped back off balance and grabbed his neck.

"Gris, what are you doing?" she protested, her voice louder.

"Moving us to a place where we can put our feet up and you can be less tense."

"But we're not finished!"

He stopped in his tracks and looked at her in his arms. He smelled coffee and sugar on her breath. "Okay, what else do you want to talk about?"

When she didn't speak, he continued toward the living room.

"Gris, you're going to drop me," she complained.

"I haven't so far. But I can, if you prefer." He had a wide grin on his face, happy she was not resisting him. They were on the mend.

Gris stood over the leather couch and held her out. She gripped his neck tighter.

"Gris!" she warned, her voice much louder.

He spun on one heel and dropped down into the couch where she bounced in his lap. He leaned back against the arm and put his feet up on the coffee table. He scooted back on the cushion and pulled her against his chest. She leaned in and let him kiss her hair.

"Nice," he whispered.

She twisted to get more comfortable in his grasp then stilled. He put a hand at either side of her head and pulled her face down to touch his lips to hers.

"Hon, I don't ever want you to think my work comes first," Gris told Audrey who digested his apology. He waited for her response.

"Yeah, well, I guess we all get caught up in life, our work and our passions. No one is saying you're not dedicated to this cause. You've become one of the best-known great white shark scientists worldwide. You've become a great champion. Every cause needs a champion. Sometimes we become buried in our work, and we don't even realize it's taking over our lives. I guess the challenge is to not let our passion become an obsession."

Gris reflected on last summer. It had been chaotic at times, the press intrusive. Eight long weeks, and then life resumed to a normal pace, but he had to admit it had been a miserable eight weeks.

He wanted to move on. They had talked it out. He understood her unhappiness, and he was determined to keep their private life private. He thought about how much he loved his wife. She was his best friend and his greatest love.

"Life sucks without you, Aud," he spoke softly into the curve of her ear. She turned and looked deeply into his eyes before kissing him lightly on the cheek. "Ditto."

~

Kyle checked his phone as he stepped out of the Marine Lab Laboratory with the lab results for the blood and tissue samples. The chemical analysis on the VSAT tag and toggle wouldn't be available for another few days.

His voice mail flashed red with a message from Detective Ellis. Ellis's message was short including the result of a background check on Jon Stevens and a question, had he driven by to check out the Stevens' grandparents' home to see if anyone was staying there.

Kyle hadn't. But now he wanted to. Unfortunately he only remembered the road name, but no house number. Then just as Ellis ended his message, he stated the house address, 9 Goose Neck Road.

Located more than a mile from the beach and ten miles from the Kelley home, Goose Neck Road was first settled by cranberry bog owners and later cultivated into small vegetable, three-acre horse farms with homes constructed at the rear of the properties. Now in the middle of summer, much of the land was densely wooded and private with many small dirt roads winding off Goose Neck Road.

Kyle looked at his watch and contemplated calling Brodie again. "C'mon, Brodie. Where are you when I need you, when I need that cocky attitude?" he whispered.

He decided while the sun was high in the sky he'd visit the property. Approaching the dirt road that led to the house number, Kyle decided to take a covert approach to the grandparents' property. He'd park his truck in an adjacent driveway where the house appeared deserted with its windows still boarded from the winter. Then he'd walk through the woods, remaining under cover to see if anyone was staying at the house.

Leaving his truck unlocked, Kyle cautiously approached the rear barn through the side woods about 50 feet off the dirt road. At first the property appeared uninhabited, but as he dodged behind a barn at the back of the property and crouched to catch his breath, he heard a voice. Getting his bearings, he scanned the layout of expansive backfields and woodlands. From there he had a clear view of the house and covered porch. As he rounded the side of the barn, the voice of someone talking on the phone grew louder.

Keeping his body low, he listened. The voice sounded familiar, like Jon Kane. Whoever it was seemed to be engaged in a heated discussion.

After a few minutes, Kyle retraced his steps along the side of the barn and waited. His heart beat fast, his pulse throbbing at his wrist. He'd rushed to the property without a good plan. He needed a plan. So he took a moment to think about his next few moves and any consequences.

First, he'd look in the barn for anything unusual or suspicious. If he found nothing, he'd creep under the windows of the house to check on who was home and talking on the phone.

Kyle moved back to his original position and gathered his wits, his heart rate settling back to almost normal. He gave himself another minute to collect his thoughts when he heard a muffled sound and the scraping of a metal post along a concrete floor. The sound came from inside the barn. Then he heard a rocking of the metal post and a slapping of metal on the concrete floor. It stopped. Then started again. Someone was scraping a chair across the concrete floor.

Staying low to the barn windows, Kyle backed up along the side of the barn away from the main house and shuffled into an empty horse paddock that gave access to the interior of the barn. He shifted his eyes across the stall floor and peeked through the iron rails separating one stall from the next. He leaned forward to get a better look. His heart plunged to his feet at a frightening sight.

Tied to the metal chair was a slender figure, a girl with a black hood tied over her head. Her arms and feet were bound to the chair by rope. He swallowed a

gasp as he took a better look.
Was the girl Lucy?

TWENTY TWO

Take Me Home

Kyle's stomach flipped as he contemplated whether the person tied up in the chair was his girlfriend. Even if she wasn't Lucy, he still had to help her.

He rethought his plan and how he could let the girl know he was there and reassure her that he was a good guy and meant no harm. Whoever she was, he had to get to her, untie her and deliver her from this nightmare.

He walked around the side of the barn once more and shuffled under the windows toward the house. He could hear the man's voice, now out of control with anger as he spoke on the phone. It was definitely Jon Kane.

Kyle turned back and moved back to the paddock fencing and stall door. He stepped into the stall and crouched to remain hidden incase Kane came in. He was in the stall next to where the girl was tied up.

He had two approaches: walk through his stall door to the interior hall and through her stall door to get her, or try accessing her stall through the closed paddock door to her stall. He needed to see if it was bolted shut. He decided to try the paddock door since it provided an uninhibited access to the woods from the barn.

Stepping through the paddock fence, Kyle tried jiggling open her exterior stall door. It was locked. He

239

would have to use the more complicated approach.

He heard her whimper. It was muffled, and he realized she was likely gagged.

He contemplated answering.

His heart broke just hearing her cries. He couldn't stay quiet.

"Lucy," Kyle whispered in a low, strong voice. "Is that you? It's me, Kyle. Babe, please, shhh."

She answered with a wistful whimper and nodded her head up and down under the black hood.

He stepped back into his stall and crept along the floor to push on his stall door. It didn't budge. He moved back and pulled it toward him. It swung open.

Finally, he thought to himself.

He took a step forward and heard some footsteps approaching from outside. Eyeing an open door across the barn aisle, he pushed it open and slipped into the darkened room.

Heavy boots scuffed the concrete, and a key scraped open a lock to a stall door which creaked open. Kyle pressed his face against the wall of the room where he hid. He could feel the light switch below under his hand.

"Smart girl not to try to escape. Someday I'll let you go. But not yet, not until I get my fill." It was Kane's voice.

Lucy whimpered as Kane walked toward her in heavy boots and ran his finger up the inside of her bare right thigh to the edge of her shorts. She startled at his initial touch then began to tremble as he moved his finger up her leg and finally Kyle heard a muffled cry when he moved his finger under her shorts.

The sight of Kane touching Lucy made his blood boil. With the hair prickling the back of his neck, Kyle clenched his fist and focused on what steps he needed to incapacitate Kane and free Lucy. He shuffled back from the door in the darkened room and found a heavy hammer at his feet. A sledge hammer. *Perfect.*

Raising the hammer over his shoulder, Kyle watched Kane with his back to him and watched Lucy wriggle away from Kane's touch.

As Kyle put his hand up to push the door open, a blaring ring interrupted Kane's next move. As Kane moved toward the phone on the wall in the barn's aisle, Lucy sighed with abject relief.

"That goddamn Bigelow. Told him not to call the house phone," Kane snarled.

Lucy heard the phone ring in two locations, one in front of her and one faintly in the distance coming from the other building. Kane turned back to Lucy and growled, "Don't you move an inch." The phone rang a third time.

"You hear me!" he blasted and she froze at his words. He sprinted out the stall door toward the house.

When Kyle heard the barn door open and the screen door to the house slap shut, he placed the hammer on the floor. He waited quietly hidden in the room for a moment before he moved. He was certain from the smell of leather and hay that he was in a large storage closet. He brushed the wall and unintentionally flipped the light switch. Startled by what he found, he fixed his gaze on one card table loaded with odd items. What the hell was it?

He took a moment to look around at the rest of the room. At eye level mounted on the back wall were pommel racks holding English saddles. To his right along the wall were five pegs holding different bridles with reins. A hook with laden with various worn halters all sizes and colors.

He glanced back at the card table where the contents were completely unrelated to anything else in the tack room: a chair with white painter's coveralls draped over the back, a table masked off with newspaper set up with a bucket of metal fish tag toggles, paint brushes, wire cutters, needle nose pliers, and a half-full metal can of orange liquid. Spread across the newspaper were 25 or more newly painted, fluorescent-orange toggles. To the right of the table on the floor lay a messy pile of detached whip wires. Kyle shook from his trance and pulled out his phone. He tapped five photos of the scene and flipped off the light.

Time to get to Lucy.

Kyle slowly creaked the tack room door open and noticed Lucy's stall door was now ajar, the key still slid into the lock. He took two long steps out of the room and into the stall. He gently slid his hand onto Lucy's thigh where the man had run his finger. He wanted to rub away his scent and intensions.

She jerked in fear. "It's okay, Luce. It's me, Kyle." He drew out his pocketknife.

She nodded as he knelt in front of her. His heart ached at the sight of her trussed up with a black hood over her head.

"Stay still, Luce, while I get you free."

He flipped open the knife and cut the hood's ties. Slowly, he dragged it over her head and saw the relief wash over her face at the sight of him, her face wet with tears. She winced as she tried to adjust her eyes to the late afternoon sunlight. He lifted one finger to her lips as a signal to remain quiet. Then he cut her hands and legs free, flipped the knife closed and slowly peeled the duct tape off mouth. He got halfway, when she reached up and nodded that she had it.

He cupped her elbow to help her off the chair when her legs buckled. He caught her half way to the floor. He considered giving her a chance to walk on her own when he heard noise outside.

"Sorry, Luce, but we need to get moving." In one fluid motion, he lifted and slung her over his right shoulder. "Hang on to my back," he breathed out at the scuffing sound of boots approaching the barn.

As the main door unlatched, Kyle took two long

strides out of one stall, turned and dodged right through another to the open paddock. He lifted the metal loop at the paddock fence and ran toward the back woods, thanking his lucky stars that Lucy was a slight girl on the thin side.

"Stop! You stop there, or I'll shoot your girlfriend," Kane bellowed from inside the barn. But Kyle didn't stop or glance back. They were at the edge of the woods now and had only a few more steps before they would be obscured by the long late afternoon shadows.

Kyle heard a gunshot ring out from the barn, followed by a soft cry from Lucy.

"Grab my back as we jump," he told Lucy as he took a final leap into a narrow burrow where he lay her down, then lay over her. He heard footsteps on the grass as he reached and slowly dragged leafy tree branches over them. Two more gunshot fired to the left about 80 feet away. Kyle heard footsteps running toward them then stopped.

"Think you can get away from me, huh? You don't know me. I never lose. When I find you, and I will, I'll make it so no one ever recognizes the likes of you again. Not when I'm done severing you into tiny pieces and feeding you to those man-eating sharks you love so," he snarled as he stalked forward. He swiveled to the right and Kyle heard him slide the silencer onto the end of his pistol. He moved away for a few minutes, now past them.

The sun was low in the sky but wouldn't set for another hour. In the woods, darkness would be their ally. For another ten minutes Kyle and Lucy remained motionless as they heard Kane pace by them three more times, then walk toward the dirt road.

Lucy took a deep breath. Leaves and dirt were raining down on her face from tree limbs and underbrush Kyle used to conceal them. He looked into her eyes and saw fear. He continued to hold them, when she finally breathed out and relaxed her shoulders a bit. He gave her a crooked smile and then laid his cheek against hers. He could hear her breath slowing.

In the distance Kyle could hear the arrival of police cars. Someone must have called in the gunshots. He heard Kane answering their questions, explaining he thought he heard intruders. Knowing he would be tied up with the officers for a while, he slowly removed the brush and lifted Lucy to her feet. They remained crouched until Kyle was sure they could get away without detection. He listened as the police officers used their radios and decided the distraction and noise would mask the sound of their escape through the crackling groundcover.

Gingerly, they stepped away from the burrow in the opposite direction from Kyle's truck and police cars. After five minutes, they'd made a half circle around the police scene and stepped out onto the intersection of Goose Neck Road to Compton Lane, about a half block from where he had parked his truck.

Without even glancing back at the police cars, Kyle opened his driver's side door and helped Lucy climb in. He noticed a small hole from a bullet on the passenger's side near the windshield wiper, but he didn't tell Lucy.

She slid onto her seat, where she blinked in confusion-and her eyes filled with tears. Kyle climbed in, cranked the truck to life and eased it down the driveway. Not wanting to call any attention to them, he slowly rolled his truck toward Compton Lane where he saw Brodie speeding his pickup truck down the dirt road toward Goose Neck Road.

Brodie flashed his megawatt smile as he locked eyes with Kyle, passing them before pulling a quick U-turn. Kyle floored it to the main road.

After a few minutes when Kyle was certain only

Brodie was tailing them, he pulled off the road near the edge of a large freshwater pond and let the truck idle. He turned to Lucy and quickly scanned her face, her neck, her torso, and her legs. With two hands on either side of her face, he looked deep into her eyes, brimming with tears. He shook his head as tears welled up and streamed down to her jaw.

Kyle glanced quickly through the rear window then back to Lucy, "I think were alone." He pulled her into an embrace, holding her as if he hadn't seen her in a year.

He pulled away and kissed her lips gently, then more forcefully, moving on to kiss away the tears on her chin, then her cheek, and finally each eye. Her tears now came full strength, and he couldn't keep up, so he found her lips again. She gasped for air and he put a few inches between them.

"I got you. I got you, Luce," he repeated, pulling her into another embrace. The familiar words turned her soft cries to sobs. "You're such a tough girl, so strong, so brave. I wasn't going to stop looking until I found you. I just couldn't concentrate 'til I knew you were safe, Luce."

"I know! All I could think about was you." Her words came out as a squeak through the sobs.

Kyle pulled some leftover napkins tucked into the door compartment from breakfast and wiped away her wetness just as Brodie pulled his truck up behind them.

Kyle rolled down his window as Brodie approached them.

Laying Lucy against his chest to quiet her and calm her breathing, he greeted Brodie.

"Finally got my message, huh?" he asked his best friend.

"Sorry, man. I was with Alicia and my phone was off," Brodie confessed.

Kyle shook his head. "Could have used your

brawn in there. But it all worked out."

"Who the hell took her?"

"This maniac named Jon Kane. A real winner. I think he'll be spending a little time with the police officer tonight explaining why he was firing off his Glock at us."

Brodie raised his eyebrows and shook his head in disgust.

Kyle continued. "Had a gut feeling it was him. Came here when Detective Ellis told me he could be staying at his grandparents' house."

"I'm so glad you did." Lucy spoke so softly into his neck, her words were barely audible. He squeezed her to assure her she was safe as he swallowed past the lump that had built in his throat since hearing Detective Ellis affirm that she wasn't in the pub "Please take me home," she whispered.

"Luce, that's too dangerous right now. That could be the first place he goes to find you. We need to get you to a safe place, where he would never go."

"He's right, Lucy. The dude might go there looking for you," Brodie agreed.

"How about your home?" she asked Kyle.

He shook his head, "No. I'm sure he's already staked it out too."

"Then where?"

"I think I know just the place."

~

Gris Kelley stood outside the Marine Fish Laboratory and waited for the press to quiet down. He had told Kyle he would delay the conference but later received a message from Marine Fish Laboratory headquarters requesting he provide some explanation to quell public concern. Now it was 6:30, and he was in front of a small group of press to answer questions.

Three microphones were angled into Gris's face as

he began. "While two miles offshore yesterday, we came upon a near-dead white shark. Named Giant Greta, she was the 44th shark tagged in the program. The crew off New Jersey tagged her about three weeks ago.

"She is the third great white shark found stranded in the last two weeks for which we completed necropsies. As with the first, the cause of death is still undetermined while we await results from tissue, organ and blood samples."

"Why are you telling us this now when you told us just a three hours ago that you needed to wait for the results?" one reporter called from the rear of the group, his tone frustrated.

"It is my understanding that there is not only some confusion, but quite a bit of concern out there. So we are hoping this brief statement will resolve any confusion and help alleviate public concerns," Gris tactfully responded.

"Can you tell us if there was any evidence of hook and line capture or injuries from long line?" a reporter asked.

"We did not find any marks on any of the sharks that indicated either. At this point we are looking at death from possible starvation, pollution or toxins, or ship collision at sea," Gris added.

"How would a shark die from starvation in an area so rich with seals?" another reporter shouted.

"Sometimes sharks fast when they feel sick in order to redirect their energy to healing. For all of these fish, you couldn't miss their discolored livers and empty stomachs. They also had a number of parasites throughout their bodies, a sign that they were not recovering from whatever ailed them."

"What changes the color of a shark's liver?" another voice asked.

"Some diseases and infections, types of cirrhosis and reaction to toxins in their environment. We came upon all of these sharks in a moribund state, meaning they were near death and likely to pass within the hour. All did die just after we either towed them into the harbor or removed them from the beach where they stranded. So all the sharks were in the beginning stages of decomposition for the necropsies. We are trying to rule out whether the discoloration was a result of decomposition or something else.

"Can you show us the liver or is it already gone for testing? "The reporter continued.

Gris chuckled. "Umm . . . no. Actually a shark's liver is quite large. It accounts for about a quarter of the fish's body weight. We only took a sample. So for these fish, which ranged in size from 10 to 14 feet in length, their livers weighed in at 300 and 500 pounds."

"So do you think these sharks died of a disease or from something in its environment?" a different reporter shouted.

"It is not clear what the final cause of death is yet for any of them. When we know, you'll be the first we'll call." The reporters laughed softly at Gris's canned remarks.

TWENTY THREE

A Safe Place

Kyle waited for his mother to answer the phone as he struggled to stay under the speed limit driving away from Goose Neck Road.

Having identified Kane at the property, he now knew with whom he was dealing, a suspicious, unpredictable lunatic.

"This guy's totally unstable," he said beneath his breath. "I won't trust him if he was the last person on Earth. He stalked you at the pub, then kidnapped you, went crazy on the phone with Bigelow, then tried to hunt us down with a gun."

"You say something?" Lucy asked.

"Yeah, I don't trust this Kane dude to not come looking for us." Though he hadn't yet heard the details of Lucy's harrowing experience, he would do whatever it took to keep her safe.

An unexpected voice answered his call. "Who's there?" Kyle asked with an edge to his question.

"Hey, son, where are you?" It was his father who knew nothing about Lucy's abduction. "Mom's here, and we're making dinner. Kyle? Are you okay?

Kyle heard his mother's peaceful humming in the background stop when his father said his name.

"No." Kyle shifted his eyes to Lucy as she unbuckled her seatbelt and slid across the bench seat and under his arm. He gave her a squeeze. "We're not okay." He glanced into his rearview mirror to see if Brodie was still on his tail. He was.

"Dad, I didn't tell you because you were on the harpoon boat, and well earlier today, I . . . uh . . . well, I just found Lucy. She was kidnapped earlier . . . today—around noon, shortly after I saw her at the pub."

Kyle heard his father's sharp intake of breath. "Oh, Kyle, I'm so sorry. I wish I had been here to help."

"It's a long story, Dad, and I will, or actually Lucy will tell you about it later, but right now I need help to keep her safe in case her abductor comes looking for her.

Kyle waited a moment to allow his father time to process the serious information.

"Because I'm pretty sure he's going to be angry when he sees she's gone from where he tied her up."

"Okay, listen to me," his father voice changed to a take charge, controlled tone. "I will call Detective Ellis. I want you to go to his office at the Sheriff's Department. It's a Safe House. Do you know where that is?"

Kyle shoulders sagged with relief. He was hoping his father would call Ellis. "At the sheriff's department on Leggett Road?"

"Yes, that's the location. It's after hours so the front door will be locked, but all you have to do is ring the doorbell and they'll let you in. I'll call him now to meet you there. It'll be a good place for you to file a report and for us all to talk."

For the first time in the last hour, Kyle was able to breathe easy. He pulled up to a stop sign and looked into Lucy's eyes to reassure her.

"Kyle, did you hear me?"

"Yes. Yes, Dad, I heard. I'm on Brad Street now. I think I need to turn left here to get over to Leggett Road, go about two miles and then turn right. Is that the place?"

"Yes. You've got it. We'll meet you there."

"Ok, we're headed there. Brodie is behind me in his truck. So tell Ellis he'll be with us. And we'll need a first aid kit for Lucy. She's got some scrapes. And Dad?"

"Yeah?"

"Bring your laptop. I have a disc with the test results. I think you'll want to look at it while we're there. Maybe you can make some sense of them."

TWENTY FOUR

Not Your Fault

Kyle watched Lucy drink a third glass of cold water while they waited for his parents and the detective to arrive. She gulped it down as if she hadn't tasted any liquid in the last 48 hours, then reached for a fourth.

"Whoa, Luce, how 'bout you take a break from the water?"

Lucy stared at Kyle like she had been zapped with a bolt of electricity.

Brodie turned to his friend. "Hey, Kyle, maybe she hasn't had anything to drink today."

Lucy's eyes filled with the tears she had been working so hard to contain since her breakdown in the truck, and Kyle was instantly sorry that he'd just vented his own stress at her.

"Oh," Lucy said in a soft voice. "Yeah, sure." She looked down at her feet.

Kyle walked toward her and gathered her in his arms. "I'm sorry. I didn't mean to bark at you . . . that came out all wrong." He pulled her into his chest, and she quietly swallowed her tears. He drew her tighter into his body and sat down on the couch with her on his lab. He tucked her into his shoulder.

"Maybe if you tell me what happened, it will help." He waited, giving her time.

Brodie sat across the room shaking his head at his friend's suggestion then looked at the floor.

After a long silence, Lucy started to speak, hesitantly at first. "It was so scary being in the black hood . . . darkness," she stammered. "His voice was angry and mean. I didn't know if he was going to hurt me or touch me." She shivered.

"Did he touch you?" Kyle clipped, his voice tight as Brodie listened.

"He pushed me around and told me he would kill me if I tried to get away. He said he liked to look at my legs in my shor . . . shorts, and he ran his finger up my legs and under the hem of my shorts." She stopped and squeaked out a sob.

"Did he try to trip or kick you?" Kyle said through a wave of intense anger. He needed answers.

"No. I mean, when he was trying to get me into the truck, I fell down a few times and bumped my head and my knees. But I don't think he deliberately tried to trip or kick me. It's hard to tell because I was in darkness.

"He threw me into the truck because I was trying to fight him off. He was so strong I couldn't get away from him," she told Kyle and Brodie who were mesmerized by her description.

"Did he ever get past the hem of your shorts, or molest you? Because if he did, I swear I'll kill him." Kyle's jaw clenched, his eyes molten black.

"No, he didn't have time," she said with relief.

Kyle studied Lucy's face and knew what she was thinking. "It's not your fault, Lucy, you know what he did, kidnapping you, wasn't your fault, right?"

Lucy remained quiet with her eyes fixed on the floor ahead of them.

Kyle placed a finger under Lucy's chin and moved her face so he could look directly into her eyes. "He is a demented, impulsive whack job. I'm not sure of his reasons for targeting you. But I have a feeling it has to do with the work Dad and I do with the white sharks. And if it is, then Dad and I are to blame for your assault. It's not your fault. You are a victim, and I am sorry that happened. Do you get that?"

After she nodded with obvious reluctance, Kyle tucked her back into his shoulder, and she took a deep breath. It wasn't long after that she nodded off in the warmth of his arms until Brodie's voice broke the silence.

"I'm going head out. You and Luce going be okay?" Brodie asked in a low voice.

"Yeah, man. Thanks for coming to find me and Luce."

Brodie nodded and gave him a brotherly handshake. "Call me when you land."

"Sure will."

Brodie walked out the door just as Detective Ellis walked in. "You guys found each other." He stated the obvious."

Kyle shifted Lucy off his lap, and they stood to face the detective. "You could say that. Guess you got Dad's call." Kyle noticed Lucy's body trembling.

"You okay, Luce?" Kyle spoke to her softly while the detective watched.

"Just a little cold, and I feel jumpy," she whispered.

"She's probably still in shock, Kyle," he detective interrupted. "From your father's brief description, it sounds like she had a harrowing time with Mr. Kane. Lucy, you are safe here at the department. No one can get in here. I heard on the police scanner that Kane was taken in on firearm charges. He'll probably be released on bail, but not for a while. First he needs to be charged and brought in front of a judge," Ellis explained.

"So he's being held at the police department?" Kyle asked.

"Yeah, they have a couple holding cells. He'll either be transported to our department to bring him before the judge or have a judge see him on rounds after he reviews the police report's details.

Lucy trembled at the thought of Kane back on the streets again.

"There you all are!" Audrey's warm voice entered the room as she walked straight to Lucy with open arms. She enveloped the teenager who didn't resist or meet her eyes. Gris putdown his laptop case and stepped sideways past his wife to hug his son.

"I brought the first aid kit. Kyle told us you got pretty scraped up during your ordeal," Audrey talked into Lucy's hair when the girl didn't step back." It was pretty clear she needed a parent to assure her that she'd survived and no other harm would come to her.

"Look, I brought some fudge brownies with cream cheese icing," Kyle's mother added and her son's eyes lit up with anticipation.

"When's the last time you had a meal, Lucy?" Gris asked with a concerned look.

"A while . . . it's been a while." She licked her dry lips just thinking about the brownies.

"Well, I also brought chicken sandwiches for you, too, because I wasn't sure if you'd eaten," Audrey added as she set Lucy free to drag a small cooler along the floor. As she unzipped the top, Kyle dug out a CD jewel case from his pants pocket. He passed it to his father.

"Can we go somewhere, like a conference room where we can set up the food for the kids and I can look over the test results?" Gris asked Ellis.

"I thought you'd never ask." He guided the group down the hall to a clean but austere conference room with swivel chairs and a massive table. Computer hookups were available at the top of each seat.

Gris plugged in his laptop and slid the CD into the side. After ten minutes of flipping from one file to the next, he called Audrey to his side. He needed her opinion on some of the off-the-chart results.

Gaining her B.S. in chemistry, Audrey had a

strong base of knowledge of how chemical compounds, natural toxins and contaminants worked in the environment. The year after she graduated, she took her first job running tests at a water analysis lab prior to landing a job in finance. She had a good eye for connecting the dots between statistical relationships and science.

He clicked through folder after folder on the laptop trying to locate Chang's files. Finally, he located a folder named "Unfamiliar Findings." Tapping it open, he found the blood, muscle and liver results Chang had referred to on the phone.

"Chang wasn't kidding when he said there are some odd synthetic chemicals showing up in these tissue samples," Gris said softly as he scrolled through the data sheets. He rubbed his forehead and shook his head, then continued to scroll. He stopped and blinked his eyes. Again he shook his head.

Finally he told Audrey, "Look at these numbers. They're totally abnormal. See how elevated the heavy metal concentrations in the muscle samples around the dorsal fin area are compared to other muscle areas?

Audrey scrutinized the findings. "I know we don't find heavy metals of this range in water samples, but do most fish or at least sharks carry high levels like these?"

Gris shook his head. "You're right, metals can run high for some fish and sharks, but never like this. And look," Gris switched to the next page. "The whole blood is off the charts, as well, with high levels of multiple human pharmaceuticals. It doesn't make any sense. Those levels aren't possible in nature."

Audrey nodded. "You're right; they look high."

"Here," Gris drew her attention to more elevated numbers. "The shark would have to be swimming around in a tank filled with antidepressants and birth control pills to have these levels," he continued while

Audrey darted her eyes back and forth and tried to keep pace with Gris' questions.

"What about the liver samples?" she asked.

Gris pointed to the liver results. "All these sharks were either beached or found floating. All have degenerated livers and high levels of botulinum toxin in their muscle tissue, and in nearly every other organ we examined."

"Botulinum toxin? As in Botox?" Audrey eyes went wide with alarm.

He nodded.

"But can't even tiny levels of Botulinum toxin in a person or animal cause instantaneous death?"

"Bingo."

"Are these recently tagged fish, or were they tagged in Florida?" Audrey asked as she caught sight of Kyle and Lucy quietly consuming the platter of finger sandwiches.

"All were recently tagged by the New Jersey crew this past spring. Greta came from wintering in Florida. We found her with the remains of a tether from an older PSAT tags on her put in last fall by the Florida crew. But after six months the tag popped off her and unloaded its data via satellite when it hit the surface. She was tagged for a second time in May by the New Jersey crew with one of the new VSAT tags," Gris confirmed.

Audrey shook her head as she adjusted her eyes to the numbers and data results. "You lost me. I thought you used PSAT tags."

"We do, but we've been trying out a new video tag called a VSAT tag, video satellite archival tag that uploads data and video via satellite each time the shark breaks the surface."

"So all these fish were recently tagged?"

Gris nodded. "And all had the appearance that their dorsal fins were sliced off," he added.

"What? Sliced off? Like sliced, like cut off, like

done in finning?" she asked with obvious skepticism.

Gris nodded.

"Really? I find that hard to believe. You have any pictures of these dorsal fins?"

Gris clicked open photos taken from different dead sharks. All had their dorsal fins jaggedly sliced and all appeared in varying stages of decomposition. Some appeared cut near the base while another was missing its tip and what remained flopped to the side. But all appeared partially decomposed. Audrey looked over Gris's shoulder as he flipped from photo to photo examining the fins. She moved closer to the computer screen.

"Can you enlarge that photo—there?" She pointed to the area at the base of the shark's dorsal fin where the tag was set. "It almost looks like the skin was burned or scorched during its removal. See how the tissue appears singed or cauterized?"

Gris nodded as he squinted at the image before flipping to the second photo and the third. "Actually, I never termed these fins as cut or sliced. In fact, that's what I told the NOAA agent when he questioned me for his ongoing finning investigation."

Audrey's body stiffened with the thought of an ongoing investigation into finning and Gris being interviewed by federal agents.

"Most of these fins don't look cut to me. If anything they look like they were burned, then probably festered as they rotted away with decomposition," he concluded.

"So what do the other fins beside the dorsal fins look like?" she asked.

"Frayed, but not even close to the state of deterioration as seen on the dorsal fins." Gris showed her several photos and she agreed. "These fins may have started with a slice, but more likely they look like they were seared on the outside or even from the inside," he continued.

"Seared from the inside? Like spontaneous combustion?"

Gris shot his wife with a curious look. "I wasn't really thinking spontaneous combustion. But now that you mention, it could be like that."

Audrey paused for a moment. "When you first told me about the sharks dying, I was thinking that maybe these fish died from being in contact with a pollution source or by eating some highly toxic prey, and as time passed, the items they came in contact with, slowly killed them," she said.

"You could be right." Gris was opening his mind to extreme options. He stared at the test results "I mean, look at these results. These things don't happen to sharks in the natural everyday world, at least not yet. Sharks don't swim around for long in this kind of sickly state with these levels of multiple human pharmaceuticals in their blood, not to mention botulinum toxin in their organs and body tissues, or with ragged decomposing dorsal fins. And they don't survive long with gaping sores where their dorsal fins once were."

"Any significance to why they are marked with a letter?" she asked Gris.

"You'll have to ask your son that question. He thinks they may be birthmarks or genetic markings." Gris shrugged then pushed the palms of the hands into his eyes and rubbed. He stepped away from the computer and, head down, began to pace the floor.

Audrey knew he was thinking of cause and effect relationships and how chemicals could impact shark functions.

Kyle left the table at the back of the room when he saw his father pacing. "So what's the verdict?" Kyle tossed the question to his parents. Gris caught his eyes and shook his head in frustration. "Sorry, we were eating. Thanks again for bringing the food, Mom. Did you need us?"

Gris ignored his son's question and continued to pace.

"Finding this many synthetic chemicals in one fish at the same time . . . it's almost like these sharks all attended the same party and chugged the same cocktail," Gris mumbled as he scratched his head.

"Maybe they did," Audrey joked in answer to his unlikely statement.

Gris stopped in mid-stride and looked at Audrey.

"What?"

"You're right. You're absolutely right," Gris cried out.

"Right? Right about what?" Audrey threw her hands up in confusion.

"These sharks all drank the same cocktail," he exclaimed.

"Gris, you really have lost your mind," Audrey said, chuckling at his idea. "Where would great white sharks go to get served this kind of cocktail? I mean who would ever serve them?" She was still laughing to herself while she imagined a picture of sharks sitting on barstools waiting to be served a cocktail. "A person would have to be insane or at least some kind of crazy lunatic to serve up that kind of cocktail," she added in all seriousness.

With every word Audrey spoke, Gris nodded his head faster and faster.

"Gris, why are nodding your head at me?" Audrey wanted to laugh again as she watched her husband's head bob up and down.

"Because none of the chemicals that were found during testing would be present in a shark at the same time unless they were put together in some sort of lethal cocktail. They've never been grouped together like this in other studies. None of them have familial or linked relations to one another. It has to be that these chemicals are seen here together because they are all part of a cocktail given in some way to these sharks.

Audrey cocked her head, waiting for more of an explanation. When he offered none she turned to Kyle and Lucy who were walking to join them. "I feel like we're in the twilight zone here. Is this possible? Are there really people out there who want to kill off sharks with a lethal cocktail?"

"Well," Gris explained, "having met over the years a lot of professionals and laymen who asked the question why protect them, I have to say not everyone agrees they need protection. I'm sure for every advocate, there is a skeptic."

"During the past 24 hours, Lucy and I have certainly experienced the actions of one particular skeptic, or more like a lunatic," Kyle added.

His father's eyes narrowed as he considered Kyle's cryptic comment about Kane.

"How? Tell me how you think these sharks get this kind of poisonous cocktail?" Audrey asked.

"Good question. I have some ideas about who could have been involved in a plot to kill off the sharks, but I don't have any evidence," Gris said.

"Then tell us who would have motivation to want these sharks dead?"

To her surprise, Kyle answered, "I actually made list after I got that text from Lucy's abductor about 'No more updates' on the great white shark deaths. It seemed odd that the person who had Lucy didn't want the public to know about the great white sharks dying. So I made a list of those groups or people who might want to hurt them."

Kyle pulled out his phone and flipped to his note app, showing it to his parents. They both squinted.

"That's impossible for us to read, Kyle," Audrey said. "Can you send it to my email so we can open it on the laptop?"

Kyle tapped a few keys on his phone then waited for his father to open the file.

Pro-shark
Commercial fishermen (eat seals who commercial catch)
Environmental activists (save species)
Scientists (gain knowledge)
Federal and state agents (legally bound to protect)
Tourists (curiosity seekers)
Recreational fisherman (chance for observing
Sharks in the wild, hook on line)
Tag or equipment companies (benefit from sales)
Finning industry buyers (more fins available, more $$)
Elected officials (boasts local economy)

Anti-shark
Commercial fishermen (eat fish, damage gear)
Business owners (scare away tourists, loss of income)
Lifeguards (job hazard)
Surfers (risk of injury or death)
Tourists (closed beaches, no swimming)
Elected officials (scares away tourists)
Dive boat owners (scares and eats divers)

3 groups anti great white sharks:
Business owners, lifeguards, surfers

Gris studied Kyle's short analysis and agreed with his son's results. The only group that didn't gain any benefits from the arrival of the great white sharks was business owners. Lifeguards and surfers couldn't be considered because the fish simply posed a job hazard, not a threat to their financial status.

Gris thought back to the recent town meeting and Bigelow's rant of how no local business in their seaside town could possibly show earnings or survive great white sharks roaming its waters.

"This is helpful, Kyle," Gris said, breaking his son's attention away from his phone where Kyle was shuffling through the rest of his texts.

"I think I know who may be motivated," Gris said.

Kyle's eyes widened at the same moment, and he nodded agreement.

Gris raised his eyebrows, "You too?"

"Yeah, and I think I have the evidence to prove it."

Gris cocked his head with anticipation.

"When I was trying to get Lucy out of there this afternoon, I forgot about the pictures I took while I hid in the barn. Kane had been yelling at someone on the phone when I got there, so I hid in the barn where I found Lucy. When I went to help her, Kane walked in, so I hid in the tack room which was dark. The phone interrupted him, and he started ranting about Bigelow calling him at home. Kane took the call in the house, which gave me time to get to Lucy. When I went to leave the tack room, I bumped the light switch on. What I found was weird. Take a look." Kyle extended his phone which displayed the photos.

Blinking his eyes open, his father pushed the phone aside. "Kyle, again, I can't make out much of anything in that picture, except maybe some items on a table. Can you send it to the laptop?"

A moment later, Kyle stooped between his parents' shoulders as they gawked at the revealing photo of the table with painted fluorescent orange toggles laid out to dry and a nest of discarded tag whips at its side.

Audrey turned to Gris with a look of complete confusion. "Am I missing something here?"

"Yes. But I think our son found the smoking gun. My guess is that these toggles hold the answer to why these great white sharks are dying."

TWENTY FIVE

That's A Little Harsh

Jon Kane handed his payment to the bail clerk and moved to the next line for the sheriff to dispense his personal belongings.

"One brown wallet with four hundred thirteen dollars and fifty cents, one silver Rolex dive watch, one navy long sleeve shirt. That's all we have for you Mr. Kane," the deputy slid the items across the counter.

Kane was seething from the events of the last 24 hours. Not only did he have a bloody hole in his arm from a sharp toggle that wouldn't stop throbbing and likely held future ramifications, but the girl he'd kidnapped was missing, the police had been called to his driveway and seized his Glock, silencer and most of his magazines of ammo, and he'd been charged with carrying a firearm without a permit, firing a handgun within the town limits and public endangerment. He was just lucky they didn't know about the girl he'd tied up in his barn.

Hailing a cab, Kane thanked his lucky stars that his juvenile record had been expunged. If he'd still had his felony record on file he wouldn't be walking free on bail. Instead he would have been handed a free pass to an automatic 10-year sentence in prison.

Kane leaned forward and gave the cab driver directions to Joseph Bigelow's 5-star resort. He handed the driver a $100 bill and told him to wait for him at the curb. Exiting the cab, Kane drew in a deep breath to contain his anger as he moved swiftly toward the inn's front desk. He waited a few seconds then provided the receptionist his name.

"I'm Jon Kane here to see Mr. Bigelow immediately. It's urgent," he snapped.

The receptionist left the counter and entered a side office to check with her boss and returned with a well-versed excuse. Bigelow was not unavailable.

Kane smiled at the pretty 20-year-old blonde, nodded thanks and burst past her into Bigelow's office.

"Mr. Bigelow . . . I apologize for the intrusion . . . but he just ran past me . . . ," the receptionist said from behind Kane.

Bigelow held up his wide right palm. "Ah . . . Mr. Kane. Did we have an appointment?" Using a white linen napkin, he dabbed frosting from an afternoon snack at the corner of his mouth.

"I need to speak with you on an urgent matter," Kane bit out, his jaw clenched. His arm left arm was still wrapped in the white gauze bandage.

"I'll permit it, Ms. Hendrickson. You may go." Bigelow waved her out of the office.

Bigelow's eyes roamed over Kane and locked onto the gauze bandages wrapped on his left bicep. "What is it?" he snapped.

"This?" Kane acknowledged, pointing to his arm.

Bigelow didn't respond.

"*This* is a bandage covering the hole where a shark tag stabbed my arm. One of the tags with the fluorescent orange toggles."

Bigelow's eyes widened, and he let out a soft snicker. "You're serious?" the billionaire asked with disbelief.

"Do you remember assuring me that these tags would never pose any harm to me or others?" Kane stepped toward Bigelow until he was flush against the front of the massive desk. "Do you?" Kane's voice boomed across the short distance.

Bigelow leaned back in his leather chair and picked a morsel free from a back tooth. "Humph. Did I say that, Mr. Kane? I don't recall saying all that. You may want to have your hearing checked. Our company has a very good health plan you may want to take advantage of for that." Bigelow smugly dismissed the accusation.

Kane's mouth dropped open at Bigelow's response, then snapped into a flat line as he clenched his back teeth. He paused for a moment to answer Bigelow's arrogant suggestion.

"If that's what you suggest, I'll have a doctor look at my injury, draw some blood to check for any toxins...tell him how I received the hole and then share the blood results with the press and . . ."

"Mr. Kane, don't waste my precious time." Bigelow cut him off mid-sentence. "Why are you here?" He pushed the empty plate aside, looked at his nails, and then shuffled some papers on his desk.

Kane considered his response and in that moment, decided he was finished with working for Bigelow. Time to settle his pay and disappear.

"You have until tomorrow morning at 9:00 to deposit the final payment we agreed on into my overseas account." Thrusting his chin forward, Kane leaned in over Bigelow's wide walnut desk. He smelled vanilla sugar on Bigelow's breath.

"You can't be serious," Bigelow scoffed.

"Never been more serious in my life. You have 'til 9:00 tomorrow or 3:00 pm Switzerland time," he specified.

"And what if I am unable to meet your childish deadline?" Bigelow said, leaning back in his chair.

"You mean you don't deliver? Then there will be consequences. Deadly consequences."

Bigelow sat up in his chair. "You know I can't reach my people to move that kind of money by then."

"If the payment is not in that account at 9:01, you can expect the unexpected and a detailed letter to authorities linking your name to the entire scheme."

"Hold on, Kane. That's a little harsh, don't you think?" This time Bigelow's words were edged with alarm and he came across as whiney.

Kane tossed his head back and cackled. "You want harsh? Just cross me, and you'll get harsh." His eyes narrowed and he turned serious once again. "Remember, by 9 or consequences will befall you."

"You're bluffing." Bigelow sneered at Kane.

"I'll leave it up to you. It's your call, Bigelow. Your call and your life." Kane whirled about and strode out of the office, leaving the door standing wide open.

TWENTY SIX

Kaboom!

Knowing Joseph Bigelow wouldn't honor his end of the contract, Kane took his time that evening planting and wiring all the explosives necessary blow Bigelow's resort sky high.

The next morning, with one hour of sleep, Kane reached the Swiss bank authorities to ask if anyone had called in or executed a large transfer of funds into his account. All authorities confirmed no such activity had been requested or approved. Kane called two more times with no transfers received and gained his final update from bank authorities at 8:56. No transfers were scheduled for the next hour and none had been received into his account. The update didn't surprise him. But it did add fuel to his raging anger. He was glad he'd stayed up all evening putting his plan in place. He was now ready to move on it.

Drinking his third cup of coffee from the front seat of his car, he waited, staked out in Bigelow's resort parking lot. At 9:12 am, he watched Bigelow wheel into the parking lot in his sleek Porsche 911 Carrera, park it behind some large bushes and push the button to raise the car's roof back in place. He watched Bigelow lean across the passenger's seat to collect his briefcase before opening his door.

Bigelow stepped out and met Jon Kane's steely eyes. He jumped back against the car then stood stock still as Kane pressed the muzzle of his semiautomatic

Glock with a silencer to his neck.

"Step away from the car," Kane said in a low steely voice.

Kane pushed the pistol into the resort owner's roll of fat that jiggled from his chin, loving the surge of power he got from the terror in Bigelow's eyes.

"Now real nice, Bigelow, we are going to walk to your office. If you make any attempt to flee or signal anyone for help, I will shoot you at point blank range. I have yet to see anyone survive a close shot to the head. Do you understand me?" Kane's jaw flexed with anger.

"Answer me!" Kane barked.

"Yes, yes, whatever you say," Bigelow assured him.

"Start walking." Kane dropped the Glock to Bigelow's ribs and pressed in two inches. Bigelow's breath hitched and Kane saw a wince of pain in his face from the pinch of the gun.

Together, they started the slow walk toward Bigelow's office, just past the resort's front check-in foyer. The place was not as busy as Kane had hoped.

In a further effort to conceal the gun from view, he pulled out Bigelow's shirttail and pushed the gun into his fat folds until the tip rubbed at his ribs two inches from his spinal column. Bigelow sucked in a short breath at the change in position and stumbled as they approached the front door.

"Don't try anything stupid," Kane said.

The front desk was empty which made it easier to have Bigelow press in the combination to open the door.

Once inside, Kane slammed the door behind them and twisted the interior lock. Bigelow abruptly dropped to his knees and begged. "Don't shoot. Please don't shoot me."

"Shut up," Kane snapped.

"My people, they are working on the transfer. I'm

telling you the truth! Only a little more time, and it'll be done."

Kane moved the gun to Bigelow's temple. "That's bull," he snarled, "and you know it. I've had enough of your lies. You never had any intention to transfer the money, and for that, Bigelow, you will pay. You will pay dearly." His voice was filled with malice.

"Get up, you slob." Kane pulled at Bigelow's flabby biceps but it was impossible to lift the 260 pound man. "I. Said. Get. Up." He pronounced each word clearly.

After a minute of trying to get his feet under him, Bigelow grabbed at the mahogany, liquor cabinet door handle and pulled himself to his feet.

Kane shoved the man forward with the muzzle of the gun. Bigelow moved toward his desk and before he could sit down, Kane grabbed his wrist and twisted his arm into a right angle behind his back. Within a few seconds Kane had a thick rope around the man, completely confining him to his chair. A cloth across his mouth kept him silenced.

"The bottom of this chair is rigged to explode if you try to roll forward, to the side or backward." Kane's details were presented in a blasé manner, as if he were talking about the features of a new car.

Kane walked casually to a stereo cabinet and folded back the doors to peruse the music selection. He chose Beethoven's Symphony No. 5 in C minor.

"I have some business to take care of," Kane said as he turned up the volume. "Remember, now, one wheel rolls and kaboom!" Kane raised his hands in the air like he was tossing confetti to the ceiling. Then he turned, locked the office door behind him and strode with confidence out of the lobby.

~

Detective Ellis insisted Kyle and Lucy spend the

night at his home. He had two empty bedrooms on the second floor of the gray-shingled cottage abandoned by his kids, now away at college.

After an hour of watching the illuminated bedside clock, Lucy walked through Kyle's open bedroom door and climbed in the side of his bed, wrapped in her comforter. He woke up when her weight hit his mattress.

"I can't sleep. The nightmares keep coming. Is it okay if I stay here," she asked.

"Of course," he nodded and squished to the left to make room for her. He pulled her closer and tucked her small frame under his shoulder. He listened to her breathing slow with each breath she took. After 10 minutes, the rhythm of her breathing told him she was finally asleep.

Lying in the same bed together was new for them. Sure, they'd curled into each other on a couch for a good movie or even a nap, but never lay together in bed. Surprised by his feelings, none of it felt awkward or wrong. Instead it felt right.

His mind was filled with thoughts of Lucy and her brave attitude facing Kane and surviving the day's events. He admired the courage she'd mustered to get through. He wondered how many other girls her age, hooded, gagged and tied up would have coped as well in the same situation.

He rolled toward her. The moonlight shone through the side window casting a glow into the room. He could see her face perfectly, her dark long lashes resting on her cheeks, her lips slightly apart and her forehead completely relaxed. He pulled her into his chest and continued to listen to her breathing, even as the pulse of ocean waves unraveling against the shore. Before long he gave into the rhythm as it coaxed him to join Lucy, and he, too, fell off to sleep.

Kyle awoke late in the next morning to the lyrical whistles of bobwhites in the salt marsh and the sight of his striking girlfriend still sound asleep on his chest. Having seen her in the morning light, he knew he'd never fall back to sleep. He pushed the memories of the previous day from his mind and tried to focus on something good.

He hadn't been surfing in more than a week. The thought sent a jolt of enthusiasm through his body. Surfing was one of the best remedies to cleanse tension from his body. Eyeing Lucy carefully, he slid out from under her and replaced his void with a second pillow. She nuzzled it and continued to drift along in sleep.

He tiptoed from the bed and shimmied his board shorts up over his boxers while contemplating how the waves were this morning. He pulled a small sheet of paper off the bureau and wrote a note to Lucy on the flat top of the windowsill, when a huge puff of dark grey smoke caught his attention. It billowed to the sky several blocks to the north across from the fish docks.

He stopped writing and squinted at the sight, then heard the whine of fire trucks as they wheeled down the town's main street toward the smoke.

"Where you going?" Lucy asked. Her voice was husky with sleep.

"Oh" he spun around. "I didn't mean to wake you. Go back to sleep. I'll be back soon. I'm just going to check the waves, maybe see if Brodie's already out there. Mrs. Ellis is downstairs. She said your father called last night and will be at your house later today."

Lucy nodded at all the information so early in the morning. She gave him a wide yawn and he watched as she stretched like a heavy-eyed cat, then curled into the extra pillow. Her sleepy expression and mussed hair captured his eyes when a loud blast that resembled the bang of fireworks broke his daze.

"What was that?" Lucy asked, recovering from a jump that put her on her feet right behind Kyle. He was turned and looking out the window. He decided he needed a better view so he lifted the screen and leaned out to see what caused the blast.

"Looks like a one of the big houses or a resort in town is on fire," Kyle answered.

Three more loud explosions shattered the silence and shook the house. "It's definitely coming from that fire about four blocks away." He moved aside to let her have a look.

"Is it safe?" Lucy's voice was inquisitive though wary.

"Sure, have a look," he guaranteed.

Lucy leaned out the window to see a fire raging four blocks away as flames leaped to the sky. "Holy cow! Is that the Lawson estate?"

"I don't think so. It's further up the road. Looks like it's across from the town docks."

"Is it the town fish docks?" Lucy asked, concerned for his father.

"I don't think so. See over there," he leaned in and pointed. "You can see the boats lined up at the fish docks. Looks like business as usual. If a fire were going there, you wouldn't see a boat in sight. They'd all be headed offshore far, far away from the fuel dock."

For a moment it was quiet.

"Hey . . . um . . . thanks for letting me climb in and take over your bed last night," Lucy said. "I . . . ah, tried to run from the nightmares . . . "

"Anytime. But you know you don't need to thank me. You'd do the same for me"

"Yeah, well, your super brave girl wasn't very brave last night."

He reached for her and said, "Happens to all of us . . ."

Three more loud blasts rocked the house and shook the window glass to the 1920 home.

Kaboom! Boom, boom. The roar of more sirens

followed the blasts.

"Kyle? Lucy? Are you hearing this?" Mrs. Ellis called up the stairs.

Kyle walked to the top step. "Yes, ma'am. Have you heard what's on fire?"

"Mark called and said it's Bigelow's resort near the fish docks," she answered.

Kyle nodded as his eyes widened. He remembered how angry Kane had been when Bigelow called him on the house phone when he found Lucy in the barn. He stopped and thought back to the bizarre scene of the painted toggles on the table in the tack room and his text demands to stay quiet and give no information to the press.

"You okay, babe?" Lucy asked Kyle.

Kyle didn't respond.

~

About 40 minutes later Kyle heard his father asking Mrs. Ellis if Lucy and he were awake.

"Can anyone sleep with this kind of noise?" she asked with a chuckle. Kyle heard her walk to the foot of the stairs. "Kyle, your father's here."

Kyle took the stairs down two at a time 'til he reached his father at the foot of the stairs. To Kyle's surprise, Gris hugged him warmly.

"Everything okay, Dad?"

"You got a minute?" Gris asked.

Kyle nodded, and Mrs. Ellis offered them coffee, then led them to the screen-in porch at the back of the house where they could talk.

"Kyle, I'm sure you heard the blasts this morning."

Kyle nodded.

"I've been with the FBI and Sheriff's Bomb Squad over at Bigelow's resort, or at least what remains of the resort. Someone pulled the fire alarms at the resort about 8:00 this morning, forcing all the patrons to evacuate and to alert the town's fire department. A truck was sent down to check out the alarm system. At first, the fire chief said it was likely a system malfunction. But when the chief went to investigate, Mr. Bigelow could not be found, and his office was locked.

"The fire chief was finally able to find the manager and open the door to Bigelow's office where they found him tied and gagged in his office chair. Right away the chief saw the chair was rigged with explosives."

Lucy walked in as Kyle's father finished his sentence. She stood next to Kyle and asked, "What's going on?"

"Dad was just telling me about the fire and Mr. Bigelow," Kyle said, then patted the seat next to him on the chocolate-colored linen couch.

"Go on," Kyle encouraged his father.

"As the two approached Bigelow, the first bomb went off in an adjacent building. It was the first of seven, all triggered on timers that essentially leveled every resort building, except the main one that houses some offices and the check-in desk.

"After the first bomb exploded, the chief called for police backup, the bomb squad and the FBI. The bomb squad was able to disarm the wires attached to Bigelow's chair and evacuated the premises. When he was leaving he told the FBI and local police that Jon Kane was responsible for the bombing.

"But there is more to the story than just bad blood between those two. Seems Mr. Kane and Mr. Bigelow had an arrangement...an arrangement that nearly got Bigelow killed and will likely put Jon Kane on the FBI's most wanted list."

"Okay," Kyle said, his eyes wide.

"I don't yet have all the pieces to the puzzle of how they fit together, I mean between Kane and Bigelow.

After he initially blew off steam about accusing Kane for the bombing, Bigelow went silent and still isn't talking until he sees his lawyer. At this point, I guess the FBI is taking over the investigation from local police and fire. I guess they do that when people are kidnapped and bombs are planted and people are rigged to explode." Gris shook his head in disbelief. "If Kane's left the country, Ellis said the FBI will turn it over to the U.S. Marshall's to bring him in. I mean if they can find him."

"They could start by looking at hospitals. Kane got some poison in him when the tag snagged his arm. He's bound to show some symptoms," Kyle mused.

"I'll pass that along to the Ellis," Gris nodded. "Bigelow was lucky the fire was contained to all the buildings on the resort property except the main inn where he was tied up. Though it didn't burn, it's in bad shape from all the other building blasts. They'll have to level all of it and start over."

Kyle and Lucy looked at each other, thinking the same thing. Tying and gagging were the methods Kane used to restrain Lucy, so it wasn't inconceivable he used the same method on Bigelow. But why?

"So what's Kane's role in all of this and what kind of arrangement did he and Bigelow have?" Kyle asked.

"That still needs more unraveling. But I'm afraid Dr. Chang's theory was probably on target. I talked to Ellis at the scene and he said Kane, at that moment, was likely fleeing the country on a flight out to Europe, the Caribbean or South America. He'd collected his commission checks yesterday and likely embezzled money from the tagging company," Gris added.

"So that's Kane's crime, that he embezzled money?" Kyle asked.

"That and possibly that he bombed Bigelow's resort and conspired to poison the white sharks."

"I knew it, I knew it. I knew Kane was bad from

the first time I met him. I felt it in my gut!" Kyle's voice escalated with each statement, and he jumped to his feet.

"Ellis apparently met with the company's CFO and the lead tag engineer of Smart Fish Acoustics yesterday," Gris continued. "He learned that there was no proprietary magnet system on the VSAT tags, there was never a need to activate anything, and when Ellis showed the engineer one of our video tags, the engineer said the product he distributed was never issued with the toggle painted fluorescent orange."

Kyle shook his head as he reflected on the tack room at the barn and the table set up with toggles and paint.

"This morning when I was at lab headquarters I spoke to Dr. Chang about the tests conducted on the video tag that he sent out earlier this week. He said the only thing found unusual was the orange paint on the toggle. It wasn't actually paint, but a poison adhesive that dissolved once implanted below the shark's skin. From there, the poison likely entered the shark's bloodstream, leading to cirrhosis of the liver, nerve damage, brain damage, loss of appetite and destruction of the central nervous system and in some cases asphyxiation.

"Why, why kill the sharks? Why would anyone want to kill something that great?" Kyle was working hard to control his anger. But he felt himself teetering on the edge and thwarted the urge to punch a wall.

"Like I said, Kyle, we're still trying to pull all the pieces together. But without Bigelow talking, this could take some time," Gris explained.

"So will sharks continue to die?" Kyle asked.

"As far as we know, the only tags that had the orange toggles were those delivered to New Jersey and Cape Cod. Florida's tags were normal, as were North Carolina's."

"So how many more could die?"

"Only seven were tagged by the New Jersey crew, and so far we have recorded seven deaths here on Cape Cod. We only tagged one with a VSAT tag here on The Cape and she was named after your Mom, Audrey Marie." Kyle winced. "So we are close to the end."

"I hate that these sharks have been targeted. I just don't get why," Kyle said again.

"Neither do I. Do you remember when you were a boy and we talked about how people kill sharks for many reasons. When you were younger, it was all about bravado and showing off for other fishermen. But the reasons behind these deaths are probably different. People are not so much motivated about proving their strengths and abilities these days. Now it seems like those who kill are motivated by money. They kill whites for the price that their large fins can land. They kill them for the high price their jaws will bring. Perhaps this time is no different. While I think the majority of the people here in our culture want to save or protect these sharks, there are always going to be some who don't. Likely those people are motivated by greed, by money, but not the kind of money you are thinking, like how much they can gain from selling the shark's jaws or fins. Instead, these people see the sharks as a threat that could cause them to lose their money. By killing off the white sharks, they think they are eliminating a chance of losing business or income. Once the sharks are dead, they think their business will thrive once again."

Kyle thought about his father's words. He knew he was right. It was the Bigelows of the world who saw these unpredictable, wild white sharks as a threat. It would take time to prove it, but he knew in his gut that his father was right about the killings.

"So is there any good news in all this?" Lucy chimed in, leaning back on the sofa.

"I guess the good news is since Kyle and I stopped

using the VSATs after tagging only one shark, no others can be harmed. Ellis told me the CFO of Smart Fish Acoustics offered to replace all our tags and provide three new boxes to the tagging program to finish the summer and cover all of next summer. Even better, it's actually just the start of the great white season for Cape Cod. These sharks will likely be here for another two or three months. So we'll have plenty of time to tag and collect data," Gris finished and turned to meet his son's eyes.

"Terrific," Kyle said loudly and sarcastically, clowning with his father as he rolled his eyes back and flopped down next to Lucy on the sofa like he'd been shot.

Lucy grinned as she watched Kyle kid his father, working hard to sound serious but failing.

Kyle saw Lucy grinning and took a swipe to grab her but missed when her dimples, now etched deeply into both cheeks, distracted him. Her diminutive expression had the ability to stop him in his tracks and even blur his father's news of how the season was just starting.

TWENTY SEVEN

Brain-numbing Cold

"You coming?" Kyle asked as Lucy finished packing a canvas bag with a towel, a jug of water and peanut butter sandwiches.

"Of course," she answered. "Did you want to go alone?"

"No, not at all. I want your company. I just didn't know if you want to rest some more."

"Well, I didn't say I would go swimming, but I will come watch you surf and maybe catnap on the warm sand. Besides, the ocean air will probably help wash away those nightmares."

He agreed it would help her forget and give her resolve to move forward, away from the awful memories of the last few days.

Thirty minutes later, Kyle plowed his feet through the warm sand behind Lucy. He looked ahead and counted the number of waves in each incoming set. The largest waves rolled in at six feet, while most reached only four to five feet in height as they crossed over the submerged outer sandbar and created a small trough of warmer water with their backwash near the beach.

Lucy picked up her pace after she dropped her towel and sandals at their usual spot and continued without delay toward the waves. His eyes on her, Kyle dropped his board in the same location and stopped to watch Lucy tear away her sundress and continue toward the water.

Kyle scanned the horizon on the left and the right, then ran to catch up. When she heard his footsteps she turned back and flashed him a white-teeth smile, dimples included, then took off running down the beach for the water. Kyle stumbled forward when he slowed down to avoid running her over as she stopped to cast him a look.

A look that asked, "Aren't you coming?"

Kyle sprinted toward her, scooped her over his shoulder and dove headfirst into the icy water.

She surfaced, coughed out a mouthful of water at him, then screamed, "Kyle Kelley, you know I don't go in the water before August. Did you really think I planned to dive in?"

He laughed at her annoyance. "My bad, I must have misread your longing looks my way!" He continued to chuckle as she groaned at his response. "Luce, this is the perfect cure for numbing out those wicked thoughts from earlier this week. Come on. Let's swim."

He dove underwater, tugged at her bikini top and pulled her under to join him. She shot to the surface again when the cold water hit her temples like a vise. The water was so cold she swore it would numb her brain. At least, she hoped so.

Soon her feet were numb, and she no longer felt the stabbing sensation of the cold temperature spearing through them. She swam toward Kyle, then worked hard to tread water.

"See, it's not so bad. You get used to it after a while," Kyle said with a convincing nod.

She laughed loudly at his ridiculous remark, "Yeah, when your body turns numb?"

He moved closer. Her lips were tinged a blue-purple, and she was trying hard to keep her teeth from chattering.

"Alright, alright, I get the message; you're cold. Let's get out and warm you up. Then I'm hitting the waves."

"Good by me," she nodded as she rode a couple white water waves ashore. With numb feet she stumbled in the sinking wet sand up the shore and knelt on the sand when she saw her towel. "Luce, stand up. Let me get that," Kyle said steadying her and wrapping her shoulders and torso up in the oversize beach towel, then hugging her to transfer his body heat.

"Ah, much better," she said through chattering teeth. She closed her eyes. He let her go for a moment, spread his beach blanket and dropped her onto it like a bundle of kindling.

"Want your hot chocolate?" he asked. She nodded, her eyes still closed. "It's near the bag. The lid's still on." She nodded again, her eyes still closed.

"I'm going to head back in for some waves. You good staying here?"

Lucy nodded a third time, still not opening her eyes.

When Kyle laughed at her serene expression, she opened one lid to peek at him. Then closed it and grinned, showing him her cute dimples.

Mmmm, those dimples are like a magnet. Hard to walk away from.

She flattened out the sand lumps beneath the towel before snuggling into the blanket. Any moment now, she'd drift off to a nap.

Once he was assured that Lucy was safe, Kyle grabbed his board and splashed into the surf, all their worries behind them.

EPILOGUE

Survivors

130 miles southeast of the Cape Cod at Oceanographer Canyon

"There," Annie Morris pointed 20 feet ahead. "It's a dorsal fin," she exclaimed to her father.

Mancini heard her call out and signaled aloft to the first mate Cam who nodded when spotting the robust shark and immediately throttled the engines back to match its speed.

Still in a leg cast and using crutches, Annie had finally taken Gris up on his offer to come aboard the harpoon boat for a great white shark-tagging trip before the end of summer. Seeing Audrey Marie, one of the earliest tagged sharks of the summer, reappear on his computer screen after vanishing for two months, Gris scheduled the trip for Labor Day weekend. Audrey Marie's timing provided not only a final trip before nearly all the white sharks migrated south, but also allowed the group a glimpse at how great whites hunted the deep canyons off Cape Cod.

Annie's call to come aboard was no surprise to Kyle, who had visited her at the hospital 72 hours after he rescued her from the shark attack. Having survived three reconstructive leg surgeries, and awakened on the day after the third, she declared herself a shark advocate. Actually she used the term 'ambassador' when she spoke to the press. When questioned how soon she would return to surfing, she said she would likely be on dry sand in a cast the remainder of the summer. But she pledged she'd never ditch surfing and would pursue it again when she was physically able.

Her uplifting news served as a stark reminder that not all were quick to give up their allegiance to the species and a passion for the ocean. Gris had known several shark bite survivors who were never able to escape the months of night terrors that followed such an incident. For those, such nightmares made it impossible for them to ever return to the healing water of the ocean or even glimpse a shark from the safety of a boat cabin or aquarium wall.

Now the holiday weekend, the trip would likely be the last of the summer season, as many of the sharks had moved offshore and south during the last week of August. Knowing this, Mancini agreed to the long-range trip plans, inviting the Kelley family, including Gris and Audrey, Annie and her father, and unexpectedly Kyle and Lucy from college as well as Lucy's father. The latter three had decided to join the trip at the last moment, boarding at 7:30 am.

After many hours of steaming southeast of Cape Cod, Cam heard the spotter plane pilot radio the position of a large 14-foot great white shark located about a quarter mile ahead. It was swimming southeast beyond the South Channel at the outer edge of Georges Bank toward Oceanographer and Lydonia submarine canyons about 130 miles southeast of the Cape Cod Canal.

Oceanographer Canyon, known to be rich in marine life, ran 6,600 feet deep and was frequently blanketed by Sargasso seaweed, a curse for fishermen, but a blessing for great white sharks that prowled it for larger fish like skipjack, mahi-mahi, yellow fin tuna and porpoise.

Within minutes the harpoon boat caught up to the spotted shark.

Gris walked forward to the harpoon pulpit from the wet lab. "It's Audrey Marie, the first shark we tagged this season. Just saw her green light flash on our computer. I'm working on her video now. She was our only VSAT tagging."

No time for hunting, Audrey Marie's belly looked swollen, showing a girth more than six feet across. She swam in a familiar undulating manner at a relaxed rate of two knots. At first Gris did a double take and looked to Kyle. "Do you remember her being this wide across?"

Kyle shook his head. She was either swollen from a recent meal or laden with pups. The presence of the boat didn't deter her attention to her cruise path.

"She looks pretty banged up, Gris," Mancini called out. "Her head and torso have a number of scratches and her dorsal fin's frayed and leaning to the right."

"Where do you suppose she's headed?" Annie asked.

"She doesn't appear to be in search of food. Hard to say," Gris said.

Gris looked to his right when he heard Kyle taking photos with the digital camera.

"Let me guess, you see a letter marked on her fin," Gris teased his son.

Kyle pulled back from the lens. "Matter of fact the letter M or W depending on its orientation."

"Made any sense of all the other letters?" Gris asked Kyle as Lucy wove fingers through Kyle's side belt loop.

"We came up with NABCAL, CANLAB. Also, LANCAB or LABCAN. Then there's BALANC without its final Letter E. Or maybe..." Lucy stopped when Mancini's voice interrupted her.

"What's the letter you're missing?" Mancini asked.

"Letter E," Kyle answered.

"You say you saw the letter M on Audrey Marie?"

Kyle nodded.

"Maybe your letter M is really a letter E when flipped on its side. Ever think of that?" Mancini asked.

Kyle glanced back at the digital photo on the camera screen. "You think? Do you think their deaths are telling us that the VSAT tags were disrupting nature's BALANCE?" Kyle whispered to his father.

"Or it could be a genetic anomaly. I guess it's anyone's guess, son."

Mancini looked to the starboard side. "Fall back, fall back, Cam. She's slowing down."

As Audrey Marie reduced her speed, she rolled to the side and back, giving everyone aboard a glimpse at her laden belly. "She's definitely carrying pups," Gris confirmed.

Giving a final swish of her tail, Audrey Marie slowed to a glide in the water. Once still her body began to sink below the surface first three feet, then eight, then 12, then 15 feet until Gris saw one last flicker of her white belly and she was out of sight. He ran to the laptop in the wet lab to watch her from her VSAT video tag.

"Mancini, Audrey, everyone can see her on the monitor descending into the canyon?" he called from the lab.

The group crowded around the laptop screen and watched in silence. With the boat engines now off, all that could be heard was the gentle slosh of waves lapping the hull as it floated with the current.

After fifteen minutes, everyone watched as Audrey Marie propped herself onto a ledge along the side of Gilbert's Canyon about halfway to the bottom that lay 900 feet below the boat. The only lighting available at that depth was the lighting provided by the video camera.

Standing in a circle behind Gris and Kyle, the group focused their attention on the screen as they watched Audrey Marie awaken and circle one last time. She settled again on the ledge floor. Listing to one side, she rested momentarily, fluttered her tail and rolled to the right. The water became murky with a brown spiraling fluid.

Within seconds, to the shock of all, five small pups emerged from the mist, darting into the camera then bumping off to the side. The tag bobbed in a jerky motion as more pups began to swim around their mother in the smoky darkness far enough away to snap free from their umbilical cords before starting their ascent to the surface.

Remaining in a reclined position, Audrey Marie did not move.

"I'm not too sure how much longer she'll be able to remain still without water flowing over her gills for oxygen," Gris said with grave concern.

Enamored with the sight of the birthing, the group didn't hear him, but instead counted aloud with Mancini the number of pups now ascending away from the camera lens toward the glistening sun. Lucy cooed at their adorable size and shape.

"I think I counted eleven pups," Audrey reported.

When the video lost the shape of their bodies, the group looked at Audrey Marie now completely still on the ledge.

"We just witnessed the first live birth of a white shark," Gris stated in a sad tone.

"Isn't that a good thing?" Lucy asked.

"Yes, Lucy, a wonderful thing. In fact, a moment of a lifetime. No one has ever seen the birth of a great white shark," Gris answered somberly.

"Then why do you sound so sad?"

"What's happening to her?" Annie asked at the same time.

"Audrey Marie hasn't moved for at least two

minutes now. I get the feeling this was Audrey Marie's last journey," Gris said.

"Last journey?" Audrey asked her husband, hearing his melancholy.

"I'm afraid so. She was the only white shark our Cape Cod crew tagged with the new VSAT tag that had the coated tag toggle. She is the last of the eight sharks, seven from New Jersey and one from Cape Cod to die from the poisoned toggle."

Gris was right. It was Audrey Marie's final journey. The video camera fluttered with movement from a deep current as she lay on the ledge floor rolled to her side.

While experts theorized that most female sharks likely select birthing locations that would allow young pups access to shallow water nurseries quickly, away from large prey, Audrey Marie had purposely selected a deeper remote habitat to birth her pups. It was a place where her pups could ascend and then find cover beneath the blanket of protective Sargasso seaweed and find plentiful baitfish to nourish their growing bodies.

Kyle thought about how smart Audrey Marie was to select the shallow canyon from where her pups could ascend and survive while gaining a peaceful resting place for her to die before any predator could find her.

Gris watched his son. He knew he was considering the huge shark giving life in exchange for her death.

"She was one dedicated mother, huh?" he asked Kyle who quietly nodded. "To think how she lasted just long enough to make her journey, give birth to all those healthy pups all before sinking to her death in the canyon."

"It's a miracle," Lucy added, looping her arm through Kyle's while he exchanged glances with his father.

"Yes, it is. Though bittersweet," Gris said.

"Well, then, having lost those eight great whites to the tainted tag toggles, I think we're fortunate to have counted eleven pups from the great Audrey Marie. Let's hope they're all girls so they can eventually carry their own pups," Lucy finished.

As the pups continued their ascent to the surface and beyond the view of the camera lens, the group moved to the upper deck.

Within minutes, Lucy pointed off the starboard side, "I think I see small shark dorsal fins at the surface over there!"

"You sure do," Gris agreed.

Kyle leaned into the rail, trying to make out the young whites slicing through the shadows cast by seaweed, rich with bait fish.

Gris put a hand on his son's shoulder. "The pups are already hunting. A good sign."

Together, father and son watched the newborn white sharks swim off in separate directions to begin a hunt that would last them a lifetime.

The End

About the Author

Amy Adams grew up in New England, spending each summer on the outer beaches of Cape Cod. After earning her master's degree in marine policy, she migrated to Florida with her husband, a fisheries biologist who studies sharks. Working as an environmental writer, she recognized a notable shift in the public's perception of sharks since the release of Peter Benchley's novel Jaws in 1974. That said, she also found very little non-scientific reading material publicly available to effectively learn about the species and its sometimes tangled relationship with people. Seeking to fill this gap, she wrote this novel to provide shark conservation information imbedded in an engaging story format - of interest to readers who may not have current interest or knowledge of white sharks and to shark enthusiasts as well.

To increase financial support for white shark scientific research and understanding, she is donating a portion of her profits from **Tagged** to the Atlantic White Shark Conservancy, a non-profit organization established to support white shark research and education programs to ensure that this important species thrives.

Visit her at ***www.AuthorAmyAdams.com*** and ***www.Tagged-thebook.com*** for updates on the next books in the **Great White Adventures *series***.

Read on for a sneak peek of Amy Adams' next novel.

Supplementary

TAGGED 2

Book Two in the Great White Adventure-series
Coming soon from Yellow Dog Printing LLC

"Hey, Brodie, just heard on the news about the capsizing!" Kyle Kelley gave Brodie Gilmore a friendly slap on his right shoulder after he caught him opening his truck door at the town fish docks.

Brodie winced. "Take it easy, Kyle!" He cupped his right elbow wrapped in a brace.

"Oh, man, I'm sorry," Kyle startled at his friend's reaction. "What happened? You hurt?" He hadn't noticed the brace.

Brodie stepped out and walked with an unhurried, measured gait from his truck to the commercial fish house. He sank heavily onto a bench and exhaled. His Coast Guard uniform was crumpled and stained. Kyle took a closer look. "Did you have a run in with a coffee machine?"

"I wish it were that simple," Brodie sighed. "The knockdown happened early this morning near the entrance to the inlet."

The two friends surveyed the fish dock where they'd spent so much time together as teens. The early June air was brisk with a steady onshore breeze beneath a blue, cloudless sky.

"Hey I'm sorry. How bad does it hurt?"

"It's not too bad, more a nuisance," he said then grimaced as he shifted his arm away from his side to rest at his waist.

"Tell me about the knockdown. The report on TV said the crew was caught by surprise while heading offshore for a search and rescue. Were you in that 42-

foot response boat your station picked up a couple years ago?"

Brodie nodded.

"Were you at the helm?"

"No . . . I mean yes . . . I mean. The Bos'n was at the helm. I was with him and two other crewmen. We were headed out on a search and rescue call for a fisherman overboard a few miles offshore in heavy surf."

Now staring, Kyle listened to his friend recall the incident.

"We were headed offshore through the breaking waves at the inlet when our boat knocked down."

"Knocked down, huh? Like all the way over, or just a sideways type of roll and then back up?"

"No, it was a complete roll. A total 360."

"Sideways or pitch pole?"

"Sideways."

"The TV didn't give any details. So how'd it happen?"

"Heading out of the inlet we hit a huge wave, then hit something hard. I thought it was a rock or a sandbar."

"The inlet next to the big sandbar where all those seals lounge?"

"Yeah, right there at the south entrance."

"Dad told me over the past week when heading offshore early mornings to tag, he's seen a bunch of great whites bellying up to that sandbar at dawn, lurking in the shadows to chow on horsehead seals at slack tide."

"Humph. That might explain what my Bos'n said he saw."

"What'd he see?"

"Said he saw this strange thing bump up against our windshield when we rolled under."

"Strange like in a rock, or weir? What kind of strange?"

"Just after we all felt this jarring thud against the boat's hull and we began to roll backwards and sideways, my Bos'n said he first saw the head, then the gill slits and finally the torso of a massive great white smash against the boat's windshield. He even said the impact made him flinch thinking it would break through the glass."

Kyle's body tensed, anticipating the rest of Brodie's story.

"For me, it was total pandemonium in there, like complete chaos once the boat tilted sideways, then turned upside down, then spun us back upright."

Kyle shook his head as he listened.

"I'm not sure how my Bos'n saw all that with the shark. He admits it was chaotic, but for him it was hard *not* to see it three feet in front of him. I guess it was the thump of the shark's head hitting the windshield that caught and held his attention until the boat turned righted when it disappeared. He said he thinks the shark's first impact against the boat's starboard side started the knockdown."

Brodie paused and moved his arm into a more comfortable position. He looked back to Kyle.

"He. . . uh. . . you're not going to believe what he saw. Probably think the dude's crazy."

As if the story could get any more exciting, Kyle cocked his head in expectation.

"You know my Bos'n, Malcolm Short. He's been around a while at this station. He's no rookie, says it like it is, a real straight shooter."

"Yeah, I know Malcolm. A little too straight-laced for me, but yeah I know him. What'd he see?"

Brodie contemplated whether he should share the bizarre observation the Bos'n claimed.

"C'mon, cough it up. What'd he see?" Kyle persisted.

Brodie hesitated. "Brodie. What. Did. He. See?" Kyle enunciated each word.

Brodie cleared his throat and said, "Malcolm told me when he first got a glimpse of the fish's head he thought it had red eyes. Said he could be wrong. It was chaotic underwater. The water was turbid with froth and bubbles. Even though everything was moving fast, I remember it like time slowed. When I think of it now, it was like we were in slow motion. Then before we knew it, the boat was upright in its normal, vertical position."

Kyle's eyes widened, his mouth dropping open. Brodie's description resembled scenes from a creepy nightmare . . *a massive white shark with red eyes.*

"Wow, that's quite a story. So it wasn't some rogue wave but instead some crazy, red-eyed white shark? Is that Malcolm's claim?"

"Yeah," Brodie tipped his eyes down hearing the doubt in his friend's voice. "Sounds extreme, huh?"

"Yeah, extreme," Kyle agreed wondering if his father had seen the television story or spoken to any crewmen.

"After our tumble, the boat righted so fast. Unfortunately the incident sent two officers who were still securing gear, bouncing around the pilot house."

"They at the hospital now?"

"Yeah, both have concussions. The new guy, who just arrived from Puerto Rico on his tour, has a broken wrist. McCormick sliced his chin open and dislocated his shoulder."

Kyle cringed at the injuries. "Brodie, that sounds bad. You sure your wrist is okay?"

"Yeah. I had X-rays. It's just a simple sprain. No fractures, just minor stuff. I'll live." Kyle patted his friend's shoulder, only this time gently.

"At first when we righted, I was riding this adrenaline rush. I mean, I was shaken, actually a lot shaken. But it wasn't until Malcolm and I dropped off the two for transport to the hospital, our vessel was put in Charlie status, and after we briefed the new boat crew that they told us they were short crew. He said all of our crew needed to follow procedure and be assessed for any injuries and cleared. But he also explained without two others aboard the search and rescue mission would have to be aborted.

"So of course you raised your hand and volunteered. Am I right?"

"Kyle, they said it would be 'aborted.' What would you do? Hang 'em out to dry? Make them all abort the mission?" Brodie pinched his brow together and let out a heavy sigh.

"Don't they usually do some sort of debriefing or hold you for observation before they just plunk you back on a new boat and whisk you offshore again?"

"Yes, but these were extenuating circumstances, and there was a man awash at sea overboard. I'm sure if Risk Management knew what we did next they would have a field day. Our asses would be hanging high. But without us, they would've aborted.

"You said that," Kyle nodded.

"Mission aborted and dude still fighting for his life in the water until a different station was able to respond." Brodie's voice climbed two octaves by the time he finished explaining.

"Long story short, Malcolm and I signed some sheet saying we were unharmed in the knock down and good to go. Then we headed back out. It was when we cleared the inlet that my wrist started hurting."

Kyle shook his head. "I have to admit, you're dedicated." Kyle smiled at his friend.

"Shut up, dude. You won't admit it, but you'd do the same."

"Malcolm tell anyone else about what he thinks he saw?" Kyle asked, praying the Bos'n kept the weird description to himself, at least until he was able to inform his father.

"Not yet. Our Ops Boss told him to be available for a statement to command center to be used in a press release. But I'm not sure he'll share the part about the red-eyes. Sounds totally made up. I think he'll be too worried that he'd get hauled in for a psychiatric evaluation."

Kyle rubbed his chin at the thought of the press getting wind of Malcolm's story and the white shark's aggressive behavior. It was news that could certainly stir concern over the coming summer weekend and kickoff of tourist season a week away.

"I need to get to Dad," Kyle mumbled.

"What's that?" Brodie asked.

"Oh . . . ah . . . nothing." Kyle turned on his heels, deep in thought about how to reach his father offshore.

"Hey, where are you going? I thought since they gave me the rest of the day off we'd head out for some chow."

Kyle turned around, running a hand through his hair. "Oh, right. Can we do it another time? I just remembered I've got to get a message to my father."

"Can't he wait 30 minutes while we eat and catch up? I mean you know I asked for this location on my tour of duty so that I could get back here this summer—you know, to relive a little bit of our childhood together."

Kyle smiled at his best friend's comment. Brodie was one of those lifetime friends that he could go two years not seeing and when they got together again, he'd just pick right up from where he left off without a blip.

"Ah, man—I'm sorry," Kyle paused. He needed to reach his father before the news broke. "Can I meet you for a beer later at the Hoolihan's Pub? Say 9:00?"

~

Stay tuned at *www.AuthorAmyAdams.com* and *www.Tagged-thebook.com.*